RABBIT'S FOOT LUCKY

Deborah Marcum

For my family... For all the patience, putting up with my
while writing a book outside my comfort zone.

CONTENTS

RABBIT'S FOOT
LUCKY

MONDAY, FEBRUARY 14

The furious flames had completely engulfed the tiny house sitting on the edge of town. A small crew of firefighters only worked to contain the scene. The structure was unsafe to enter, and nothing could be salvaged. Mason Dean stood back from the inferno, sweating in his gear despite the freezing temperatures. Since the town of Bartlett didn't see many house fires, he stood with his fellow first responders, mesmerized by the hypnotic flames licking the cold night sky.

As he lifted his arm to wipe the moisture from his face, he noticed a slight movement in his peripheral vision. It came from the small, decrepit shed that stood at the back of the property. There it was again… Something moved in the doorless entryway. Mason slowly backed away from his crew to see what caught his eye.

After peeking his head into the opening of the shed, he was surprised to find a child sitting on the floor. She made herself as small as possible in the corner as her wide eyes beckoned him to keep her presence a secret. Looking back over his shoulder, he made sure his teammates weren't watching him. Mason eased into the creaky shed to speak to the child.

Quietly, he asked, "Are you hurt?"

She didn't answer aloud, but she shook her head.

"Do you have any family in the house?"

Again, no audible answer. Just another head shake.

Mason kept his voice low and asked, "Where are your parents?"

This time, he could barely hear her answer. "Mommy said if this ever happened that she's already dead."

Surely, he didn't hear her correctly. Figuring the girl was suffering from shock, he tried another approach. "Will you come with me? Let me help you, and we'll find your mom."

Opting to not answer, the child adjusted her position to look away from him, giving Mason a glimpse of the black and white bunny in her lap. "Is this your pet?"

"It's just me and Ginger now. When they find us, they'll kill us too." The voice sounded ominous, especially coming from a child who could be no more than five or six years old, close in age to his own daughter. His heart broke for the girl.

Despite the juvenile source of the information, Mason knew he had to take it seriously. "I'm your friend now. If you'll trust me, a few of my friends will keep you safe." He extended his hand towards the girl. Timid fingers slowly reached back.

Nothing good happens after midnight. Kennedy knew this, but she answered her phone anyway, mostly just to stop the incessant ringing. Unknown numbers brought their own level of aggravation.

"Hello," she grumbled, her voice not disguising the fact that the ringing phone disturbed her slumber.

The woman greeted her by name, dismantling her sleepy theory that this was a wrong number. "I'm trying to reach Kennedy Hughes. Is this she?"

Sitting up in bed, wondering who could be calling her after one in the morning, Kennedy tried to shake off the sleepiness. "This is she. Who is this?"

"This is Marla Jamison with Child Protective Services. I apologize for the late call, but I was given your number by the Emergency Animal Clinic."

Child Protective Services? Emergency Animal Clinic? That raised more questions than answers. Even though Marla couldn't see through the phone, Kennedy shook her head in confusion as she responded, "What can I do for you?"

Marla Jamison took a minute to explain her situation. "There's been a house fire tonight, and a pet rabbit has been orphaned. The Emergency Animal Center said that you rescue animals and might help us out."

By this time, Kennedy was fully alert, still befuddled over why a CPS agent was calling about a rabbit. "Of course, I can help. Do I need to come get the bunny?"

"No, please stay where you are. We'll bring it to you."

By two, Kennedy had gotten dressed in jeans and a sweatshirt and waited for the bunny to arrive. She turned on the television, but she couldn't find any breaking news about a fire in the area. Just more ridiculous stories about the ridiculous new president of the United States. Kennedy got tired of hearing his spiel. Mocking him aloud, she muttered, "I just became president, and I love to hear myself talk, and I'd rather travel around the country than sit in the White House to do any actual work." She switched the TV back off.

In case Marla or whoever needed some coffee, she brewed a whole pot. Milo, her brindle pit bull, gave a little woof when he saw headlights appear through the front windows of the house. Kennedy didn't know what to expect, but two vehicles to deliver one rabbit seemed a bit excessive. A stocky lady got out of the sedan that pulled into her driveway first. She might've been fifty-ish with dark skin that might be appearing darker in the dim light. Leaving Milo at the door, Kennedy slid on her house shoes and went outside to greet her.

"Hey, you must be Marla. I'm Kennedy. Do you have the bunny in a cage or something?" She watched her own breath condense in the frigid air as she tried to glance into the backseat of the sedan.

Offering her hand, Marla answered in a maternal voice, "The bunny is riding in the SUV behind me. I'll get her now."

After they shook hands, Marla went to the back door of the idling SUV, leaving Kennedy standing next to the sedan. As the door to the SUV opened, the dome light illuminated the cab of the vehicle. Kennedy noticed the driver with his head turned to peer into the backseat. He wore a BFD sweatshirt, so he must've been the Bartlett fireman on the scene. He had a nice profile, strong jaw, and chiseled features. If Kennedy had to be interrupted after midnight, at least the handsome man offered a nice vision.

Marla eventually came away from the vehicle with a bunny in her arms. No cage. No kennel. No box. Kennedy found it odd that the man would allow a bunny to ride freely in his backseat. After gladly accepting the black and white bundle of fur from Marla, Kennedy prepared to go into the house.

"Do I need to sign any adoption papers? If you or the delivery guy need a cup of coffee, I put on a fresh pot," she offered, inwardly hoping the handsome fellow in the SUV might visit for a few minutes. Normally, Kennedy paid no attention to the opposite sex. She never offered attention, nor did she require it from a man, but this particular guy piqued her interest. Any man who went out of his way to ensure the safety of an orphaned bunny might be worth meeting.

Marla returned to her still-running sedan. "No paperwork, I just wanted to make sure someone compassionate gave the rabbit a loving home. Thank you for helping us out tonight."

Kennedy turned to take the bunny inside, but before she

made it to the front door, a small voice pierced the silence.

"No, I want to stay with Ginger!"

Kennedy turned back, surprised to see a small girl practically tumble out of the backseat of the SUV and run towards her. The fireman also rushed from the vehicle to chase after the girl.

A few minutes later, Kennedy settled in the living room of her house with Marla and the fireman. A baby gate was set up to close off the kitchen where Milo sat attentively, hoping for a chance to visit with the bunny and child. The girl, filthy and disheveled, cuddled with Ginger on a blanket on the floor in the corner of the living room, feeding fresh parsley to her beloved pet. Now that everyone was settled, explanations were in order.

Speaking quietly so as not to upset the child, Kennedy got the conversation started. "You didn't tell me the bunny's owner was a little girl. Don't you think she needs to keep her pet close by?"

Marla had taken off her pea coat and sat on the couch, clutching a mug of coffee with an expression of fear on her face. In the light, Kennedy could see the worry lines etched in Marla's almond-colored forehead. These lines were just as deep as the smile lines framing her mouth. Working for Child Protective Services must be difficult. Every happy ending for a child in the system started with a terrible beginning.

When Marla answered, she used her own hushed tone, "I don't like it either, but the fewer people who know about her, the better. We don't know everything about what happened with the house fire. Since we assume it was arson, we're going to put her into an emergency foster home, and that's easier to accomplish without a rabbit in tow. With everything she's gone through, we wanted to make sure the bunny was safe for her peace of mind."

"What's her name?" Kennedy didn't like being lied to, but she could see the situation was unorthodox.

Marla still spoke quietly. "We don't know. She doesn't really answer any questions. The paramedic assessed her at the scene and said she's suffering from a mild shock. Separating her from the bunny might not help the situation, but we need to get her to safety. I wasn't even informed about the child until she arrived at the fire department."

Kennedy turned her attention to Mason, the fireman, sitting in the chair to her right. He hadn't said a single word aside from a brief introduction, but it was time for him to contribute to the conversation.

His rich, deep voice answered without anyone asking him a direct question. "She's in fear for her life. I found her hiding in a shed behind the house, so I had our paramedic check her out, and then I snuck her away from the scene in a blanket. She rode back to the station in the engine with me and my crew, and we called Child Protective Services from there. Whatever's going on, it's best that the general public doesn't know where she is."

Kennedy could smell the lingering smoke on his clothes, proof that she was, in fact, awake. "Have you not been able to find her parents? Or whoever she lived with in the house?"

Marla shrugged her shoulders and replied, "I really can't go into detail with you, but it's safe to assume this girl is now an orphan. I'm taking it upon myself to keep her safe in the meantime."

Any level of threat against the small child made Kennedy feel defensive. Speaking fervently but still quietly, she pleaded with Marla, "So, you think she's in fear enough to sneak her away from a fire scene, and you don't want anyone to know where she is... But if you put her in a foster home, can't people track her through your paper trail? Will the foster parents be able to defend her from whatever she's in fear of?"

Again, Marla shrugged. Kennedy could tell she shrugged

from defeat and not indifference. "There aren't a lot of fosters readily available, and I don't have another option."

"The hell you don't!" exclaimed Mason.

His outburst caused the girl to whimper.

Kennedy and Marla spent a few minutes on the floor with the child, cooing and soothing her back to a calm state. Even though kids weren't her specialty, the little orphaned girl tugged at her heartstrings. Mason hovered over their shoulders as if he wanted to help, but Kennedy blocked his access to the frightened child.

After a few minutes, the girl quieted down. Kennedy's new package of arugula was now being fed to the bunny one leaf at a time, while the girl regained her contented state. The women moved back to the couch, where Kennedy made eye contact with the fireman and asked, "Mason, what other option does she have?"

"None," interjected Marla. "We have discussed this, and there's no other option."

Keeping his voice in a lower register, Mason responded, "Marla, you didn't see how she looked at me. I wouldn't have snuck her away from the scene if I thought the threat was imaginary. You need to skip the paperwork and let me take her home." Turning his attention to Kennedy, he further explained, "I'm registered as an emergency foster, but they have rules against girls going home with single men. My daughter is six, and Gracie would help this girl acclimate to a new setting until we can find some of her family."

Kennedy briefly wondered what kind of woman would leave a hot fireman like Mason but swiftly got her mind back on track. "Marla, I know y'all only came here because of the bunny, but I have to agree with Mason on this. She needs to keep her bunny with her, and she could really use a friend her own age about now. If there's even the slightest possibility that someone dangerous is looking for her, it sounds like keeping her off the record is for her best protection. What can you do to help her out?"

Marla's face took on a different expression, as if she couldn't decide between screaming or crying. "I have rules, Kennedy, and I don't have another option. Along with finding a foster family who is willing to take her tonight, I need to ensure they'll keep her off the records for a couple of days until we can sort this out. Regardless, the bunny must stay here. I already have my work cut out for me, so unless you're personally going to sign up to be an emergency foster, you don't even have a say in the matter."

"Sign me up." Speaking before thinking wasn't a problem Kennedy usually suffered from, but the compulsion to help outweighed any logical thought. "What do I need to fill out?"

Marla and Mason both stared at her in bewilderment.

"I'm serious. You can inspect my home, and I'll sign whatever forms are needed so you can check my background. I am begging you, don't advertise where this girl is staying. Come by every day and check on her if you want, but don't jeopardize her safety. She'll be fine with me."

Marla held out her hand towards Kennedy and said, "Give me your driver's license." Without further acknowledging Kennedy, Marla pulled out her cell phone to make a call. "Hello, Officer Walker, this is Marla Jamison. I need you to do me a favor off the record… yes, can you do a background check on Kennedy Lynn Hughes?" The exchange with the officer lasted less than five minutes. Marla never specifically told the officer why she wanted the background check performed, but she hung up the phone to make sure she had Kennedy's attention.

"Obviously, that wasn't an extensive check, but Officer Walker knows you and is willing to personally vouch for you."

Mason spoke up before she could continue. "I've worked several scenes and investigations with Officer Walker. He's a stand-up guy."

"I'll allow it for the night, Kennedy. Now, I'll have to do an inspection of your home. Do you have clothing or anything for this girl to change into?"

Clothes for a kid? She had a couple of Halloween costumes for her dog, but that wouldn't suffice. In a split second, Kennedy came up with a solution. "My neighbor keeps her nieces all the time, and they have a closet full of clothes that should be her size. I'll just go borrow some. Go ahead and inspect my home; nothing is off limits. I'll be right back." After putting Milo in the backyard for the home inspection, Kennedy rushed out to retrieve the necessities.

Once outside, the blast of cold February air slapped Kennedy in the face. Before her neighbor went out of town last week, she asked Kennedy to keep an eye on her house. Fortunately, she wouldn't have to wake Pennie to enter her house at two in the morning. Then she considered what she just signed up for. A child. In her twenty-six years, she never once felt the tug of a single maternal molecule. No biological clock. No baby fever. What just happened?

She knew what it was like to be an orphan. Even though she was eighteen when her parents died, she learned quickly how to survive on her own. This little girl would need guidance and support and all that parental stuff. Maybe Kennedy could find a helpful video on YouTube to instruct her throughout the process of being a guardian.

She punched in the code to the garage and entered Pennie's house, escaping the frigid temperatures for a few minutes. Kennedy wondered about her neighbor sometimes. Pennie was friendly and outgoing, but she sure had trouble deciding what kind of man she wanted to date. After a summer fling with a cop, then a quick relationship with a scientist, she suddenly got back together with the cop to go live on a houseboat for a while. Kennedy didn't understand what it was like to be flighty or co-dependent like that.

Regardless of how Pennie chose to live her life, Kennedy would be in her debt for a while. Officer James Walker, Pennie's brother, just gave a personal reference to Marla on her behalf. And now, she would be borrowing personal items from Pennie's house without permission. Kennedy never knew what it was like to have siblings, but she felt a pang of jealousy anytime Pennie's brothers and sister came around. Even though they always seemed to be having a blast, Kennedy always politely refused invitations to join them for get-togethers.

Right now, she simply felt grateful that Pennie gave her the alarm code to her house. Who would've guessed that Kennedy would need to pilfer some kid's clothing in the middle of the night? Using a garbage bag, she borrowed two of everything she could find. Pajamas, dresses, pants, shirts, coats, undergarments, socks, shoes, and hair bows. She even took a teddy bear from the bed. Pennie was generous to a fault, so Kennedy knew her neighbor would have no problem lending this stuff to the little girl in need.

Being sure to re-arm the security system, Kennedy rushed back to her own house ten minutes later, feeling a bit like a crooked Santa with a sack full of plunder. She walked into her own living room to find Marla already seated back on the couch, writing in a notebook. It probably wouldn't take ten full minutes to inspect her twelve-hundred-square-foot, sparsely furnished house. Mason sat on the floor next to the child, encouraging her to speak.

"Well, I have clothes and stuff. What do you think, Marla?" Kennedy asked breathlessly.

"The variety of snakes and stuff you have disturbs me, but

the only problem I have that pertains to the foster situation is that you don't have a bedroom set up for her. Otherwise, your home is fine. I didn't even find a stash of alcohol. The front room looks like it should be a dining room, but it's full of plants. What's that about?"

Kennedy walked to the front room and explained to Marla all about her springtime project. "Normally, I'd just keep these few animals in here, but this is also where my garden begins each year. These are all the seeds I'm germinating. The peppers, tomatoes, and squashes do better when you start them indoors. These larger plants are ones I'm propagating from the garden last year since they performed so well." She proudly displayed hundreds of seedlings, knowing only the best of the vegetables would be planted in her own garden, while the rest would be given away. Marla must have thought these were marijuana plants or something; the relief on her face was noticeable. They walked back towards the living room where Kennedy kept talking.

"I have three bedrooms. Two of them just store supplies for foster animals, but I can consolidate that stuff into one room. By the end of tomorrow, or today, or whatever this is, I'll have a room set up for her. We just need to get a little sleep first."

Marla and Mason both nodded. Mason offered the most appreciative look when he said, "Thank you for doing this. I'm here to help; please call me if you need me." He took out his phone and got her number before he left. Marla gave Kennedy a very maternal hug before she left. It had been eight years since Kennedy felt a hug like that, and it flooded her with warm emotions.

"Okay, sweetie. Why don't we let Ginger go to bed for the night? Then you can get cleaned up and get some rest too." Kennedy tried her most comforting tone, and it worked. She allowed Milo back into the kitchen before turning her attention back to the girl.

The child sat up, acknowledging that she heard Kennedy without saying a word. She obediently picked up the bundle of fur and looked expectantly at her new mother figure.

Kennedy had already prepared a kennel for the bunny before they arrived, so she grabbed it from the next room. The cage measured two feet by four feet, and it had been lined with paper. She added a litter box, along with a cardboard box filled with timothy hay for Ginger to munch on, and the bunny went in the cage without hesitation.

The little girl seemed pleased that Ginger took to her temporary home so well, so Kennedy tried to encourage her more. "I think tomorrow, we can set up a bigger home for Ginger after we get your room set up. Do you think y'all will be happy staying with me for a while?"

Still smiling just slightly, the girl nodded.

"Good. I'm going to get a bath ready for you. Do you need help washing your hair or anything?"

Another nod.

During her tenure as a veterinary technician, Kennedy had bathed many a dog and cat. She even bathed the occasional snake and ferret. This would be the first time she ever bathed a kid. While water filled the tub in the hall bathroom, she made sure soap and shampoo were available. Remembering she had some bath bombs that a coworker gave her at Christmas, she brought them for the kid to enjoy too.

The girl cooperated with the bathing process and allowed Kennedy to scrub the smoky smell from her hair. Kennedy spoke soothing words about bubbles and warm water, just filling the silence and letting the girl get used to her voice, much like she would do with a frightened puppy.

She had to drain the dirty water and fill the tub again to ensure the girl actually got clean. The child expressed fascination with the bath bombs and seemed to immerse herself in the experience. Kennedy took the opportunity to see if the girl would open up.

"My name is Kennedy. You can call me Ken if you want. What do you want me to call you?"

The big, sapphire-blue eyes looked up, and the girl spoke so softly that Kennedy read her lips more than she heard her voice. "Joy."

Kennedy took a deep breath and smiled at the headway; her heart flooded with happiness that the girl trusted her enough to say one word. While Joy dried off, Kennedy found some underwear and warm pajamas for her to wear. She then took the time to blow dry Joy's long hair, which turned out to be brownish blonde now that the filth had been washed out. Since the little girl seemed to savor the attention, Kennedy brushed her hair for a few extra minutes after it had dried. Using a spare toothbrush, they finished the bedtime preparations. Finally, it became time to find sleeping arrangements for a few hours.

Milo loved kids, but she didn't know if Joy loved dogs. The girl still wasn't talkative, so Kennedy led her to the baby gate and asked if she wanted to pet Milo. Joy boldly reached through the gate, causing Milo to respond with massive tail wagging and slobbery kisses to the tiny hand. Feeling comfortable, Kennedy removed the gate and asked Joy to follow her to the master bedroom. Milo followed without being asked.

Kennedy carried Ginger's cage with her so they could all get settled in the small master bedroom. Joy and Milo took the bed. Ginger took the floor next to the bed. Kennedy got out an extra blanket and took the floor at the foot of the bed. By the time she got comfortable on the floor, Joy and Milo were sound asleep, spooning each other.

Kennedy glanced at her phone. 4:37 a.m. Maybe she could catch a few hours of shuteye before the sun officially rose over this Monday.

Instead of going straight into a peaceful sleep, Kennedy went straight into dreamland. Even during slumber, her brain attempted to make logical sense of what just happened. Her brain told her that the activities of the last few hours wouldn't allow for peaceful rest, and she should've expected the fitful sleep. After her subconscious escorted her to the next phase of dreamtime, the imagery didn't consist of the orphaned girl or the black and white bunny. The images were much more disturbing.

The fireman. Mason Dean. His dark hair was cut close on the sides and slightly longer on top. Despite the winter season, his tanned face and thick lashes made his honey-colored eyes almost glow. Eyes that seemed to see right through her. The fire department sweatshirt didn't reveal much, but he stood at least six-foot-three with a lean build. He exuded strength as well as exhibiting monumental integrity with the handling of Joy and Ginger.

Then her brain remembered Joy. During the next phase of her dream, Kennedy's brain reminded her that the kid would be hard work. A room needed to be set up. Basic supplies needed to be purchased. She needed to buy a kid's toothbrush and toothpaste. Not just any toothpaste, but something kid friendly. A mental checklist of kid supplies occupied her subconscious during the remainder of her sleep.

By eight that morning, Kennedy woke up wondering why she felt anxiety about toothpaste. The only thing she vividly remembered from her dreams was the image of Mason Dean. There was no time to fixate on the hunk; too much needed to happen. Wiping the sleep from her eyes, she got up from the floor to find that Joy and Milo were already awake, the girl lovingly petting the pampered dog in the middle of the king-sized bed.

"Good morning, Joy. Are you ready to get up? You can help me feed the chickens and the other critters." Kennedy tried to look eager about her morning chores, eliciting a smile from Joy.

After getting Joy dressed in some jeans and a sweater that were just a tad loose, they went outside to let the dozen hens out of their coop. Her subdivision of Bartlett, a suburb of Memphis, Tennessee, didn't officially allow chickens. Kennedy made it a point not to keep any noisy roosters and to pass out eggs to her neighbors, so no one would complain about her backyard flock.

Joy carried a bowl of grapes with her and squealed with delight when the chickens surrounded her, begging for a treat. The little girl's giggles were contagious, causing Kennedy to laugh along as she refilled the food and water containers. They gathered the few eggs from the nesting boxes and went back into the warm house.

Kennedy had taken the opportunity to snap a few candid pictures of Joy gathering eggs and feeding grapes to the chickens. She sent the pictures to Marla with a message.

All is good so far.

Marla replied with a smiley face emoji.

While Milo ate his kibble, Joy ate a bowl of Frosted Flakes at the table with Kennedy. The galley-style kitchen had a small eating area, but a two-seater pub table was the only thing that fit in the space without overpowering it. Up until this morning, Kennedy never even needed the second chair.

Between bites of cereal, Kennedy asked a few questions to see if Joy would speak. The questions were only met with smiles, nods, and head shakes. She didn't feel like forcing a conversation would be fruitful, so Kennedy kept the topics light while maintaining a calm tone. They moved back to the living room after finishing the quick breakfast, where Kennedy turned on some cartoons to occupy the child for a few minutes.

Letting the Smurfs take Kennedy back to her childhood, she thought of how things used to be... And how things were now. A dozen years ago, the same kitchen held a table for four. It seemed crowded, but she loved being close to her parents. *Crowded* was never a problem back then. The carefree childhood and worry-free days before becoming an adult had faded to a distant memory.

Back to the present. Kennedy shouldered all the responsibilities that went along with being an adult, and now, she'd be shouldering the responsibilities of spontaneous motherhood as well. Since Joy appeared preoccupied with the cartoon, Kennedy needed to take care of her own morning routine.

First, a shower. Kennedy patiently waited for the water to heat up before she jumped in. A glance in the mirror revealed dark circles under her aqua-blue eyes, a direct result of the fractured sleep. Her dishwater-blond hair fell halfway down her back. She never bothered to color or style it since a ponytail or a braid were always appropriate for her casual existence. Thanks to her active lifestyle, along with the manual labor of gardening and working as a veterinary technician, she had toned arms and legs. In fact, Kennedy was proud of her body. At five-foot-nine, she felt statuesque and confident.

The hurried shower allowed Kennedy to be back in the living room in time to see an episode of *Dora the Explorer* starting. Leaving her hair wet, she decided she could handle some inside chores before tackling the errands of the day. After feeding her menagerie of critters with crickets, pellets, and salads, she rejoined Joy in the living room. The child seemed to be mesmerized by the show, so Kennedy waited for *Dora* to end before she suggested anything else.

She also took the opportunity to respond to the text from her neighbor. Pennie's alarm system notified her that the garage opened in the middle of the night. Kennedy assured her that everything was okay, and she only needed to borrow a few necessities. At some point, Kennedy would have to come up with a plausible explanation of why she had a kid without sharing all the details. If Joy were in any danger, Kennedy would have to keep her true identity secret. Not that she knew anything about the kid's identity herself, but Joy being the lone survivor of a housefire might not be information she needed to share with anyone. Finally, *Dora* finished exploring, so they could get the day started.

"Joy, we have to set up a bedroom for you today. Do you want to pick which room you want?"

Without speaking, Joy obediently followed Kennedy to the tiny hallway where they could see into the two smaller bedrooms. Since her parents' death, the rooms had never been set up with beds. A few kennels were stacked in one, while a few aquariums were set up in the other. The colorful king snake in one of the aquariums captured Joy's attention, and in an instant, her face was pressed against the glass.

"Do you want to hold the snake?" she inquired softly.

Without a sound, Joy nodded. Kennedy unclipped the screen top and gently picked up Medusa. The little girl fearlessly accepted the five-foot-long slithery creature and grinned from ear to ear.

"How about we make this your room, and Medusa can stay in here with you and Ginger?"

Another silent nod, but the grin remained on her face. Kennedy left the girl sitting on the floor with the snake while moving the extra tanks into the other bedroom. It only took ten minutes of moving to get the room emptied of everything except for Medusa's aquarium. Then she swept the floor to get ready to move furniture into the space. Internally, Kennedy wasn't sure how she felt about letting Joy have this room. Seeing the girl in the same bedroom where Kennedy spent her childhood years might evoke too many haunting memories. Pushing down the flashbacks, she tried to refocus on the current situation with the child.

"Do you like the color?" The light-sage wall color was chosen because it was in the clearance section at the paint store, so it wouldn't hurt her feelings to pick out something new. As expected, Joy nodded in agreement with the color. Kennedy moved the rabbit cage into the room, thankful that Ginger was far too large to become a tasty morsel for Medusa the snake.

The small room left enough space for a twin bed and a dresser. Maybe a tiny desk or toy box could be squeezed in. The plantation shutters covered the window, so curtains were never necessary. If Joy stayed longer than a week or two, they might have to add some curtains and wall decorations to add some personality to the space. The closet only held extra blankets, so they were quickly relocated to the adjacent bedroom. Now, they needed to find some furniture.

Looking at her Jeep Wrangler in the garage, Kennedy reconsidered the idea of furniture shopping. How could she get a bed or anything else back home? *Oh yeah!* Her neighbor left the keys to her truck with Kennedy and requested that she drive it occasionally to keep the battery strong. A few minutes later, Kennedy and Joy drove to the Salvation Army in the jacked-up Ford truck since thrifting would be the best solution to find furniture on a budget.

The selection of furniture was plenty to choose from without being overwhelming. With Joy sticking close by, they came across a beautiful daybed that reminded Kennedy of the one she slept on as a child. She shook off the feeling of nostalgia when Joy expressed interest in a twin-sized bed with a wrought-iron headboard. They quickly found a tiny table that could be used as a nightstand and a three-drawer dresser. A child-sized wooden desk might fit in the room, and for thirty dollars, Kennedy didn't pass up the deal. Fortunately, the Salvation Army sold new mattresses, so they got all the furniture they needed in one stop.

The gracious workers at the store helped load the purchases in the truck and secured it all with twine. The fact that she would have no help unloading it would be a problem for later. When she got home, Kennedy backed the truck up against her garage before they switched to the Jeep. More shopping remained. Maybe a neighbor would help unload the furniture when they got back.

Once Upon a Child offered great clothing on consignment, and God must have been working this miracle in advance… They had a clearance sale. Once Kennedy found out Joy's size by having her try on a few items, she bought almost every shirt, coat, dress, sweater, jacket, pajamas, and pants that might fit. After they checked out, Kennedy knew they had purchased over a hundred items, but they all managed to fit into three bags. Kids clothing certainly didn't take up much real estate.

They moved on to Walmart. Some things simply must be purchased new. Joy stayed quiet throughout the trip, but she lit up at the sight of the soft pink bedding set. After loading the bed-in-a-bag into the cart, Kennedy took a guess at her undergarment size and picked out a variety of socks and shoes too. They eventually found themselves in the pet supply section of the store. Kennedy explained that a small dog playpen would make a great, spacious area for Ginger inside her bedroom. Joy offered another smile without a word. A few more pet supplies joined the overflowing cart.

Despite the crowded basket, Kennedy still needed to get some toothpaste for the girl. Why was she so worried about toothpaste? They also picked out some kid friendly bath soap, shampoo, *Dora the Explorer* bubble bath, and other toiletries.

Finally, they made it to the checkout.

Joy remained wide-eyed, seemingly out of sorts with all the activity. Kennedy had no way of knowing what her life experiences had been up until now or if the girl was still dealing with shock. To keep communication open, Kennedy continued to narrate their movements, giving Joy the opportunity to stay engaged. When she mentioned lunch, there was no response. Kids, in general, gladly ate chicken nuggets, so Kennedy relied on her old faithful for a quick meal.

A drive-thru Chick-fil-A lunch hardly delayed their progress, allowing them to make it back home by two. Not bad. Kennedy cut tags off the clothes, while Joy watched more cartoons. She eventually got a load of clothes going in the washer. Not one to waste the opportunity, she chose to use her neighbor's washer for the bedding. Marla sent a message just checking in, and Kennedy replied that everything was going smoothly so far. The only problem remaining had to do with the furniture... It was time to figure out how to get it all unloaded.

The small table and desk were no problem. The mattress, however uncooperative, made it into the house with some effort. One piece at a time, the bed frame was transported into the house as well. Kennedy's fingers hurt from the cold as she eyed the final item remaining in the truck. As she stood behind the truck, contemplating the dresser, a red Suburban pulled into her driveway. The sunshine reflected off the windshield, obscuring the driver, until the door finally opened to reveal Mason when he stepped out. Then an adorable girl jumped out of the passenger-side backseat.

"Looks like you could use some help?" Mason asked, shielding his eyes from the sun.

"A little help would be nice," Kennedy managed to answer calmly despite her racing pulse. Why did she react so strongly to his presence? "Let's introduce the girls first."

Joy and Gracie sat on the couch watching *Dora* together a few minutes later. Milo sat between them, soaking up the attention from the children. Kennedy marveled at the similarities and the differences. The girls were about the same size, both with golden-brown hair. Gracie watched TV with honey-colored eyes like her dad, while Joy had sapphire-blue eyes. The biggest difference had nothing to do with genetics, though.

Gracie's face possessed a healthy glow. Her vibrant personality was almost visible. She seemed to have a perpetual smile and an inquisitive, fearless nature. The thick mane of hair on Gracie's head was shiny and full of body. The swoopy bangs and wispy layers were a cute yet manageable style for a six-year-old. Her outfit of a pink sweater, cream leggings, and fuzzy boots had been put together perfectly. The beautiful little girl obviously inherited her good looks from her gorgeous dad.

By contrast, Joy looked pale and delicate. No exuding personality. She didn't seem particularly bashful, but she certainly wasn't outgoing, remaining silent for the most part. Her long stringy hair needed some attention and deep conditioning. The ill-fitting clothes, even though they served their purpose for today, only made the girl look more frail. Kennedy only had experience with animals, but she could tell this particular rescue needed some work. Now that she could clearly see the deficiencies, she could take direct actions to improve Joy's quality of life.

Back outside, Kennedy redirected her attention to the handsome fireman. Now out of earshot of the girls, they could talk freely.

"She's only spoken once so far when she told me her name is Joy. The whole time we ran errands, she only smiled and nodded. Hopefully, Gracie can help her open up a little."

Mason smiled. "That's a start. She's smiling and not crying at least. We might need to be worried that she isn't processing the whole situation, but I don't know the best way to approach any of that proactively."

He jumped into the back of the truck, and Kennedy took notice of his perfect backside hugged by his jeans. As Mason pushed the dresser towards the tailgate, Kennedy watched his muscles flex, visible under his form-fitting, long-sleeved knit shirt. She had seen good-looking men before, but Mason was the epitome of magnificent. She snapped out of it in time to help him lower the dresser to the ground.

After they worked together to haul the last piece of furniture into the house, Mason unexpectedly stayed to help her put the bed together. They positioned the bed at an angle, coming out from the corner of the room. The dresser went against one wall, while the desk went against another. Mason lifted the snake's aquarium off its stand and moved it to the top of the dresser. Clearing out the aquarium base created a little more space in the room. The bedroom looked acceptable for Joy by the time they got it all arranged.

While Mason stayed with the girls, Kennedy relocated the truck to where it belonged next door and moved all the bedding into the dryer. Back home, she moved all the clothes to her own dryer. She took a few minutes to set up the animal playpen as Ginger the bunny's new home in the corner of Joy's room.

Gracie expressed some interest in Medusa the snake, spurring Kennedy to remember her manners. She introduced Gracie and Mason to the rest of her variety of animals. Pickles the rat, Yams the hamster, Eragon the bearded dragon, Princess the ball python, Kasey the corn snake, Rimshot the tarantula, and Cleo the scorpion. She explained that anytime a pocket pet gets surrendered at the clinic where she works, she would bring it home. Rescuing animals was her thing, so it made sense that she readily agreed to invite Joy into her home.

Even though the endless cycle of chores distracted Kennedy from the time, her stomach reminded her that she needed to find some dinner. Taking a seat for a moment, she tried to determine a good dinner plan. "So... I'm getting hungry. Were y'all planning to stick around for dinner? I was thinking of ordering pizza."

Mason smiled. "We didn't really have plans. I guess we weren't the Valentine's dates you expected, but we'd love to take you two out for dinner."

Kennedy had completely forgotten about Valentine's Day. It was just another day for her. Dating was never a priority, not that she ever had any real relationship with a man. In fact, she couldn't recall ever being invited to any real Valentine's dinner date. Of course, Mason only invited her because he wanted to help with Joy. No reason to think the fireman might be personally interested in her.

"I didn't have a date anyway, and we don't want to interrupt your daddy-daughter time. We can just order a pizza so y'all can continue with your plans." As much as she appreciated Mason's kind attempt to include them, she tried to gently back out of his invitation.

Mason smiled again. Goodness, he had a nice smile. "It's hard to believe you didn't have a date, but we're just going to find a deli or some other restaurant that won't be crowded. We insist that you join us."

A half hour later, the four of them waited in line to order dinner at Jason's Deli. Kennedy felt distracted by all the things she still needed to get for Joy. Fortunately, Mason had a spare booster seat in the SUV for her. It never even occurred to Kennedy that she needed one. What had she done? This wasn't as simple as housing an abandoned bunny. This was a kid. No instruction manual or checklist included.

Joy still hadn't spoken that day, and she appeared overwhelmed with the restaurant setting. Just like Kennedy was out of sorts with the parental setting. At least Gracie appeared perfectly at ease, along with her dad. She showed a great deal of astuteness for her age as she ordered a grilled cheese sandwich with a side of fruit.

Gracie turned to Joy, pointed out a picture of the sandwich, and asked, "Would you like the same thing I'm getting?"

Joy smiled and nodded. Kennedy felt a load of gratefulness at the sweet gesture. Mason and Kennedy added their sandwich requests, and he paid the bill, while she took their order number. Even though only a few empty tables remained, she managed to claim a spot and display the number placard to serve as a beacon for their food. Mason proactively filled drink cups for everyone before joining them at the table. While they waited for their dinner, Kennedy wanted to spend a few minutes engaging Joy to see if she would say anything. "Joy, have you eaten here before?"

She shook her head. No.

"What's your favorite food?"

She shrugged her shoulders.

"Did you like the chicken nuggets you ate for lunch?"

She nodded. Yes.

Kennedy made eye contact with Mason. If he could read her mind, he would know she needed help. She had no capacity to manage this situation. What did she get herself into? Buying a bed and some clothes… That was easy. Developing a relationship with Joy… Not so easy. She feared things might get worse before they got better.

Keeping his tone calm, Mason offered some assistance. "Everything's still really new to Joy. She just needs a little time and encouragement." Turning his attention to the little girl, he asked, "Joy, will you tell us if you need anything else? Are you okay right now?"

Joy nodded. Yes.

Mason continued, "Remember, we're your friends. We want to help you and keep you safe. Do you remember my name?"

"Mason," Joy whispered.

"Very good. Do you remember her name?"

"Ken," she answered, barely audible.

Mason kept the momentum going, if the two words could be considered momentum. "The weather will be warmer tomorrow, and I'm taking Gracie to the zoo. Would you like to go with us?"

Joy nodded.

"I need to hear you say it. Would you like to go with us?"

"Yes."

The server brought the food at that time, giving them something else to focus on. Kennedy was impressed that Mason found a way to interact with Joy, but he should have run the zoo thing by her first. Once everyone started eating, Mason addressed her concern.

"I wasn't sure if you had to work tomorrow. What's your schedule look like?"

Kennedy replied, "I work ten-hour shifts Wednesday through Saturday. My days off are always Sunday, Monday, and Tuesday, so I don't work tomorrow."

Again, with his gorgeous smile, Mason said, "Then you're free to go to the zoo with us... Unless you want a few hours to yourself while I take the girls."

The Memphis Zoo ranked as one of the top zoos in the USA, so Kennedy rarely missed a chance to visit. She hesitated because the idea of spending a day with Mason and the two little girls seemed dangerously close to family time. She hadn't experienced any semblance of family time since before the death of her parents.

While Kennedy considered how to answer, an older lady stopped on her way through the dining area and commented, "What a beautiful family! The girls look so close in age; you must've had them back-to-back."

Laughing at the absurdity, Kennedy responded, "Yeah, it seems like they both got here at the same time." The lady moved on with a chuckle, and Kennedy reconsidered the zoo.

"You know if I go to the zoo with you, everyone's going to think we're a family. More comments like that one. Doesn't that make you uncomfortable?" Kennedy inquired.

"Absolutely not. I don't care what people think. Maybe, in a small way, we are a family. I can pick y'all up around ten in the morning, and we can eat lunch at the zoo?" He said it like a question, but Kennedy had the impression he wouldn't be accepting "no" as an answer.

Against her better judgement, Kennedy agreed. She only survived this long by keeping relationships at bay. Being hurt emotionally couldn't happen if she prevented the emotions to begin with. She seriously had no idea what she was getting into here.

Gracie managed to entertain them for the rest of their dinner. She giggled and laughed at her own jokes, causing Joy to brighten just being in her company. Mason and Kennedy didn't get a chance for any small talk once Gracie took over, giving them a mealtime refreshingly devoid of any serious topics.

After dinner, they all returned to Kennedy's house. Mason watched TV with the girls while Kennedy put the clean sheets on the bed and put away the clean clothes. As she sorted the clothes,

Kennedy realized they didn't get any toys, coloring books, or anything to mentally stimulate Joy. She also realized she didn't have a babysitter for when she returned to work on Wednesday. Geez, this motherhood deal would be difficult.

She returned to the living room, shaking her head and mentioned to Mason, "You know, I didn't get any toys today. And now I know she needs a booster seat. Maybe I need to skip the zoo tomorrow and get some more things for Joy."

Instead of Mason answering, Gracie piped up. "We brought some stuff. Daddy, let's get the toys."

They went outside, leaving Joy and Kennedy waiting in the house. A minute later, Gracie brought a humongous stuffed bunny to Joy, and the expression on Joy's face was priceless as she accepted the fuzzy doll. Then Kennedy took her turn being astounded as Mason brought in a large tote full of toys and books. They went to Joy's room and unloaded all the goodies, including several décor items. Mason screwed a small hook into the ceiling and hung a mesh canopy over Joy's bed, making it worthy of a princess.

Kennedy was astonished, feeling all kinds of appreciation yet unable to come up with words to express herself. "This stuff is perfect. I don't even know what to say."

Mason pulled her back to the living room, leaving the girls in the bedroom to sort through the toys. Once they were seated next to each other on the couch, he said, "You don't have to say anything. What you did, keeping her out of the system, that's a big deal. I promised her that I'd keep her safe, and I was so angry when Marla wouldn't let me bring her home. If you didn't step in, who knows what would've happened. I really do feel like she's in danger."

Kennedy knew she committed to something big, but she had trouble wrapping her head around the idea that anyone wanted to harm Joy. "Do you really think someone dangerous is looking for Joy? She's just a kid."

"I really do. She isn't talking right now, but her mom warned her something like this might happen. We don't know the full story, but I intend to find out and keep her safe in the meantime. I took off work for the next two weeks so I can be available for whatever she needs."

The thought of the studly fireman hanging around for two weeks made Kennedy slightly apprehensive. Something akin to affection stirred inside her, but she couldn't focus on that feeling while concentrating on Joy. "For now, I need to think of an explanation for why I all of a sudden have a kid. Anyone who knows me also knows that I was an only child with no cousins or anything. My parents died when I was eighteen, and I don't have any other family. Assuming I don't need to tell people that she survived a recent house fire, I need something plausible to tell them."

Slowly nodding in agreement, Mason suggested, "Maybe you can say she's a distant cousin of some sort, and her mom died. Child Protective Services found you through family records, and you agreed to foster Joy to keep her out of a group home. Even as we speak, I know Marla is looking for Joy's family, and who knows what she'll find?"

"I'll stick to that story and try to stay vague to anyone who's curious. For Joy's sake, I hope Marla finds her real family and that there's no real danger."

Before the conversation progressed any further, Joy and Gracie joined them in the living room, both stifling yawns. It seemed that the longest day ever was taking its toll on the children, and Kennedy concurred.

"It looks like I need to get Gracie home. We all need some rest, but I'll be here at ten in the morning to pick you two up for the zoo," Mason said as he got up, stretching a little from his own long day.

"Joy, will you please go put on the pajamas I left on your bed while I walk Mason outside?"

Joy obediently returned to her room. Kennedy followed Mason and Gracie back out into the cold night air. Knowing the routine, Gracie jumped into the passenger-side backseat of the SUV and proceeded to fasten herself into the booster seat. Mason opened his driver's door, while Kennedy, again, felt herself at a loss for words.

"So... um, thanks for dinner and for bringing the things for Joy."

Turning back with a smile, he replied, "Thanks to you, for taking care of Joy. It's been a while since I've enjoyed Valentine's Day, but tonight was great."

He followed up the endearing statement with a warm hug, and Kennedy soaked it up. She returned the hug briefly before he backed away. "See you in the morning," she whispered softly.

She waved as they pulled out of the driveway, partially blocking her eyes from the headlights. The surge of emotions was more than Kennedy knew how to handle. The light scent of his woodsy cologne clung to her, reminding her of his embrace long after they drove away.

"Okay, Ken. Shake it off. Get into mom mode," she told herself as she walked back into the house. She found Joy in her room, wearing pajamas, sitting on the floor next to her bunny. Milo sat with her. He had long since been desensitized to pocket pets, and he acted like he was the size of a bunny rather than a seventy-pound pit bull.

"I need to put the chickens up. Then we can finish getting ready for bed."

Joy nodded in response. Kennedy returned several minutes later to change into her own pajamas. She wanted to develop a nightly routine with the girl, so they started by brushing their teeth together. Then she tucked Joy into bed and read *Sleep Book* by Dr. Seuss from the stash of books that Mason donated.

"It's time to sleep now, but we'll get up early to take care of the animals before we go to the zoo." Kennedy kissed her on the forehead and turned out the light, thankful that Gracie donated a princess nightlight to plug into the corner of the room.

Instead of exiting the room, Kennedy turned back, standing in the doorway. "You know I'm right across the hall if you need me." She could see Joy nod in the soft glow of the nightlight.

TUESDAY, FEBRUARY 15

Kennedy awoke around six, feeling trapped. Literally, not figuratively. Her blanket held her tightly on both sides, preventing her from sitting up or rolling in either direction. Finally opening her eyes, she found Milo on one side and Joy on the other. Neither budged despite her struggling. After some repeated nudging, Milo finally jumped down and stretched on the floor so Kennedy could creep out of bed.

She took care of the hens and fed all the pocket pets, thankful that Joy stayed asleep the whole time. Shutting the door to her bedroom, Kennedy took a shower, trusting Milo to keep Joy company. The bathroom mirror showed an image that concerned her. Kennedy didn't wear makeup daily, and she rarely styled her hair. Today might be a good day to change things up from the plain Jane in the mirror.

She spent a few minutes blow drying her long hair before ironing it flat. Kennedy added a little mascara and a touch of bronzer to emphasize her high cheekbones. She hesitated a moment before applying some tinted lip balm. Pleased with the finished product in the mirror, she turned her attention to clothes. *Feminine* might not be the best way to describe her wardrobe. Skinny blue jeans, white t-shirt, black leather jacket, and high-top sneakers would be her best choice for the day.

Time to focus on the kid. Kennedy had never spent time with children, and she assumed they mostly woke up fussy and bratty. After some gentle prodding, Joy surprisingly got out of bed with a pleasant expression on her face. They ate another bowl of Frosted Flakes together before proceeding with anything else.

Bath time elicited more smiles and giggles from the girl, and Kennedy treated Joy's hair with a deep conditioner. She added a little mousse before she dried it. Joy seemed to relish the attention. Kennedy felt her heart melting as they bonded over the simple routine.

Joy sat still for a few extra minutes while Kennedy French braided the top section of her hair and then finished by gathering all her hair into a high ponytail. The mousse helped the ponytail look full of body. Joy's face still had a pale complexion, but Kennedy couldn't bring herself to apply bronzer to a girl who could be no more than six years old. A little time in the sun would eventually introduce some natural color. Thankfully, they would both be getting some sunshine that day.

Joy's outfit mimicked Kennedy's. Blue jeans, sneakers, white T-shirt, and a black cardigan sweater. Maybe she'd never considered kids before now, but the feeling of having a little mini-me was borderline exhilarating.

Mason would be there within an hour to pick them up, so they put Milo on a leash to take him for a quick walk. The warmer weather today provided a wonderful break from the cold snap of the previous week.

As they walked, Kennedy tried to lure Joy into a conversation.

"Hey Joy, do you know what kind of bird that is?" she asked, pointing at a blue jay.

Joy shook her head.

Dang it. She kept trying. "That's a blue jay. Blue is my favorite color. What's your favorite color?"

Joy shrugged her shoulders.

Dang it again. Remembering how Mason got her to talk last night, Kennedy tried again with a more direct approach. "Joy, remember, I'm your friend. Please talk to me and tell me your favorite color."

"Pink."

"Thank you for telling me. Do you like your hair how I fixed it?"

"Yes."

Freaking one-word answers. This was frustrating, but Kennedy accepted it as progress. During the journey through the neighborhood, Joy continued to answer a variety of questions that only required one-word answers. She felt some relief that the girl seemed to know names of colors, as well as identifying squirrels and a few other items. Before now, she had no way of knowing what all Joy knew or didn't know. Did her mom teach her things? Or *Dora the Explorer*?

Although the walk only took a half hour, company arrived while they were gone. Kennedy could see the dark sedan parked in the driveway when they rounded the corner to her block. Immediately, she panicked and wondered if the vehicle brought imminent danger. She moved in front of the girl as if she might shield Joy from what was coming. Before her heart beat out of her chest, Kennedy recognized Marla standing by the car. The instinctive reaction to protect Joy must be what the *Mama Bear* comparison was all about.

Marla greeted Kennedy with a hug and informed her that unscheduled visits were still required even though the foster situation was off the books. Then Marla did a double take.

"Her name is Joy," Kennedy said.

"Is that really you?" Marla inquired.

Joy nodded.

Kennedy intervened, "She needs to hear your answer, Joy."

"Yes."

Marla's inquisitive gaze alternated from the adult to the child. Curious as to why Marla behaved this way, Kennedy took another look at Joy. The walk in the sunshine brought a little flush of color to Joy's cheeks, and the healthy glow made her unrecognizable, along with the clean, appropriately sized clothes and styled hair. She no longer resembled the shell of a child who walked into her house only thirty-two hours ago.

Rather than stand in the driveway, Kennedy motioned for everyone to come inside. She encouraged Joy to show her room to Marla, and then she turned her attention to making a cold brew caramel coffee. Looking at the ingredients, she was reminded of when she was kid. Her mom would prepare her the children's version of the beverage that was more milk than coffee, but she loved it. To pass on the tradition, she mixed a mostly milk version of the cold brew for Joy.

Marla spoke first when they all met back in the living room. "I'm impressed with the room. That's quite an accomplishment for one day. I knew you had your hands full yesterday, so I didn't bother trying to visit." She turned her attention to Joy. "What's your favorite part of the room?"

Joy looked like she wanted to answer but couldn't find the words. Kennedy tried to help her along. "What's your favorite? Is it the bed, the nightlight, or the desk?" She continued to use a reassuring tone.

Shaking her head, Joy opened her mouth to speak again. It took a second, but she managed to say three words instead of one. "Dusa the snake."

Thrilled with the response, Kennedy answered, "I think Medusa likes you too."

Marla indicated that she wanted to talk to Kennedy

privately, so they found another cartoon for Joy to watch so the adults could move to the front porch.

"Her name isn't Joy. It's Jillian Olive Young. Maybe Joy is an acronym, but it's not her given name. Her mom's name is Destiny Rose Young. She's been living off the grid for years, but we found her birth records. Joy turned six in November. No father was listed on the birth certificate. Doing some basic math, it appears that Destiny quit her job as a clerical specialist for the City of Memphis while she was still pregnant. She started working for cash, doing odd jobs, cleaning houses, and taking her baby with her. I spoke to the landlord of the little house she rented, and Destiny told him she was hiding from an abusive ex. He allowed her to rent the house using cash, and she paid him for the utilities, so nothing had to be put in her name. He said she used a burner phone, so her number changed frequently. I found all this out just doing my own research."

"That's kind of scary, but did you get a hold of her mom? She must be worried sick!"

Marla paused and stared at the ground for a moment. "She's dead. Her body was found behind a gas station last night. Someone shot her and dumped her body. The gas station isn't far from the house, but it's just inside the Memphis jurisdiction. A friend of mine is a detective for the MPD, and he shared some information with me off the record. He doesn't know about the girl yet, and I told him I wanted to help find Destiny's next of kin, so he wouldn't be suspicious of my interest in the case. So far, they haven't uncovered any family or any abusive ex-boyfriends, but she must've been hiding from something. They also haven't found any emails or other forms of communication. Her car was registered in her name, but she used her old office address on the registration. Doing this kind of research without alerting anyone can be difficult. I don't get to use all my resources. In the meantime, I do want to maintain the assumption that Joy's life could be in danger if anyone finds out where she is."

Secretly, Kennedy still hoped that Joy's father would step up and give his daughter a loving home, but that now seemed far-fetched. "Okay, well, I'm just going to tell people that she's a distant cousin of mine, and I took custody of her because of a family emergency. I won't even go into detail if anyone asks, but I know she'd be happier with her real family if you can find some relatives without putting her in danger."

"I'm doing all I can without letting anyone know a child is involved. Maybe my friend will let me know something else soon, or I can uncover something on my own."

At that time, Mason pulled into the driveway with Gracie. Mason greeted Kennedy with a hug, and it warmed her heart more than she wanted to admit. Gracie went inside to join Joy on the couch to watch TV for a few minutes, giving them privacy for Marla to recount the same facts with Mason. They all agreed to keep Joy's existence confidential for the time being, and hopefully, she would find a peaceful resolution in the near future.

While they talked, a newer green Bronco slowed to a stop in front of Kennedy's house. The three adults watched with caution as a tall man in his twenties stepped out of the vehicle. It only took a second for all three of them to recognize Officer James Walker from the Bartlett Police Department.

"Good morning, y'all. After the cryptic background check Monday night, I figured I might need to check on Kennedy. Is everything okay here?"

"Of course, James. Thanks for checking on me." Kennedy had no idea what she was allowed to share, but the officer must have assumed more was going on than meets the eye.

"Okay then. I told my sister I'd drive through the neighborhood and check on her house anyway. Good to see you, Mason," James said as he exchanged a handshake with the fireman. "And Ms. Jamison, I kind of hoped I'd never see you again since that one baby was surrendered to our police station a couple of years ago."

Marla chuckled a little before she answered, "That's the only Safe Haven baby I've ever handled, but she was adopted very quickly. At least she got a happy ending."

With the pleasantries out of the way, Officer Walker bid them adieu and left.

Shortly after, Marla also left after she said goodbye to Joy and Gracie, leaving Mason and Kennedy standing outside. "I talked to my buddy, Police Chief Lawrence from Bartlett PD last night about the arson investigation. He didn't know anything new, and he still doesn't know there's a kid involved. I bet Officer Walker suspects something, but he won't call any attention to our situation."

"Who all does know about her?" Kennedy asked, curious of how they were keeping it all secret.

"Aside from me, you, and Marla, the only other people are three of my fellow firefighters and the paramedic who checked her out at the fire station. My coworkers fully appreciate the sensitivity of this information, and no one will find out about her from them. No one else knows she exists."

Kennedy opted to change the tone of the conversation. "Joy's settling in good, but she's still hesitant about talking to me. Maybe she can tell us more as she opens up. I think the best plan right now is making her feel safe, and I'm doing the best I can without actually being equipped for the job."

Then Mason gave her a smile that put all others to shame. "You're doing an amazing job, Kennedy, and most women don't have the balls to do what you're doing. Just look at her now. She looks like an honest-to-goodness girl instead of the zombie from a day ago. I know firsthand how tough it is to be a single parent, so I want to help, and Gracie can help too."

Before Kennedy allowed the gooey, schoolgirl-crush feelings to take over, she suggested they get on the road to the zoo. Gracie did most of the talking in the car, and by the time they arrived at the zoo, Gracie had already impersonated every animal she could think of. The silly noises made everyone laugh, including Joy. Kennedy thoroughly appreciated the distraction from anything more serious than what the fox says.

Once inside the zoo, Joy and Gracie led the way. Just like *Dora*, they wanted to explore everything, but they only managed to see all the big cats before lunch became the priority. In the Cat House Café, Gracie influenced Joy's dining option again, leaving both girls eating cheeseburgers from the kids menu. Joy responded to a few questions about their adventure so far, but all her replies remained brief.

With full bellies, the girls slowed down their pace on the trek through the rest of the zoo. They grinned and imitated animals along the way before coming to a playground. Gracie took Joy by the hand, leading her to the jungle gym. Mason and Kennedy plopped down on a bench where they could watch the girls play. No one lingered, giving them the opportunity to speak candidly.

"You never told me why you think her life is in danger. You said you snuck her away from the scene in a blanket, but I don't know why everything happened like that." At this point, Kennedy felt entitled to know more about the situation.

Mason stared straight ahead without actually focusing on anything, his face tightening into a grimace. "I found her hiding in an old shed on the property. She was so frightened. I asked if her mom was inside the house, and she said no. What she said next is the crazy part. She said, 'My mom told me if anything like this ever happened, she was already dead. And if they find me, they'll kill me too.' I could tell she was serious. Her mom prepared her for this day, but we don't know who's after her. It's hard to fight off an enemy you don't know."

39

Taken aback, Kennedy's focus shifted to the giggling girl climbing onto the statue of a hippo. Who would want to kill an innocent child? Why would a six-year-old ever need to be in fear for her life? Some Mama-Bear-level anger filled her. "What did her mom do to endanger their lives like this?"

"No one knows yet, but she really didn't want to be found."

Kennedy couldn't wrap her head around the situation. "But she told Joy about the danger? She knew they were in trouble but didn't reach out to anyone for help? She knew she might get killed but left no plans to get her daughter to safety? I know Destiny is dead, but what kind of mom does that?"

In her anger, Kennedy stared ahead at the girls, her hands angrily gripping the front of the bench on either side of her lap.

Turning his gaze back to Kennedy, Mason opened up on a personal level she didn't anticipate. "Some moms are just selfish. Gracie's mother chose drugs over her daughter and husband. We tried rehab and interventions, but she never could kick the habit. Pills always came first and divorcing her was the hardest decision I ever had to make. Gracie didn't need that influence. Plus, she deserves a family she can rely on for safety and security. It's been two years, and Bethany hasn't once asked to see Gracie. I don't even know where she is anymore. Between me and my family, Gracie has all she needs."

Kennedy felt a surge of respect for Mason. "I couldn't imagine growing up without my mom, but Gracie looks like she's adjusted well. Do you think Joy will adjust that well?"

She almost jumped when Mason put his hand on top of hers and said, "She'll be fine. She has you."

The tender moment was something she purposely avoided her entire adult life. There she sat, gripping the front of the bench, and not knowing what to do with her hand that Mason just covered with his own. This kid and this handsome firefighter were knocking chinks in her armor. Kennedy mentally tried to reinforce the wall around her heart.

"Mason, I'm barely enough for me. I don't know about relationships, and I'm sure not equipped for full-time motherhood. I stepped in for her immediate needs, but I don't have any kind of network for her long-term care. Marla really needs to find Joy's family."

"Look at everything you accomplished in the last twenty-four hours. Don't doubt your abilities to adapt. I'm going to help, and so is Marla. She's looking for Joy's family, but the process might be slow because she's keeping it off the record. Just remember, you're not alone in this."

His words were so comforting, but Kennedy had been alone for years. She no longer had the wherewithal to think in terms of family and close relationships. Counting on people, developing bonds… That was so far outside her comfort zone. History taught her it was far too easy to lose loved ones, steering her to devote her time to animals instead of people.

She didn't have a chance to respond before the girls were ready to explore the rest of the zoo. They finally decided to head home when the sun faded. By the time Mason pulled into Kennedy's driveway, both girls had drifted to sleep in the backseat. Kennedy unlocked the front door and then accepted another warm hug from Mason before she scooped up the sleeping Joy to carry into the house.

Forty-eight hours ago, Kennedy was alone. Now, she truly realized the degree of her aloneness. Since the sudden death of her parents, she had been in survival mode, standing on her own two feet. Kennedy against the world. Other than a few awkward blind dates forced by well-meaning coworkers, Kennedy had never even been on a date with a man. No real first kiss. No one to ever call a boyfriend. She was fine with that… Until now.

Joy, Mason, and Gracie resurrected emotions that she'd buried so long ago. Maybe that wasn't accurate. These emotions were completely different from anything she felt with her parents. Instead of resurrecting emotions, they spurred some kind of new emotional creation. Sitting on the chair, Kennedy watched Joy's chest rise and fall gently in her slumber on the couch. She knew beyond a shadow of a doubt that she would give her life to save Joy's if the situation ever called for it. Thinking about Mason's genuine character and the way he showed up without having to ask... Kennedy felt her walls crashing down.

Attempting to shake off the feelings, Kennedy got up to do some basic housekeeping and cook a late dinner. After preparing the pouch of just-add-water potato soup, she woke up Joy to eat a bowl with her. It seemed like a good time to approach a conversation.

"Joy, did you enjoy the trip to the zoo today?"

"Yes."

"Have you ever been to the zoo before?"

"No."

Kennedy had to remember that progress had been made just by the simple fact that Joy answered questions aloud. Conquering her frustration, Kennedy patiently tried to coax the child into stringing together a few more words.

"What kind of things would you do with your mom?"

"Nothing," Joy replied without hesitation and without inflection.

Still exercising patience, Kennedy kept on, "Did you ever go to the park? Or what was your favorite store to visit?"

"I stayed home. Mommy said it wasn't safe outside."

Kennedy tried to remain calm, keeping the anger for the girl's mom at bay. "Who stayed at home with you when your mom went to work?"

"Ginger."

The bunny was the babysitter? Surely that couldn't be

true. "You didn't have a babysitter or family come over?"

"No. Just me and Ginger. We watched TV and stayed in the house like Mommy said."

Kennedy could barely stand leaving Milo alone during the day. What would possess a mother to leave a child home alone? Now that the child had volunteered a couple of complete sentences, Kennedy had no idea how to process the information. Maybe the one-word answers were better. Still not wanting to let the opportunity for a conversation to pass, Kennedy kept asking questions. "When Mason found you, he said you were hiding in a shed. What happened? Were you getting away from the fire?"

"If Mommy wasn't home when the alarm clock started ringing... I had to hide."

The tiny voice sharing such creepy information freaked Kennedy out, sending an involuntary shiver up her spine. Joy still pronounced her R's with a slight W-sound. The experiences of this week were simply not fair to the little girl. "Honey, I don't understand. Why would you hide? Where would you hide?"

"Mommy said to hide from the bad guys in the shed under the floor." Joy shared this like it was common knowledge.

"Let me get this straight... if your mom didn't get home by the time an alarm went off, then you would know she's in trouble with some bad guys, and then you would hide in case the bad guys came to your house?" Kennedy understood without really understanding.

She nodded and answered, "The alarm clock rang, so I hid like Mommy said. I got scared; I couldn't breathe." Joy paused to put her hand on her throat, remembering the lack of oxygen from two nights ago. "Me and Ginger needed air. We stayed in the shed, but I knew Mommy was dead."

"Did your mommy say why the bad people wanted to find you? I need to keep you safe, so please tell me anything you know." Kennedy pleaded with the girl. She abandoned her half-empty bowl of soup and enveloped the small child in her arms. She carried her to the couch to continue the conversation. Realizing this was the first real physical embrace she shared with the child, Kennedy felt more connected to her than she anticipated was humanly possible.

"Mommy said we would be rich, but we had to hide from the bad guys a little longer." Her L's sounded like W's this time. *Just a wittle wonger.*

"How would you be rich? What did your mom have planned?" she asked as they sat on the couch, Joy on her lap and safe in her arms.

"My daddy would pay us. Mommy said he would give us money."

"Do you know your dad's name? Maybe he can help us."

"No. Mommy said if something bad happened, then Daddy made her dead." The TH sounded like an F. *Somefing bad.*

Still holding Joy, rocking her gently, she asked, "Do you know your mommy isn't coming home anymore?"

Joy nodded her head against Kennedy's chest, fully accepting the security of the embrace.

"I don't want anything else bad to happen, honey. I want to keep you safe, and we'll figure out who the bad guys are. No one will ever hurt you or Ginger." Kennedy made a promise she might not be able to keep, but she would die trying if she had to.

Joy stayed on Kennedy's lap without talking for the rest of the night. Joy shed a few tears, but she did so quietly. The only evidence of crying was a small damp spot on Kennedy's shirt next to her heart. No heaving sobs. Kennedy was relieved that Joy exhibited this small amount of grief, hoping this could be a starting point for real healing.

They eventually brushed their teeth and went to bed, skipping the pretense of Joy sleeping in her own room. Settling in her own king-sized bed, she muddled through the tongue twisters of *Green Eggs and Ham* to brighten both their moods before bedtime, and then Joy fell asleep nestled safely between Milo and Kennedy.

WEDNESDAY, FEBRUARY 16

When Kennedy showed up for work at seven, her coworkers had mixed opinions about Joy. They all expressed genuine concern for the fabricated family emergency, but a veterinary office might not be the best place to bring a child for the day. Her coworkers certainly never tried to bring their own kids to work. Even though Kennedy knew this wasn't the best scenario, she was at a loss regarding what to do with Joy.

Angie, a fellow technician, pulled her to the side while she was dispensing medicine for an overnight patient. "Look, Kennedy, I don't think Dr. Len is going to be okay with Joy being here. She's a liability, and you can't do your job while watching her. Ms. Sue just got here, so let's see what she says before Doc arrives."

Ms. Sue, their clinic manager, was a grandmotherly type who always smiled and found a way to make everything sound like good news. Kennedy actually looked forward to what she had to say.

Sue pushed her reading glasses onto the top of her head and looked up from her desk as they entered the miniscule office. "Good morning, ladies. What can I help you with?" Her sweet expression comforted Kennedy, but the comfort was premature.

"Hey, Ms. Sue. So, I had a crazy family emergency over the weekend, and a cousin I didn't even know died. I was the only other relative that the folks at Child Protective Services could find, and now I have a six-year-old girl staying with me until they can locate her dad." Kennedy laid on the pity as much as she could, hoping for a sympathetic response.

Jumping up to offer a hug, Sue replied, "Oh dear, that's terrible. Who's watching the child today? Do you need the day off to make some arrangements for her?"

Angie cut in before Kennedy could respond, "The kid's out back walking dogs with the kennel techs right now. She doesn't have childcare, and Ken thought she could hang out with us."

Relinquishing the hug, Sue jumped back with a shocked expression. "You brought a child here? What if she gets bit? Or scratched? Or hurt? This isn't a safe place for kids." Sue stopped to regain a softer demeanor. "Have a seat, Kennedy. Angie, shut the door on your way out."

Kennedy dropped down into the chair and waited for Sue to give her a lecture. She didn't expect this response, but she had no basis to argue either.

"Okay, Ken. I know you don't have experience with children, but I'm sure you realize that bringing a child to our clinic wasn't the most intelligent decision you've ever made. If I remember correctly, you haven't taken a vacation since you started working here other than the couple of days you took to get your wisdom teeth pulled a few years ago. This isn't our busy time of year, and we can manage without you for a couple of weeks... so take vacation. Find a babysitter or enroll her in school or something. Your schedule here can be adjusted accordingly after you find childcare for her."

Vacation? Kennedy never took time off, and she would rather stick to her routines. "Are you sure she can't just sit in the breakroom and watch TV? I don't like missing work."

The look on Sue's face would indicate Kennedy implied something like locking Joy in a kennel for the day. The aggravation caused the manager to switch tones. "I'm telling you to take vacation. That wasn't a suggestion. Do you not see

that this is a big deal for you? Take the time you need to handle your business. In fact, my granddaughter is having her birthday party Saturday at the Cordova
Skating Rink. Be there at two for pizza and games. But get out of here now before Dr. Len arrives."

By eight, Kennedy and Joy headed to Walmart. She needed a booster seat and some groceries anyway. They stopped on the toy aisle to see if Joy showed interest in any games, but she seemed unable to concentrate amid the wide variety of choices. Kennedy quickly realized that Joy likely never visited the toy aisle of a store. The girl stared with a slack jaw at all the colorful games, puzzles, dolls, and other playthings that screamed for her attention. Before Joy could get inundated with the options, Kennedy grabbed some classics: a giant bucket of Legos and a variety of Play-Doh.

Once they arrived at the Jeep, Joy cooperated by sitting in the booster seat without a fuss. Home before ten, Milo was ecstatic to see them, but Kennedy felt lost. She turned on the TV for background noise and sat on the floor with Joy to construct a Lego village. As anticipated, Joy took to the colorful blocks immediately. They erected houses and buildings on the large flat square of green. For a few minutes, Kennedy felt like a child again.

The newscaster on the TV interrupted her daydream. The lady read the teleprompter with a monotone diction. "This just in... President Robert Crawford has released his itinerary for the next few weeks in his Reuniting America Tour. The Mid-South can expect a visit from President Crawford on Friday, February 25th. He will be addressing the leaders of Memphis and Shelby County and then making a stop at Graceland." The news lady tried to add some phony enthusiasm to the last statement, but Kennedy didn't buy it. The camera switched to a pre-recorded message from the pompous president himself.

Kennedy glanced up at the TV to see his big head fill the screen. "The United States needs to become united again. As the greatest nation in the world, I know we can work together to achieve this, and I'm looking forward to meeting with the dynamic leaders across our land. It's going to take dedication and a little elbow grease, but the people of the USA elected the right man for the job. I'm going to–" Kennedy changed the station. That was all she could listen to.

The president was only in his late forties, but his hairline had slightly receded, causing his face to look unnaturally large. His icy-blue eyes penetrated through the television, giving Kennedy the creeps. His self-assuredness and ego probably attracted the attention of young women with daddy issues, but his crazy eyes and arrogance repelled Kennedy. He tried to play middle of the road as an independent candidate, and she never guessed he would get elected. But she was wrong. Now, the country was stuck with him for at least four years.

She put thoughts of the ridiculous POTUS to the back of her mind as she continued building a colorful village from the little plastic blocks. Joy walked the Lego person through the village, silently showing him all the places they constructed, letting her imagination take over. The interaction thrilled Kennedy, but she eventually had to get off the floor to make lunch. Joy didn't display any pickiness about food, and she eagerly ate her sandwich, along with the carrot sticks and apple slices.

The crunch of the carrot sticks created most of the sound at the lunch table as Kennedy couldn't come up with a good way to start another conversation with Joy. She needed to learn more about her and the threat against her. How could she ask these questions without causing Joy any distress? Where was her neighbor when she needed her? Pennie entertained her little nieces all the time and bragged about being the cool aunt. And here was Kennedy… at a loss for words to connect to a six-year-old.

While lost in contemplation, the dinging phone caused both the child and adult to jump.

Mason sent a message to check on her, thinking she was on lunch break at work. She replied that her boss insisted on an immediate vacation. His suggestion that they go to the park together made her hesitate. Did he really intend to spend the next two weeks alongside her? Why was he acting so dedicated to someone he just met?

Her delay in responding to his message should've been interpreted as Kennedy needing to think about it. Instead, Mason sent another message indicating he was on the way to pick them up. She was so caught off guard, she couldn't think straight. She was still wearing her medical scrubs, and Joy still wore comfy leggings and a sweatshirt. Why did she even care what they were wearing?

Ten minutes later, Kennedy donned her favorite "I beg your Parton" sweatshirt that featured a silhouette of Dolly. Jeans and sneakers were all she knew aside from scrubs and casual tops. She picked out jeans and a cute shirt for Joy, then spent one extra minute putting pigtails in the little girl's hair. Milo watched the activity with contempt, huffing a time or two from his spot on the floor; he knew they were leaving without him again. A Busy Bone was sacrificed to appease her sweet boy as they left with Mason and Gracie.

The playground at Shelby Farms was all but abandoned at noon on a Wednesday. Joy and Gracie held hands as they descended the massive slides, while the adults watched from a nearby bench.

"I never knew this playground was here," Kennedy said in awe of the slides surrounding them.

"There's a lot more to see," Mason said, pointing to other areas past where they sat. "There's a collection of swings that way, and a tree house over there. Gracie loves the climbing ropes. And during the summer, I let her play in the sandy area that has water features."

"This place looks like a mecca for kids. Where's everyone at?"

Mason offered her a quizzical look before he answered. "It's Wednesday. Kids are in school, and parents are at work."

"Oh, that makes sense. Why isn't Gracie in school today?" Kennedy asked, feeling completely stupid that she forgot kids go to school on weekdays in February.

"I told her teacher we had a family emergency, and she'd need to miss a week or two. She's already leaps and bounds past her classmates, so I'm not concerned about her missing out on schoolwork. Joy needs Gracie more than Gracie needs help identifying sight words."

Taken aback, Kennedy realized that Mason did intend to spend the next two weeks helping her. What did she do to deserve this? Was she happy about it? Scared? Before her brain settled on any appropriate response, the two girls ran over to them. Gracie, the elected spokesman for the duo, asked if they could go climb the ropes.

Once she got a look for herself, Kennedy had to fight the urge to climb the ropes herself. Large, netted ropes surrounded an enormous tree fort. Kids who were agile enough to climb all the way up the nets could sit victoriously on the wooden deck. Gracie wasted no time getting started, but Joy seemed a little disconcerted, staring at the daunting obstacle.

Kennedy put her hands on the ropes, trying to convince Joy to join her. The girl couldn't decide how to get started, so Kennedy climbed up a few feet and turned to reach a hand down. Still appearing scared, Joy took a step back.

Mason took it as his cue to help. He moved underneath the nets and said, "Joy, I can catch you if you fall through. I'm right here if you need me."

His words were spoken to the child, but Kennedy felt them to her core. *He's right there if she needs him.* What would that actually feel like? Someone to be there for her? Obviously, Joy was more inclined to trust than Kennedy was because she immediately scrambled onto the net without assistance. Despite the head start, Kennedy and Joy caught up with Gracie halfway up the net.

Laughing loudly, Gracie stopped when they were around six feet above the ground to hook her legs on the net and drop the rest of her body below the net to hang upside down. Mason tickled his beautiful daughter, teasing her until she resumed her ascent to the tree fort. Kennedy observed Joy watching the interaction with interest. Mason must have observed the same thing.

He encouraged the girl. "Let me help," he said as he reached through the ropes to help Joy hook her legs for stability. From atop the net, Kennedy placed her hands on Joy's knees for some extra steadiness. "Now, come on down," he said, guiding her torso through the ropes. She hesitated a moment before releasing her grip. A moment later, Joy cackled from the freedom of hanging below the net. The cackles deepened into belly laughs as Mason tickled her.

After only a minute of remaining upside down, Kennedy assisted Joy in getting back on top of the ropes. They finished racing up to the fortress, and Kennedy sat on the deck, watching the little girls run around to appreciate the view from different corners of the tree fort. In typical childlike fashion, they only wanted to stay in one place for a millisecond before lowering themselves back to the net. Mason stayed below, retaining his role as the safety net under the net. Joining them on the ropes, Kennedy followed the now-brave Joy to a lower fort constructed around another tree about thirty feet away.

Now on the deck of the lower tree fort, the girls ran circles around the tree and expended energy Kennedy didn't expect from Joy. She sat cross legged, out of the way of the girls while Mason stood nearby on the ground, eye level with the deck. Eventually, Gracie hurried to the edge of the deck and ducked under the single wooden rail. "Catch me, Daddy!" she screamed as she dove off the platform, straight into her father's arms.

Joy stood in the same spot where Gracie had just jumped, holding the rail and looking at Mason expectantly. Kennedy watched with amusement, wondering if the girl would follow suit. Mason placed his daughter safely on the ground and opened his arms to Joy. "You can jump, I'll catch you," he motivated. Joy stayed still, apparently wanting to jump, but still not ready to overcome that fear. "You saw how much fun it was for Gracie. Come on, Joy," he continued.

Still remaining frozen in place, Joy shook her head just slightly, internally trying to choose fun over fear. Mason's next question caught Kennedy completely off guard. "If Kennedy jumps first, and I can catch her, would you jump next and let me catch you?"

The shaking of her head immediately changed to fervent nodding. Joy held out her hand to Kennedy, urging the adult to go first. *What just happened?* "Um, I don't think that's a good idea. Go ahead, Joy. He can catch you."

"Kennedy, she needs you to go first. Just fall backwards off the deck, like a trust fall. I won't let you hit the ground."

It was funny that she encouraged Joy to be brave, but Kennedy wanted nothing more than to chicken out. Falling for Mason... That might be happening regardless of how she chose to get off this tree fort. Reluctantly, she ducked under the wooden rail and turned around so her back was to Mason. Peeking over her shoulder, she saw Mason grinning with a twinkle in his eyes. His arms extended wide, forming a cradle, inviting her to trust him.

She faced away again and closed her eyes. Inhaling deeply, she held her breath as she fell back. In a heartbeat, strong arms held her tightly, securing her like a baby. She couldn't remember if she exhaled, but she felt breathless and weightless in the moment. Kennedy didn't open her eyes, remaining in the safety of his arms for a second longer than Joy was willing to wait.

"My turn!" the girl squealed, bringing Kennedy back to reality.

Her feet touched the ground as Mason lowered her, and Kennedy was flooded with a cacophony of emotions. She avoided any eye contact with Mason and turned her attention to Joy. Looking up, she noticed Joy bursting with excitement, and she hardly let Mason get ready before she jumped. He still caught her without a problem and swung her in a circle before setting her down. Then Gracie grabbed Joy's hand and pulled her towards the swings.

The young girls ran out of energy after fifteen minutes of swinging, and the process of pushing swings quickly zapped Kennedy of the energy she had left. When everyone discussed the appetites they had worked up, Mason suggested they find an early dinner. Kennedy assumed he would take her and Joy home, but apparently, he wanted to make a day of it. At his suggestion of Chick-fil-A, she decided a quick dinner would be okay. The fried little nuggets of chicken dipped in barbecue sauce were her weakness.

Ten minutes later, they quickly placed orders at the counter and found a small table inside the fast-food restaurant. Kennedy took the young girls to the restroom to wash their hands before the food was served. By the time they had a seat at the table, the nuggets and waffle fries showed up. Everyone dug in like they were famished. Halfway through the meal,

Kennedy's phone rang, notifying her of a FaceTime call.

"Hey, Marla," Kennedy answered, hoping the woman had some news about Joy's family.

"I went by your work, and your boss said you took vacation. Now, I'm at your house, and you're not here either."

"Sorry, I'm trying to do some things with Joy, allowing her to have some new experiences."

"Let me see her so I can count this as my surprise visit," Marla demanded with impatience.

Kennedy leaned down next to the little girl beside her and told Joy to greet the lady in the phone. Joy smiled at Marla, and Kennedy wondered if the mess of barbecue sauce on the girl's face would count against her. The phone call only lasted a minute, and they hung up without learning anything new.

In the meantime, Mason busied himself by texting with someone. Kennedy's parents never allowed her to have her phone at the kitchen table, and she could now see why that rule might be important. But she had no control over Mason. Plus, he was the one who bought her dinner. The girls remained silent while stuffing their faces. Suddenly, Kennedy felt awkward, not knowing what to talk about even if Mason did decide to put his phone down.

After only a few messages, Mason put his phone back in his pocket. He made eye contact with Kennedy, smiling as he said, "My mom's mad because I haven't brought Gracie to see her in a couple of days. Normally, Gracie spends the night with my parents while I work, so she's concerned she isn't going to see her favorite granddaughter for the next couple of weeks while I'm on vacation."

"Oh, that's really sweet. Will you take her to visit your mom tonight?" Kennedy asked, feeling bittersweet about the situation. She would want nothing but the best for Mason and Gracie, but she felt the situation was slightly unfair. She and Joy had no family reaching out to them… offering help… being a support system… missing their company.

Maybe that wasn't entirely correct. Mason was present and trying to help. Rather than fixate on her own lack of parental support, Kennedy tried to adjust her mindset to appreciate what she did have.

"Mom wants us all to come over after we eat. She made a peach cobbler for dessert, and she wants to meet Joy."

"I thought you weren't telling anyone about her. What did you tell your mom?"

"I tell my mom everything. There's no one in this world I trust more than my mother. So when we finish eating, you two are officially invited for cobbler and quality time with BB and Papaw."

BB and Papaw. Kennedy's parents didn't live long enough to earn grandparent nicknames. She would never get to see their faces light up at the sight of their first grandchild. The thought of having children never crossed Kennedy's mind as an adult, so the thought of her parents missing out on the experience never crossed her mind either. Generations of happiness could easily end with Kennedy. Was this what her life had become? A dead end?

"I don't know what's so difficult about the invitation. I promise, my mom makes the best cobbler," he insisted.

Not realizing she spent so long lost in thought, Kennedy opened her mouth to speak, but no words came out. She felt lost. Isolated. Should she cling to Mason and his family for support? What would happen when Marla found Joy's family? Would Kennedy be left alone again?

"What's cobbler?"

The softly spoken question Joy posed made the decision easy. Kennedy committed to do what was best for Joy, and trying cobbler for the first time would be best for a six-year-old orphan.

Manufacturing a smile for the situation, Kennedy found her words, "Cobbler is a yummy dessert, and it looks like it's your lucky day, Joy. Mason promises that BB makes the best cobbler in the world."

Darkness was still a couple of hours away when they pulled up to the cozy farmhouse in the older area of Bartlett. A split-rail fence bordered the acreage where a barn was nestled behind the house. The rocking chairs on the large front porch welcomed all visitors. Before Kennedy could finish taking in the scene, BB and Papaw emerged from the front door to accept hugs from Mason and Gracie.

Kennedy stood back with Joy, waiting for the loving family to finish greeting each other. Then BB turned her sights on the orphans. The twenty-six-year-old orphan as well as the orphan two decades younger than herself. The woman appeared to see straight to Kennedy's soul, and the compassion in her eyes was unlike anything Kennedy had ever experienced.

"Come here, sugar," she said before enveloping Kennedy in a tender hug. From over BB's shoulder, Kennedy saw that Papaw had picked up Gracie and Joy, holding each girl on a hip and laughing with them. Is this what family felt like? She could scarcely remember.

After being relinquished from the hug, and before unexpected tears could fully form in her eyes, Mason placed his hand on the small of Kennedy's back, leading her into the house behind his parents and the laughing girls. The aroma of a fresh cobbler dominated the atmosphere, drawing everyone into the kitchen. While BB divvied out the cobbler into bowls, she made a more formal introduction.

"It's a pleasure to meet you, Kennedy. You can call us BB and Papaw, but we also go by Becky and Ronnie if that works better for you." She chuckled slightly, moving to put bowls of steamy, peachy goodness onto the large table in the kitchen. Joy and Gracie had taken a seat on either side of Ronnie, where they were entertained by Papaw magically pulling quarters out of their ears. "The house seems empty when Gracie isn't here. One of these days, we hope to have a whole slew of grandchildren."

Kennedy accepted a spoon from BB and smiled. "Thanks for inviting us over. How many grandchildren do you have now?"

"Oh, just Gracie. The future of our full house lies squarely on Mason's shoulders."

Avoiding any eye contact with Mason, Kennedy concentrated on the bowl of warm cobbler in front of her. She couldn't be sure if Becky was implying anything with the *grandchildren* comment, but this topic of conversation was way out of her comfort zone. One thing was for sure, though… Mason's mother certainly did make the best cobbler in the world. "This is amazing!" she said over her shoulder to BB, who still scurried around the kitchen, wiping counters and checking knobs on the oven. Then she turned to Joy and said, "How do you like your dessert?"

She managed to ask the question while Joy shoveled a heaping spoonful into her mouth, but Joy managed to nod. Not pressing the girl to answer aloud, Kennedy decided it was permissible for Joy to stay silent with her mouth full of food. Everyone ate in silence for a moment while she took the opportunity to take in the surroundings.

BB didn't quite look like a grandmother. She might have been in her fifties with stylish sandy-brown hair and a sturdy build. Only a few crow's feet and smile lines aged her pleasant face, while bright pink lipstick hinted at a vivacious personality. Kennedy was immediately wrapped up in a womb of comfort sitting in this warm kitchen, surrounded by love that was practically palpable.

Papaw might be prematurely gray, but he still boasted a

full head of hair. His forehead wrinkles and gray moustache, in addition to the wire-framed glasses, certainly gave him more of a grandfatherly appearance. Even though Kennedy's parents were both forty when they died, she always marveled at her mom's beauty despite her age. Now, forty didn't seem old... fiftyish made Mason's parents downright young to be grandparents.

The kitchen itself completely embodied a grandmother's persona... Pictures and bric-a-brac featuring roosters... Plates, bowls, and mismatched mugs stored on open shelves. Kennedy felt like she was in a movie. The home had so much charm, causing Kennedy to just now realize how devoid of personality her own home was. No portraits on her bare walls. No figurines on display to suggest that Kennedy might have a whimsical side.

Her train of thought was interrupted when BB suggested they move to the den to watch *The Little Mermaid*, Gracie's favorite movie. Foregoing any conversation, the four adults and two children settled into the cushy den to watch the Disney classic. The only light in the room came from the television, along with the lowering sun piercing through the curtains. Kennedy and Mason sat on either end of the huge couch with two girls between them. Within twenty minutes, both girls were sound asleep.

Mason slowly got up and went over to speak quietly into his father's ear. Kennedy watched as he walked back towards the couch, but instead of reoccupying his seat, he came to her side, placing his hand on her shoulder and inclining his head to the side. Giving up her spot on the warm sofa, Kennedy followed him back to the kitchen.

"Do you need to feed your dog or anything while the girls are napping?"

"Are you going to let me drive your Suburban?" Kennedy asked, still amazed every time Mason displayed concern for people and animals that didn't belong to him.

"No, but I can chauffeur you there and back. Come on."

Being alone in the vehicle with Mason had her feeling uneasy. Leaving Joy in the care of someone else didn't help the feeling. Kennedy slouched in her seat, staring out the passenger window as the sun dipped lower in the sky. Houses passed by as the vehicle turned here and there without her paying any attention to the course they took.

She squinted to see through the darkly tinted windows. "Why do you have such dark tint? Isn't this illegal?"

Mason laughed. "Yes, it's illegal. It's called *police tint*, and I can only get by with it because of my firefighter tags."

She sat up in the seat when she realized they weren't on a course to her house. "Umm, where are we going?"

"I figured you might want to see the house where Joy lived. Well, what's left of the house. I can show you the shed she was hiding in. I want another look while we still have a few minutes of daylight to see if we can learn anything about her or her mother."

Kennedy still hadn't shared the creepy information she learned the previous night, but she knew she needed to tell him about it.

"Joy actually opened up a little bit last night." She bit her bottom lip, contemplating what she was fixing to say.

Mason briefly took his eyes off the road to look directly at Kennedy. "Did she tell you anything pertinent?"

She nodded. "Joy told me they were hiding. Her mom would routinely leave her home alone, but she set an alarm clock. If her mom wasn't home by the time the alarm went off, Joy was supposed to hide from the bad guys."

"Hide from the bad guys? What the hell?"

"My thoughts exactly. Joy said they only needed to hide a little longer because they were going to be rich. Her daddy was going to pay them."

"Did she say who her dad is?" Mason inquired, stealing another glance at his passenger.

"No, but she alluded to her dad being the one who killed her mom. She literally said, 'Daddy made her dead.' It was so eerie."

She stopped talking as they slowed in front of an abandoned piece of property. No neighbors nearby. The land might measure an acre, full of overgrown grass that had turned brown during the winter months. Mature trees bordered the land, isolating it from the rest of Bartlett. As Mason steered the SUV onto the gravel driveway, Kennedy saw the charred remains of a small house. It appeared more like remnants from a large bonfire except that the ashy pile didn't hint at jovial memories like a bonfire might.

As they both exited the vehicle and walked towards the rubbish, the sooty smell immediately filled her nostrils, offending all her senses. Only three nights ago, this was Joy's home. The footprint of the house was tiny; Kennedy assumed it only had one bedroom. The only discernible items in the pile were the charred appliances in the corner that used to be a kitchen. A ribbon of yellow tape surrounded the scene without offering any real security. She stood on the edge of the debris, mesmerized by what the home had been reduced to when Mason suddenly bolted across the field.

Kennedy quickly turned her head to see what he could be chasing when she saw a woman running towards the woods. Unfortunately for the woman, she tripped in the high grass and tumbled before she could make a getaway. Mason had covered the fifty yards to stand over the woman before she could get to her feet. Kennedy rushed to join them as the woman stood, catching her breath.

She didn't appear on the verge of trying to escape, so they stopped short of physically detaining the woman. As she wiped the dirt from her knees and elbows, Mason questioned her.

"Who are you? What're you doing here?"

The frightened woman glanced up, still inhaling deeply from her open mouth. Between her gradually slowing breaths, she answered, "I'm just a nosy neighbor who wanted to see the burned house."

"I don't believe that for a second. Did you light the fire, and now you're back to see your handiwork?" Mason harshly accused.

By now, the woman stood, reaching her full five-foot-three, significantly shorter than Kennedy. Her dark-brown hair had been pulled into a loose ponytail, and she wore a baggy gray sweater with black leggings that now had a hole in the knee thanks to her recent tumble. Fragments of dried grass clung to the black fabric, causing Kennedy to wonder if she had a lint roller. As a veterinary technician, lint rollers were a necessity since animal hair was a constant hazard in her work environment. Snapping her consciousness back to the present, she noticed the woman had a crazy look in her eyes, like she feared the consequences of her recent actions.

"I didn't set the fire, but I know who used to live here. I really was just curious."

"You know Destiny Young? She used to live in this house, but now she's dead," Kennedy insisted, deducing this woman might provide some insight into the mystery surrounding Joy's life. She still stopped short of sharing anything else they knew about Destiny or Joy.

"We worked together years ago. We weren't close or anything," she said, eyeballing around Kennedy and Mason, maybe looking for a way out of her uncomfortable predicament.

Kennedy could tell that was a lie. "If you weren't close, how did you know where she lived?" She decided to change tactics to see if she could lure the woman into a real conversation. "I'm only here because I'm fostering her pet rabbit. I was hoping to find a pen in the yard, or some hay in the shed so I wouldn't have to buy more pet supplies. Who are you, really?"

The woman lowered her gaze, and said quietly, "I'm Autumn Gibson. Destiny was my friend when we worked together years ago. I just can't believe she's gone."

"It's nice to meet you, Autumn. I'm Kennedy, and this is Mason. He's one of the firemen who worked the scene, and he brought me the bunny. Are you here looking for something? Maybe we can help you?"

Her quiet response sounded ominous. "I'm afraid it's too late for what I'm looking for."

"Were you looking in the shed? What's in there?" Kennedy said as she walked towards the dilapidated structure that could barely be called a shed. It had no door to open, giving her a clear view inside without having to touch anything.

The shed measured eight by eight feet, and a gaping hole in the floor caught Kennedy's eye. She knew that Joy and Ginger found refuge in that hole, hardly big enough to be considered a rabbit's hole. The surrounding weeds were no longer green, but they were bushy enough to obscure any view underneath the shed from the outside. Inside the shed, an old lawnmower, a rake with missing teeth, and a dusty garbage can all sat to one side. A wadded-up tarp laid near the hole. In the fading light, the hole was hard to see. The bad guys would easily overlook it in the middle of the night.

Not paying any attention to her companions, Kennedy crept into the shed, stepping lightly to make sure the floor would hold her. Getting on her knees, she tried to peer into the dark hole. Readjusting to use the flashlight on her phone, Kennedy took another look. She couldn't fit her shoulders through the hole to truly assess the space, but she could ascertain that it was just large enough for Joy and Ginger to hide out for a while. The tarp was probably pulled over the opening to offer concealment.

Without learning anything, Kennedy backed out of the shed. Addressing Autumn, she asked, "I was kind of hoping to find a sister or relative who wanted the bunny. Do you know if Destiny had any family?"

Shaking her head before answering aloud, Autumn replied, "No, her parents are Canadian. She thought life in the States would be more exciting, and she came to Memphis with a boyfriend when she was eighteen. The boyfriend didn't last long, but she loved living here. We both started working as clerks for the City of Memphis during the same month; that was almost ten years ago, back when she was twenty-one. After a few years, she quit, and I've only talked to her a few times since then."

"Well, it's definitely a terrible situation. Do you know if she had any other friends who might want the bunny?" Kennedy prodded, trying to keep her talking.

Autumn shook her head as she removed a piece of grass from her ponytail. "I don't know all the details of her personal life. She was a loner. She stayed off the grid on purpose, but she sent me a text last month saying she was ready to stop hiding. I met her for lunch a few weeks ago when she gave me her address. Destiny told me if anything bad happened to her, I'd need to immediately go to her house and look in the shed. I'd find evidence in the shed, and I should guard it with my life. That's what she said."

Jumping in, Mason asked, "What evidence? What was she talking about?"

"I don't have a clue. I came here yesterday and didn't find anything. I got to thinking maybe I need to search again. It's so creepy here, so I parked a block over and snuck through the trees. I didn't want to be seen, because obviously someone killed Destiny."

"It sounds like she was trying to thrust you into the middle of a conspiracy. Just be careful, okay?" Kennedy offered a little sympathy to the woman who was visibly shaken. The woman was guarded and scared, and Kennedy couldn't blame her. With nothing else to learn at the fire scene, the trio split up. Autumn disappeared on a small trail through the woods as Kennedy joined Mason in the Suburban.

Giving the heated seat enough time to warm her bones, Kennedy contemplated the events of the past few days. This kid. This guy. His kid. The potential conspiracy. Her simple routine of working and pouring herself into her rescue animals had been completely hijacked. Nothing added up, and Kennedy could only hope Marla located Joy's family soon. That would be best for Joy. What would be best for Kennedy?

"What're you thinking?" Mason interrupted her thoughts.

Switching her gaze from the window to the driver, she checked out his profile that was illuminated in the soft twilight. He was so handsome. And so heroic. Was that the correct word? Heroic? Maybe valiant or noble? What was he doing with her right now? Did he really want to know what she was thinking?

"To be honest, Mason, I'm wondering what you're doing here. I can't fathom why you've allowed this messed-up situation to interfere with your perfect home life."

The sarcastic laugh that escaped him caught her off guard. "Perfect? I'm a single dad to a six-year-old girl. There's nothing perfect about that. I work twenty-four-hour shifts, and I depend on my parents to raise Gracie in my absence. I have an apartment that's decorated with Disney characters because I don't have any better taste than that. If you hadn't have taken

Gracie to wash her hands in the women's restroom at Chick-fil-A earlier, I would've been freaking out while she washed her hands alone, standing outside the restroom door, fretting over every second she was out of my sight." He paused to let out another exasperated laugh. "I've actually had security called on me at the grocery store one time for cracking open the women's restroom door and hollering for Gracie to answer me because she took longer than I thought she should. My home life is far from perfect."

The wealth of information was more than Kennedy expected him to share. Did Mason really just look like he had it together on the outside? He seemed far too secure to be a mess on the inside. "From the outside looking in, you have affectionate parents, a precious daughter, and a handle on the parenting thing. You can act like you don't have it together, but you're strong enough to make it work and have enough strength leftover to let me lean on you. But that really didn't answer my question."

He stole a glance at her before turning his attention to the road. "Well, you asked what I was doing here, so at least that question is easy. Three nights ago, I promised Joy I would keep her safe. I don't make promises I don't intend to keep. Even if I'm burning my vacation days, I'm committed to helping. Even if I have to file for FMLA to take off longer, I'll stick around as long as it takes to ensure that Joy is out of danger."

"You don't think you'll regret the time you're investing in this?"

"My only potential regret is that I might be inadvertently putting my own daughter in peril."

Kennedy had a good savings account, but she couldn't afford to be off work longer than six months at the most. The paid-for house and the simple lifestyle never depleted her paychecks, but she certainly hadn't considered the potential for a long-term investment regarding time or money. The potential peril was something she had already gotten knee deep in whether she liked it or not. "If you took longer off work, how would you pay rent?" The pragmatic question sounded unimportant with the lurking danger, but she needed to know how he could be so confident. Maybe she could latch onto his assurance if she understood his standpoint.

"I've never taken advantage of my parents, but they're loaded. I wouldn't hesitate to ask them for help if it came to something as important as keeping a child safe."

Not only did he have caring parents, but they were loaded to boot. She couldn't latch onto that sense of security because parents, rich or poor, were lacking in her life altogether. Kennedy stared at her hands in her lap, realizing how ill-equipped she was for her current situation.

Mason broke the silence after she didn't respond. "The better question might be what are *you* doing here? We only asked you to adopt a bunny and somehow, you ended up with a kid?" Although his tone remained lighthearted, the question was valid.

Kennedy couldn't argue. That was the better question. "If I ever figure out what I'm doing here, I'll be sure to let you know."

They pulled into her driveway, bringing the conversation to a close.

Kennedy wasted no time feeding dinner to Milo, locking her hens in their house, and refilling Ginger's stash of hay. At Mason's suggestion, they leashed up the neglected dog to take him for a walk around the neighborhood. The chilly weather didn't bother Milo, but Kennedy felt the cold all the way to her bones. She had an overwhelming feeling that something huge and dangerous revolved around Joy, and she had unintentionally inserted herself into the middle of it.

The quiet neighborhood made Kennedy feel like she needed to speak softly when she chose to start a new conversation. As if her voice would carry for the whole world to hear. She always felt secure in this settled area of Bartlett but now, the thought of danger invaded her safe space.

She softly asked, "What do you think about Autumn?"

Keeping his own voice low, Mason answered, "Well, I think she has more to tell. But I don't know whether she knew about Joy or not. If Destiny told her to look in the shed for evidence, maybe she didn't know a child was involved."

"Do we need to tell Marla about this? Maybe she can use this information to help locate some of Joy's family."

"Let's think about it before we decide to tell Marla. I'd hate to put Autumn in danger too. I'm still hoping the police can find some family since I'm guessing they would want to notify Destiny's next of kin about her death."

"Destiny met with Autumn a few weeks ago. She had to have set something in motion to cause all this. It almost sounds like she was blackmailing someone to make herself a target like she did."

Mason appeared to ponder that for a minute. "Yea, that's kind of what I was thinking. Destiny thought she was safe because she lived off the grid for so long, but whoever she feared found her anyway."

"Didn't she quit her job while she was pregnant with Joy?" Kennedy took a second to fully process her train of thought before speaking again. "I wonder if this whole situation has to do with Joy and whoever her father is. Maybe Destiny was a rape victim or something."

Mason sounded disgusted when he replied, "Or maybe she was sleeping with married men. A lot of these women want a husband, just not one of their own."

Kennedy wasn't sure if that was a jab at women in general.

Rather than be offended, she prodded for an explanation. "Are you speaking from personal experience? Or you're just assuming Destiny was a whore?"

He huffed and shrugged his shoulders. "I guess that was a personal statement. Maybe Destiny was a whore, I don't know. But I know women are capable of sleeping with men to get what they want. My ex-wife wanted pills. When I had to cut off her access to our bank accounts, she resorted to trading sex for pills. That's when I had to file for divorce. She was bringing these guys into our home, around our daughter. Back to our present situation though... If Destiny wanted money, maybe she was willing to sleep around and gather information to eventually blackmail someone."

Kennedy chose not to dwell on his personal revelation. Instead, she stayed focused on their current situation. "Destiny worked for the City of Memphis. Do you think she ever came into contact with politicians who would rather pay some blackmail money than have their dirty laundry aired for all to see?"

"That sounds like a good scenario, but she worked as a clerk. We don't know what department she actually worked in. She might've just renewed car tags all day and not even come into contact with anyone important."

"Do you think we can find out without drawing attention to Joy while we're snooping around?"

"Kennedy, are you suggesting we investigate this on our own? This needs to be handled by the police."

How could she respond to that? She thought about it while letting Milo lead her down the street. Was Mason chastising her? Should she mind her own business? She sucked in a lungful of cold air. No, Joy was her business. "Mason, the police don't know about Joy. As far as we know, they're just looking for forensic evidence to tie someone to Destiny's dumped body, but her mother's murder goes way deeper than that. I'd be willing to bet that whoever pulled the trigger wasn't even the person at the center of this. Powerful people, such as politicians, have henchmen to do their dirty work."

She glanced to her right to see Mason shaking his head. Maybe he was disappointed in her response. Kennedy never cared what people thought about her, but his opinion seemed to matter now. Not to mention, she needed his help. By the time they rounded a corner to head back to her house, a few minutes had passed. She became inwardly worried that Mason would back out and not help her. The constriction of her chest made her breathing shallow. What was going on? What had become of her routine life?

Once Milo was safely inside the house, she followed Mason to get into the SUV. Over the years, Kennedy had purposely isolated herself, even though she truly thought she was insulating herself. In just a few days, Kennedy went from imperviously alone to ridiculously dependent. Mason backed out of her driveway. In her mind, she sang along with the old Journey song playing on the radio... *I'm forever yours, faithfully*. She hadn't a clue what spurred people to write songs like that before this week.

When Mason broke the silence, she startled a little in her passenger seat. "I'm not sure we need to tell Marla about everything we found out tonight. Plus, we're just jumping to conclusions about what caused this. If we tell any police or authorities, Joy's existence and whereabouts will become common knowledge. But... If we do nothing, I'm afraid Joy will have to live her whole life under the radar, always in fear of danger. That's not fair either. Let's tread lightly but see what we can find out. When we know more about what's going on, and who we can trust, then we can involve the proper authorities to bring things to a close."

The rest of the ten-minute drive was spent in silence.

They opened the front door to BB and Papaw's house quietly to find BB in the kitchen, brewing a pot of coffee.

"The girls are still asleep. I was thinking they might enjoy riding the horses tomorrow since it's still going to be a little warm. The cold front will move through by Saturday, so we need to get in all our outdoor activities tomorrow and Friday."

Kennedy wondered why BB was making plans for Joy, but then she should be glad at least somebody was. Personally, she had no idea what to do with Joy for tomorrow or any day thereafter.

"That's really sweet of you, Becky." Kennedy couldn't bring herself to call her BB. "I don't have any actual plans, but please don't feel like you have to offer to help. I signed up for this, and I'll figure it out without burdening you."

"Burdening? Nonsense. I told you I want a multitude of grandchildren, and at least I feel like I have more than one when Joy is here. You can hang out with us or go take a nap or something. The invitation is completely open."

Before she could respond, Mason answered on her behalf, "That sounds great, Mom. Will you cook breakfast too?"

"Sure, we'll see if Joy likes chocolate chip pancakes as much as Gracie does," Becky replied.

"What time do you want us to be here?"

Kennedy felt completely excluded from the decisions being made, but she wasn't positive on how to insert herself into the conversation. She just looked back and forth at the mother and son as they poured coffee and maintained their two-way communication.

"Y'all be here at nine, and I'll have everything ready." Becky finally stopped to address Kennedy. "You want some coffee, sugar? Do you want me to cook anything special for your breakfast in the morning?"

"Pancakes work for me," she relented. Grabbing the

World's #1 Mom mug, Kennedy poured a steaming cup and sat at the table next to where Mason had just settled.

"Mason got me that mug for my birthday when he was only ten years old. It's just one of those things I could never get rid of."

Kennedy stared at the mug, running her finger along a little chip on the bottom edge. "I got my mother a similar cup when I was kid."

"I think all mothers end up with a mug like this at some point in their lives. Do you still have the mug you gave your mom?"

It was a harmless question. Kennedy knew Becky wasn't trying to pry, but she hesitated before answering. "Um. I don't have anything that belonged to my parents."

"Oh dear, where did it all go? Did you lose it all in a fire or something?"

"No, nothing like that," she answered quietly, still staring at the coffee mug rather than making eye contact with her table companions.

In a true mother's fashion, Becky reached over and placed a hand on top of Kennedy's. "Tell me about it. How did your parents die?"

Kennedy never elaborated on her background in general. The fact that anyone else acted interested to hear about her background was unusual. Shrugging her shoulders and lifting her eyes just enough to see the compassion in Becky's face, she shared the events that changed the course of her life. "I was only eighteen when they died. It was the week after I graduated from high school, and we were taking a road trip to Hot Springs to celebrate... to kick off the summer. I fell asleep in the backseat, and I woke up when our car was hit head-on by another vehicle. Our little car couldn't win against a full-sized Hummer with a drunk driver. Both my parents were killed instantly, while I only suffered a little whiplash."

"Oh dear, that's traumatic. How did you handle it all?"

"I just chose to survive. I left that highway in an ambulance, completely numb. My neighbor at the time came to pick me up and bring me home. One of my dad's coworkers helped me through the life insurance process, and even though I had enough money to attend college, I used that money to pay off the house and my Jeep instead. My Jeep was my graduation gift from my parents. I got a job at Dr. Len's office working with animals as a vet tech, and I just pushed through."

While she was sharing, Becky sat in the adjacent chair and took both of Kennedy's hands into her own. Even though Kennedy wanted to avoid the pity, it seemed okay this time. She could tell this display of pity wasn't a reflex action, or surface emotion, but Becky exuded true sympathy. "So you stayed in the house your parents bought?"

Mason spoke from behind her since Kennedy had pivoted in her chair to face Becky. "It looks like you just moved into the house. You don't have much furniture or decorations."

Kennedy clenched her teeth before answering. "It's the same house I grew up in. Joy is now occupying my childhood bedroom." She paused to consider what was worse... Bad memories? Or wonderful memories that ended so abruptly like hers did? "When I came home alone eight years ago, I didn't want any reminders to bring me down, so I got rid of everything in the house. My childhood stuff wasn't needed anymore, and the style throughout the house was my mom's. So everything went away. Furniture, dishes, decorations. I put in the hardwood floors because I hated vacuuming, and I painted every room with new colors. I was an adult, and I needed a fresh start."

Mason continued to dig deeper. "But what did you start? Your house is almost empty except for the living room furniture, your bedroom stuff, and a small kitchen table. There's no pictures or anything. What've you done in the last eight years?"

Kennedy closed her eyes and exhaled. Lifting her chin high and ignoring the dull ache in her chest, she said, "I found a passion for working with animals, Mason. My home became a sanctuary for abused and abandoned animals of all kinds. What was I supposed to do?" Her nostrils flared with her indignant response.

Becky took over speaking. "You did exactly what you needed to do, sugar. Whenever you're ready for what's next in your life, you'll know it. No one else can tell you how to heal or how long it's supposed to take. I can only recommend that you look around and accept the help and affection from people who want to be close to you."

She hadn't cried about the death of her parents in years, but a couple of warm tears slid down her cheeks before she could muster the strength to hold them back.

"Mason, go hang out with your dad and check on the girls," Becky suggested as she shifted in her chair to wrap her arms around Kennedy. With Mason out of the room, Becky gently guided Kennedy's face towards her welcoming shoulder and softly stroked her hair. The tears flowed without hesitation at that point. Kennedy felt embarrassed and ashamed for the tears, but she also felt relief, like a floodgate had opened, releasing years of grief. She leaned into the woman and absorbed the condolences. Once the sniffles started, Becky relinquished the embrace to find a tissue.

It took a few minutes to regain her composure, staying seated and dabbing at the tears. Becky stood behind her now, lightly caressing her shoulders as only a mother knows how to do. Kennedy's spirit felt soothed in the warm kitchen, in the comforting presence of this woman.

Not that Mason was wrong earlier. What had Kennedy started when she made her so-called fresh start as an adult? She had rescued hundreds of animals. Did that count? Did life exist on a deeper level? Whatever she felt for Joy exceeded anything

Kennedy would have guessed was possible. The encroaching vulnerability she developed towards Mason, and now his parents, was downright scary.

She felt in a trance here with Becky, securely surrounded by a cocoon of compassion. Just like earlier at the park. For a moment, she felt secure in Mason's arms. Weren't feelings like this fleeting? How long could they realistically last before being painfully ripped away? Her brain was playing ping pong with the idea of opening up... allowing herself to get close to people again... Would it be worth it?

"Do you want to stay here for a spell? Or do you want to go home and get some rest?" Becky asked, not trying to push Kennedy either way.

"I think I need to go home," Kennedy barely whispered in return. She was sapped, emotionally, mentally, and physically.

Back in the SUV, Kennedy stared out the passenger window again. Only Joy sat in the backseat since Gracie opted to spend the night with BB and Papaw. Joy barely roused when they moved her, and she conked out again after Kennedy strapped her into the booster seat. Kennedy wasn't far from falling asleep herself... Until Mason reached over and took ahold of her left hand in his right. She was suddenly wide awake.

She snuck a quick peek at Mason who maintained his focus on the road ahead. Rather than pull her hand back, she adjusted in her seat so their entwined hands could rest comfortably on the console between them. Holding hands was new to her, but it seemed natural with him.

"Kennedy, I'm really sorry," Mason said quietly without looking in her direction. "I had no idea you were still dealing with so much grief. I guess it's apparent that I'm still dealing with residual anger. We can't erase our pasts, but we can't let our experiences dictate our future either."

"I'm sorry too. I'm not good about communicating how I feel, and I shouldn't expect you to read my mind."

"It's been a helluva week for you, too. You didn't plan on having this kid mess up your plans, but I'm here for you. And I want to see what we can figure out on our own about Joy's father or whatever is the source of the danger for her. I don't want to involve Marla or the police at all until we know what's going on. Maybe we can let the girls hang out with my parents tomorrow while we do our own investigating. Does that sound like a good plan?"

"That would be great. Thank you, Mason."

He gave her hand a little squeeze and caressed her palm softly with his thumb. Kennedy had never felt like this before. Her heart was becoming susceptible to this handsome fireman, but opening her heart was painful. Maybe she needed some WD-40 to help her heart fully open without protest. At this moment, she wasn't sure that she wanted to go home. She wanted to stay close to Mason, drawing in his resiliency and strength. And close to his parents, where love and tenderness seemed to live.

Not her house. The sterile environment with no character. Kennedy wouldn't even pretend her house was a home anymore. If she could get in touch with her own emotions and fill in the blank space that her life had become, maybe she could still have a future. The idea frightened her but exhilarated her at the same time.

As they pulled into her driveway, Mason took his hand back to maneuver the steering wheel. It was just his hand, but Kennedy felt cold in the absence of his physical contact. Her heart floated in her chest, ready to sink or ready to soar depending on whatever Mason said next.

"Let me get her," Mason whispered as he easily lifted Joy

from the backseat.

Kennedy opened the front door and motioned for him to deposit the snoozing girl into the bed in the master bedroom. Milo wasted no time joining Joy in the bed and taking his position as the little spoon, accepting snuggles from the drowsy girl. She didn't even wake completely while rolling towards the dog to put an arm over him. If Milo and Joy could find comfort with each other so quickly, why was Kennedy not able to do the same? Why did she have so much trouble accepting comfort and support from others?

What did Becky say earlier? *She should be willing to accept affection from people who want to be close to her.*

Kennedy stood in the narrow hallway, lost in thought. Mason moved past her, heading towards the front door to leave. Snapping out of her paralysis, she quickly joined him in the front room of the house.

She spoke to his back as he reached to open the front door. "My parents never used this room as a dining room. It used to be my playroom. Toyboxes and matchbox car tracks filled this space. As I got older, my parents replaced the toys with musical instruments. This is where I learned how to play the guitar and the keyboard. Both my parents were musically gifted."

Mason turned around. "And now, it's your room for sprouting seeds?" he said with a smile.

Offering that tiny bit of personal information was harder than she expected, but his smile made it worth it. "Maybe after I get my garden planted this spring, I can do something different with this space. Joy might need a playroom if she's still here with me."

"I can build her a toybox if you want me to."

Kennedy closed the few steps between them and put her arms around Mason's waist, resting her head on his shoulder. He returned the embrace and lightly massaged her back with his strong hands. She could feel him kissing the top of her head, but she wanted more than that. Why was she so scared? Her breathing became shallow, and she wondered if this was the beginning of a panic attack.

Unexpectantly, Mason's hand wove into her long hair so he could gently tug her head backwards, just enough to be face to face. Her eyes met his briefly before she slowly lowered her lashes. She didn't want the fear in her eyes to cause Mason any hesitation. One of them needed to be brave.

The first kiss was barely Mason brushing his lips against hers. Kennedy didn't know how to react, but she refused to back away. The next kiss on the other hand... It might leave a bruise... And it only lasted a minute before Mason pulled his face back from hers. His hand remained in her hair while he pulled her into a tighter embrace. Her face was now close to his neck, inhaling his scent. Abandoning her inhibition, she lightly pressed her lips to his neck.

He only allowed it for a second before he pulled back from her. She wanted his hands back in her hair, not on her shoulders where they rested now. His face was only about six inches from hers, his eyes searching hers.

"Ken, you're too raw with emotion right now. I'm not going to take advantage of you tonight, but I'll pick you up at eight thirty in the morning. Okay?"

"Okay." What else could she say? She had entered into new territory, and she could only be grateful for the quick peck he offered before reminding her to lock the door behind him.

After brushing her teeth and washing her face, Kennedy became the third spoon in the bed. She got under the blanket to snuggle with Joy. Milo stayed on top of the blanket without relinquishing his spot. Kennedy craved human companionship now, and she hoped Joy's rhythmic breathing would help her decompress.

Kennedy's brain refused to yield to the sandman. What happened tonight? Mason refused to take advantage of her. Would it be taking advantage if she were willing? What exactly was Kennedy willing to do? Could she literally experience her first real kiss and her first sexual experience on the same night? She never considered the moral implications of casual sex because she had never been sexually active. Should she think about it now?

The fact was that Kennedy would have gone all the way with Mason tonight. Holy Moly! Did she need birth control? Did she need to do a better job shaving? Did she need cuter bras and panties? Did Mason plan on sticking around for the long haul? Would he continue to be a gentleman, not taking advantage of her vulnerable state?

Her pensiveness must've caused Joy to wake up, because the silence was broken by a small voice. "Ken."

Kennedy shook off the befuddlement inside her skull to softly respond, "Hey, Joy. I didn't mean to wake you."

The girl wriggled around to find a perfect cuddling position against her mother figure. "I love you, Ken."

"I love you too, Joy." And she meant it. Her brain abandoned the muddled thoughts of Mason in favor of the sweet girl snoozing soundly in her arms. Her pillow absorbed a few more warm tears as Kennedy succumbed to sleep.

THURSDAY, FEBRUARY 17

The combination of high fifties and sunshine was the best weather one could ask for in mid-February. Kennedy and Joy tended to the chickens and other critters. They allowed Ginger to explore the backyard, where she happily nibbled on the dormant grass before they returned the bunny to her indoor playpen. Milo enjoyed a long walk through the neighborhood. Joy became more talkative during their outdoor adventure. Kennedy appreciated that the girl was speaking in full sentences, displaying curiosity about the worm on the sidewalk and the pansies blooming in a neighbor's flowerbed.

Kennedy felt refreshed. She drew in a lungful of oxygen, feeling like she was breathing for the first time in her life. Today was a new day. Joy was opening up. Kennedy was opening up. She knew beyond a shadow of a doubt that she could trust Mason. After last night, she might admit that she could trust Mason more than she could trust herself.

Her pulse elevated when she saw the red Suburban parked in her driveway. They finished the last leg of the walk at a brisker pace, and Kennedy grinned from ear to ear when she noticed the gorgeous fireman leaning back against his vehicle, smiling in her direction. She hurried into his embrace, holding him tightly and allowing the tender moment to revive the giddy feelings she experienced the night before.

As she loosened her bear hug on Mason, he pulled her back close. "Good morning, beautiful," he whispered against her ear, following the whisper with several kisses on her lobe.

The intense shivers physically shook Kennedy. She almost dropped Milo's leash, and if Mason didn't have a good hold on her, she might've fallen over. A mental note was made in her subconscious about how much she enjoyed having her ear kissed. Mason chuckled a little under his breath, probably laughing at her reaction, but Kennedy didn't care. He relinquished the hug to pick up Joy, who waited patiently for her turn to receive some affection.

"You ready to try some pancakes, Joy?"

"Yes."

Neither Kennedy nor Mason could guess whether or not Joy had ever eaten pancakes, but she was sure to love them. Kennedy moved to put Milo back in the house so they could leave.

"Why don't you bring him? Dad had to put his old lab to sleep last month, and I think Milo might be good company for him. Plus, Milo doesn't need to be here alone all day."

Every time Mason showed the slightest amount of concern for animals, Kennedy gained more respect for him. "You don't think your parents will mind?"

"Of course not. Milo's a good boy."

Good boy indeed. Milo immediately claimed the spot next to Papaw on the couch after they arrived at the farmhouse. Gracie exchanged hugs and kisses with her dad before greeting Kennedy and Joy with hugs as well.

Becky flipped pancakes on a massive griddle, while everyone said their good mornings. Trying to be helpful, Kennedy placed forks, knives, and napkins in front of six chairs around the dining room table. At Becky's request, Kennedy proceeded to pour six glasses of orange juice. The pancakes made their way to the table, a short stack in front of every chair. Gracie and Joy got chocolate chips in theirs, and Mason helped both girls with cutting up the pancakes and dispensing syrup.

Kennedy's mind wandered again. Mason was such a good father. He truly valued family and relationships. And he was so ruggedly handsome. His integrity and self-assuredness completed his status as the ideal man. He could easily find a good woman to share his life with, whereas Kennedy considered herself to be damaged goods. Maybe she shouldn't be getting so attached to him.

Getting? Never mind. She was looking at *attached* in the rear-view mirror. Completely and utterly attached. If this ever ended, Kennedy might be devastated beyond repair. Mason deserved someone with more to offer than Kennedy had. Did she even have anything to offer him? She would only ever be a leech or a parasite, accepting the affection with nothing to give back.

"Are you not hungry, sugar?" Becky asked, breaking her internal train of thought.

"Oh, yes, I'm just distracted," Kennedy told the doting woman, and then she dug into the pancakes, releasing a flavor explosion in her mouth. "These are delicious! Are you going to share your secret ingredient?"

Becky leaned in. "It's no secret. Just a little bacon grease on the griddle." Her hot-pink lips spread into a smile before she turned to Joy. "How do you like your breakfast, Joy?"

Just like the night before, Joy just nodded her head. Chocolate and syrup covered her face. The girl looked like she was in heaven. Breakfast continued with only small talk about the pleasant weather and the variety of animals Kennedy adopted over the years.

Once the plates were emptied, Ronnie stood up from the table first. "Come on, girls. Let's get some horses saddled up for you to ride today. Mason, why don't you help us get loaded before you two leave."

Feeling betrayed, Kennedy watched Milo follow Ronnie outside.

"Don't get your feelings hurt. Everyone loves Papaw," Becky told her, displaying an uncanny ability to read the situation.

"I think it's sweet. Let me help you with the dishes," Kennedy said as she grabbed a couple of plates and a handful of silverware.

Alone in the kitchen, the women started a new conversation that Kennedy didn't anticipate. Without looking up from the dish she scrubbed in the sink, Becky said, "I saw you looking at Mason earlier. I recognize that look. You done caught some feelings for him, haven't you?"

Taken aback, Kennedy almost dropped the plate she was drying. "Caught some feelings?"

"Don't play dumb. He likes you too."

"My feelings don't matter, Becky. Mason deserves someone with more to offer than I have. I almost feel bad that he's acting obligated to help me so much right now."

"I have to admit, I was concerned Tuesday when he told me he planned to spend so much time with you and Joy. He explained how he met you, and I assumed he was just infatuated because of the way you stepped up to help Joy. I was also really concerned because Mason hasn't shown interest in being serious with anyone since the divorce. Meeting you under these dramatic circumstances might be manufacturing feelings that don't really exist below the surface. Now that I've met you, it's clear that both of you need each other."

"Becky, I don't even know who I am. I've been operating on autopilot for so many years, and it's probably safer for me to stay that way. Joy will eventually be united with some family, and I'll go back to my comfort zone."

She handed Kennedy the last wet plate and *tsked* before

attacking the sticky forks with her soapy sponge. "What's holding you back from getting out of your comfort zone?"

"It's obvious that I'm not handling my grief well, even eight years later. It's just not fair that my parents were killed like they were, and I guess a part of me died with them. What's left of me needs to play it safe."

"Not fair? Lots of things aren't fair. It's not fair that Gracie's slut of a mother turned out how she did. Let me ask you this... You aren't even Joy's mother, but you would die to protect her right now, wouldn't you?"

"Without a doubt." Kennedy knew that within twenty-four hours of accepting the girl into her home.

"Your parents would die over and over again to make sure you got to live. As a mom, I can tell you that for a fact. If you died so that Joy could live, would you want her dwelling on it the rest of her existence? Hiding behind some excuses about what's fair?"

"Of course not," she replied with a new batch of tears stinging her eyes. She could predict where this lecture was going.

"You'd want Joy to live a full life. Full of love and experiences. Your parents want that for you too, Kennedy. So live. Experience life to the fullest. You're going to get hurt along the way, I can also attest to that as a mom. But all the experiences make you who you are. Don't be desensitized to life because you're scared."

Kennedy stacked the last clean plate on the shelf and then used the corner of the towel to soak up the tears before they had a chance to fall.

Becky continued speaking, giving Kennedy a chance to get it together. "You should also know we're fully armed and ready to protect those we love. Don't worry about leaving Joy here today. I don't really foresee any trouble, but we're cocked, locked, and ready to rock if trouble comes this way."

"Thank you," she choked out, still keeping the tears at bay. Kennedy saw Mason coming back to the house through the kitchen window, so she needed to get a grip on her mentality.

"Now, go see what you can figure out with Mason," Becky demanded as she took the towel from Kennedy's hand and offered a goodbye kiss on her cheek.

As the red Suburban veered down the two-lane road, Kennedy closed her eyes and leaned back against the headrest, simply enjoying the warmth of Mason's hand holding hers. She wanted to know where they were going and what his plan might be, but more than that, she wanted to make an intimate connection with someone. Silently, Kennedy willed herself to become vulnerable, to be available for love and pain and everything in between. If anyone were worth the risk, Mason would be the one.

"Did you not sleep well last night?" The deep voice cut into her thoughts.

Opening her eyes and giving him a sideways glance, she answered, "I slept fine, just thinking about our situation. How do we start investigating what's going on? Where are we even going right now?" So much for admitting what she was really thinking.

Mason offered a glorious smile in reply. "Don't worry your pretty little head about that. I did some brainstorming, and I came up with a good starting point."

Kennedy scrunched her nose and turned her face fully towards the driver. "My pretty little head? Did you seriously just say that?"

"Well, you have kind of a Resting Bitch Face going on, but I still think you're pretty."

Despite the potential insult, Kennedy laughed aloud and playfully pulled her hand out of his. Over the years, she had heard random pick-up lines and stale words of flattery from the occasional blind date, but this might be the first genuine conversation with a man that she could categorize as legitimately complimentary.

"And you're prettier when you smile like that. Now, give me your hand back so I can tell you what I came up with." He extended his right hand over the vehicle console and waited until she returned her left hand before he continued.

"The first part of my plan was easy. I found Autumn Gibson on Facebook and saw that she works in the mayor's office doing clerical support. Her history goes back to her high school days, and she's worked in the same office for the last ten years. Which means Destiny also worked in the mayor's office. If our theory is correct, then she was sleeping with someone in that office seven years ago. Since the City of Memphis is very departmentalized, we can easily look back at the administration during that time and maybe narrow down if she worked with someone who could be potentially worth blackmailing."

Astounded, Kennedy had to agree. "That's genius! So, where are we going to do this research?"

"At my fire station. My chief was one of the guys who helped me sneak Joy away from the scene that night. We're going to research on his computer since I don't have one at home, and this seems like tedious research to handle from a phone. Plus, Chief has some connections with the Shelby County and City of Memphis leaders if we need his help with anything. But first, you need to let Marla know we're busy today, so she won't try to facetime you later."

Kennedy took a few minutes to text Marla several pictures of the six-year-old proudly mounted on a quarter horse. And she was grateful that Mason took these photos since she had been oblivious to the idea of taking pictures to chronicle Joy's adventures so far.

"What did you tell Marla?" Mason asked as she put her phone back in her pocket.

"Just that we'd be trail riding, and I didn't want her to worry if we don't have a good signal. I told her I would text her later when we get back to the house in case she wants to visit or call. Marla thanked me for letting her know. That's it."

No sooner than they had finished talking, Mason pulled into a small parking area behind a one-story brick building that housed one of Bartlett's fire stations. The three garage bays were closed, so Kennedy had no view of any engines or ambulances that might be present. She had never been inside a fire station, but she had always been fascinated by the first responders since that fateful day eight years ago when a big red fire truck blocked the interstate so the jaws of life could extract her from the mangled wreckage that used to be her parents' car.

Passing through a small entry area, Mason led Kennedy to a lounge where four firemen watched golf on TV. Mason offered quick introductions, but once he introduced her as his *girlfriend*, Kennedy couldn't remember names or anything else that anyone said. They moved quickly through a kitchen towards an office that occupied one corner of the station. The engraved nameplate on the door read "Chief Rice." It reminded Kennedy of the same kind of nameplates that get glued onto high school sports trophies.

Mason rapped on the door and opened it without waiting for a reply. The older man behind the desk stood and came around to shake hands and formally introduce himself.

"You must be Kennedy. I'm Kyle Rice, the guys around here just call me Chief." She couldn't quite see his smile, but the upward movement of his bushy gray moustache provided Kennedy with enough proof that the chief was indeed smiling.

"Pleased to meet you, Chief. Thank you for helping us out today," she replied as she looked down at the shorter man. He wore a BFD ballcap and sweatshirt, but his work boots didn't add enough height to make him as tall as Kennedy.

"Anything to help this unfortunate situation. I'm going out here with the guys but come get me if you need me." The chief scurried out of the small office and shut the door as he exited.

"What do the guys think you're doing in here?" Kennedy asked.

"I told them I'm doing a continuing education course for my EMT license," he answered, "and I told them you were helping me study." He moved towards the desk as he spoke.

The computer sat on the clean desk, inviting Mason to set down the notebook he carried. He had a seat in the executive chair, and Kennedy pulled a smaller guest chair around so she could see the screen as well. The investigation was ready to commence.

"The mayor is always elected for a four-year term, so seven years ago would've been one year into Mayor Wigginton's term. He only served that one term since he lost his bid for re-election, but we can still see his leadership team from that year." Mason said all this as he pecked away on the keyboard. "Okay, here are his elected leaders. You ready to write?"

Kennedy nodded, pen in hand.

"Let's write down the names, and then we can do some more research on each one individually. First, we have Beau McFarland, the chief financial officer. Then Pam Anderson, the chief communications officer. Next is Lashonda Kinney, the chief operating officer..."

Kennedy interrupted after writing down the first three names, "Mason, if Destiny was sleeping with someone to get pregnant, it wasn't with a woman. Skip the women for now. If we run into a dead end, we can go back to research the women."

"Fair enough. The next man is Marion Childress, the fire chief. Then... Brett Jamison, the chief of staff. Most of his leadership team consisted of women, so that keeps this list short. The mayor would also be highly interactive with the thirteen council members." He clicked a few links on the computer before saying anything else. "Here's the city council from that year... eight of them were men, and they're listed with pictures."

"It's safe to say that the five black men didn't contribute to Joy's DNA. Even Mayor Wigginton himself was mixed race, so I'm not going to list him here," Kennedy said over his shoulder.

"That leaves David Maddox, Gerald Gates, and Reid Kilgore." After listing those names for Kennedy to add to the list, Mason typed in another search and clicked a few more links until he found what he was seeking. "The last group that the mayor would be highly involved with are his appointed officials. I don't have pictures here, but we can go ahead and list the men."

In the next few minutes, Kennedy added six more names to the list. John Canterbury, special counsel. Patrick Roth, public works director. Wallace Thatcher, library director. Anthony Duncan, information services director. Dustin Boothe, housing & community development director. Levi Kellerman, general services director.

"Is there anyone else who frequents the mayor's office that we need to identify?" Kennedy inquired, trying to make sure they cast a wide net for this portion of the research.

"I doubt it. All these appointed guys will have assistants who spend time in the office, but I don't think any of them would be blackmail worthy."

"That gives us twelve names to start with," Kennedy said, feeling less daunted than she did only an hour ago before they began this search. "Are you ready to see if any of these names can be ruled out for any reason?"

Mason resumed his pecking on the keyboard, while Kennedy shifted her gaze to the window. The sunshine hinted at the unseasonably warm weather, which compelled the buttercups to bloom early in the adjacent field. Across the field, six-foot wooden fences provided privacy for the backyards of the suburban neighborhood. Directly outside the window, a barbecue grill and a couple of picnic tables sat unused, even though today would be the ideal day to enjoy some outdoor cooking.

Kennedy remained mesmerized by the serene view until a bright-red cardinal landed on the table outside. Her dad was a baseball fan, a St. Louis Cardinals fan to be more specific. She thought of her dad every time she saw a cardinal, and she smiled at the beautiful red bird. The bird seemed to make eye contact with Kennedy, cocking his head to the side and giving her a renewed peace that she couldn't explain.

Was her dad communicating through a bird? At that time, a drab-colored cardinal joined him on the picnic table. The female counterpart of the red bird took her turn looking in the window at Kennedy. Then the feathered friends flew off in unison. Was she nuts? Was she so desperate for a sign that two birds on a picnic table could affect her so profoundly?

"Are you okay? You look like you just saw a ghost." Mason's voice broke her trance.

Kennedy turned back to look at the handsome fireman next to her. He had rotated in his chair to face her, and he leaned forward to plant a soft kiss on her lips. "Mason, I'm better today than I've been in a long time."

"Good," he said as he turned back to the computer. "Let's scratch David Maddox and Dustin Boothe from the list. They're both dead now."

Kennedy scratched those names and waited for Mason to

provide further instruction. It seemed strange, as she sat there. She literally felt lighter in the chair, like an unspeakable weight had been lifted. Here she was, in the middle of some possible conspiracy that put a child in danger, but Kennedy felt like she had a purpose and a real connection to something important. Something pivotal. She felt fully alive.

Mason continued his research, printing articles and clicking links, while Kennedy continued her emergence into the living world. Of course, no one could see her transformation, but on the inside, she underwent a metamorphosis that any butterfly would be proud of.

"Okay, scratch off Wallace Thatcher, Marion Childress, and Patrick Roth. They're all black guys. And then scratch off John Canterbury. He's been in jail for several years for vehicular homicide, so nothing worth blackmailing there. Even special counsel appointees can't get away with drunk driving."

"Good, I hope he rots in jail," Kennedy spouted off with more anger than she intended.

"You and me both," he said without taking his attention away from the computer. "The only other name we can reasonably remove from the list for now is Gerald Gates. He's eighty years old, so I doubt he was capable of making a baby seven years ago."

"That narrows it down to five names. You don't see anything obvious to rule these guys out?"

"Nope. We need to do some deeper digging to find out where these remaining men are now and see how likely they are to become blackmail victims."

They spent the next two hours making notes and printing articles on the five men. Three times during the two hours, tones from the loudspeaker summoned all the first responders to emergencies. Mason and Kennedy heard sirens from the ambulance or the fire engine as they left in response to the calls. Mason visibly jumped each time the tones sounded, but he settled back in the chair each time. He certainly was heroic. Ready to rush into someone else's crisis without hesitation. Always eager to help. It became clear to Kennedy that this was more than his job. This was his nature.

BB had a picnic lunch ready by the time they got back to the house. A large quilt was spread on the lawn, displaying a plateful of sandwiches and bottles of water. The girls joined BB, Papaw, Mason and Kennedy on the quilt, and everyone dug in hungrily.

To Kennedy's amazement, Gracie and Joy took turns talking about the horse ride. The larger imagination belonged to Gracie, who vividly described the evidence of bigfoot that she saw throughout the woods. Joy did take an opportunity to point out a spot on her arm where a caterpillar landed earlier. The adults laughed as the children entertained, and Milo didn't care who did what as long as Papaw kept sneaking him pieces of turkey sandwich.

What was it about this family? Kennedy couldn't believe how quickly Joy came out of her shell around these people. Her own shell seemed to be disintegrating, like ice melting in the warm sun. As she observed Joy giggling and enjoying her childhood, maybe for the first time in her life, Kennedy's chest tightened at the thought of someone wanting to harm the girl.

"You have that RBF going on again; what're you thinking?" Mason asked quietly, leaning close to her ear.

She offered a wry smile before answering. "Just about how hard I would fight to protect the ones I care about."

"Well, we can be a tag team, fighting together." His eyebrows waggled as if he might be joking, but Kennedy knew she could count on him to join her in whatever battle might lie ahead.

BB led the girls back into the house after lunch to watch another princess movie. Papaw and Milo got the horses settled in the barn. That left Kennedy and Mason free to dig into all the articles they printed earlier.

Sitting at the kitchen table, Kennedy read one after the other... notes from the mayor's agenda and city council meetings... stances on school funding... arguments over mandatory overtime for the police force... proposed honorary changes to street names... approval of special use permits for historic buildings. She was both amazed and bored by the things politicians were required to go on record about.

With only a few interesting points here and there, the hours spent studying the information only caused Kennedy a massive headache and crossed eyes. Mason finally stood up and stretched. "I can't read anymore today. This hasn't uncovered anything so far, but I know we're going to come up with something that helps. Obviously, there won't be an article about which public official was sleeping with his secretary, no smoking gun, but we'll find something that stands out eventually."

Kennedy thought about that for a second. "You're right. How the council addresses its constituents probably won't tell us anything. Maybe we can do some more recent searches of where these guys are now. What have they done since their tenure with the city? Can you find them on Facebook the same way you found Autumn Gibson?"

He continued to stretch his neck by moving it side to side as he retrieved a bottle of water from the refrigerator. "That's probably a better angle to help us study this from a personal standpoint instead of political. I was hoping Destiny's name would appear in an article, like maybe she worked closely with one of these guys on a project. When I googled her name earlier, all I got was the brief report about her death."

Kennedy took a minute to lean back in her chair,

extending all the muscles in her back. As she resumed her normal seated position, Mason moved to stand behind her and massaged her shoulders. Her immediate response was to tense up, but Kennedy exhaled and gave into the pleasure of his hands tenderly kneading her tight muscles. Involuntarily, her eyes closed, and her head drooped forward. She might have moaned, but she hoped the noise stayed inside her head. His thumbs rubbed in concentric circles at the base of her neck, evoking tingles throughout her whole body.

After only a few minutes of bliss, Mason moved his face so close, she felt his breath on her ear. "Will you give my massage technique a five-star rating?" One hand moved from her shoulder to move her hair away from her left ear. A trail of soft kisses traced the path from her ear to her neck. Kennedy knew her moan was audible that time, but oh well. *What was this crazy tingling throughout her core?*

"Come on, let's go hang out with the girls for a few minutes."

Kennedy's body seemed to be in shock from the sudden arousal, followed by the sudden end of the physical attention. After a quick check to make sure she didn't have any drool on her chin, she shook it off and joined Mason in the den. While Cinderella patiently waited for her prince to show up with a glass slipper, the two girls watched so intently, neither noticed the adults enter the room. When Prince Charming finally came to the rescue, Gracie clapped her hands as if the cartoon characters could hear her applause.

It hurt Kennedy to decline the invitation to stay for dinner, but she needed to get home to tend to her own animals. Hugs and thanks were given, and a treat was used to entice Milo to follow her outside. This time, Gracie joined Joy in the backseat with Milo between them.

From the driver's seat, holding her hand again, Mason suggested they grab burgers to eat when they get to Kennedy's house. In no time, the aromas from two kids meals and two adults meals made everyone hungry. Kennedy burned her tongue on a couple of fries during the short drive, but it was worth it.

"I guess we can eat at the coffee table since I don't have enough chairs in the kitchen." Kennedy shook her head at the conundrum she never expected. Joy and Gracie enjoyed their cheeseburgers and played with the stickers that came with their meals. Kennedy ate quickly and then put her chickens up and fed the rest of the household critters. When she finally sat back down in the living room, Mason sent the girls to Joy's room to play.

He turned on the television for background noise, and they watched a few minutes of the news before resuming any conversation. The anchorwoman spoke about a missing woman in South Carolina and a potential serial killer named the Marina Marauder.

"I hate it when they give a serial killer a nickname," Kennedy said with anger.

"Yeah, it almost validates what they're doing. Years ago, we had a serial rapist here in Bartlett. I don't remember his real name, but they called him the 'Big-Bellied Rapist.' At least his nickname was embarrassing, and he got arrested. Let's just keep our fingers crossed that the girl in South Carolina is found before it's too late."

Sighing from all the evil in the world, Kennedy tried to refocus on the current events in her own home. "We need to make plans to continue researching these politicians tomorrow. I feel bad asking your parents to watch Joy and Gracie while we're doing this, and we probably don't need to make an appearance at your fire station every day in the meantime. Do you have some good idea on how to proceed?"

Before he could answer, some dramatic sounds played from the television, signaling to viewers that breaking news was on the verge of being shared. Kennedy grabbed the controller to turn the volume down, but the picture displayed behind the news lady gave Kennedy tunnel vision. The controller dropped, along with her jaw.

"This just in," the lady said, obviously reading a teleprompter, "The Memphis Police have issued an endangered child notice for a young girl who may be the victim of an abduction in the Bartlett area. Kevin is reporting live from the scene... Kevin, tell us what you've found out so far."

The view switched to a field with the charred remains of a house and the reporter standing with a microphone. "Yes, Sarah, you can see what's left of a home behind me. A home where a woman and her small daughter lived until the house burned to the ground on Monday. The woman, Destiny Young, was found shot to death at a gas station down the street the next day. The Memphis Police are still investigating the details of her death, and the Bartlett Fire Department is still investigating this house fire as potential arson. The community is outraged and saddened tonight over Destiny's missing daughter. Sarah, please show the photo and tell our viewers how they can help."

Switching back to the newsroom, Sarah spoke into the camera again with a blurry picture of Joy behind her. In the picture, a frightened Joy held Ginger. It must have been a low-quality cell phone picture without any close-up of Joy's face. If Kennedy didn't know it was Joy, the picture wouldn't provide quite enough detail to recognize her.

"Please take a look at this picture. Her name is Jillian Young, and she recently turned six. The police have only learned of the girl's existence by this picture recovered from her mother's phone. Birth records have confirmed that Young did in fact have a daughter, but no other record has been found regarding the girl's whereabouts. As of now, investigators cannot determine whether Jillian is enrolled in school or even if she lived with her mother in Bartlett. One possible scenario is that Jillian was abducted when her mother was murdered, and the police are searching tonight to ensure that the girl is safe. If anyone has seen this child, you are urged to contact the police on the number shown on the screen."

The tunnel vision and shallow breathing made Kennedy feel weak. The newscaster moved onto another story, and she turned her head to see Mason also sitting in shock.

"Kennedy, we have to keep her out of the public eye until this is solved. Fortunately, that picture doesn't provide a good likeness of Joy, but we can't take any chances."

Choking to get any words out, Kennedy inhaled deeply and tried again. She placed her hand over her heart, making sure it was still beating since she was certain it stopped completely. Then instantly, her heart started beating so fast, she could hear her pulse in her ears. "What am I gonna do?"

"I don't like you staying here by yourself right now. Go pack a bag for you and Joy. You can stay with me for now."

"But my animals…"

"Milo and Ginger can go with us. We can come back tomorrow morning to feed the rest of the animals. Can you just leave the chicken door open at night? We'll just come by each morning to feed everyone until we know the danger has passed."

Kennedy quickly jumped up and tried to make sense of everything in her head. Clothes. Dog food. Toothbrush. She hadn't stayed overnight at someone else's home since high school. She didn't even own an overnight bag. The one time she attended an out-of-town veterinary conference last year, she had to borrow a suitcase from Pennie. Panicked, she tried to find a solution for an overnight bag.

"Kennedy, breathe. Just get a few outfits while I help Joy get some clothes together. Then we'll grab the things from your bathroom and some food for Milo and Ginger."

Fifteen minutes later, they loaded Ginger in a kennel in the back of the Suburban, along with the reusable grocery bags from Whole Foods that doubled as her overnight bags. Mason's parents had already called to make sure they saw the story. While Kennedy looked around to make sure she hadn't forgotten anything important at the house, her phone rang, displaying Marla's number on the caller ID.

"Hello."

"Kennedy, did you see the news?"

"Yes, ma'am."

"I still haven't told anyone about you or Joy, but I want to know who killed her mother before we tell the police that Joy is safe. The chatter at the police station indicates some major trouble surrounds her. I don't like this at all; I think I'm getting an ulcer," Marla said with disgust.

"Marla, I'm going to stay with a friend for a while. Please don't come to my house expecting to do a surprise visit. I'll just lay low until you let me know the danger has passed."

"As much as I hate that, it's probably for the best. I did manage to do a quick search for Destiny's family, and her parents both died a few years ago. I can't find anything else without it being extended family in Canada. We're that sweet child's only advocates right now, and I won't even try to call you again unless I have important information or until we know it's safe."

After she hung up, Mason recommended that she leave her phone at the house. They both seemed paranoid, thinking someone might try to track her through her phone. Out of an abundance of caution, Kennedy left her phone on the nightstand.

Mason punched in the code to open the gates to the

apartment complex. Kennedy hadn't even paid attention to the drive, but these apartments were constructed fairly recently, built adjacent to the new golf course at the Bartlett Country Club.

"Do you play golf?" Kennedy asked as the vehicle wound through the tightly situated buildings and slowed down for the incessant speed bumps.

"No, but I like the view. I also like knowing that another strip center won't be built next door, and the gated community seems more important now than it did when I moved in a year ago. There's a big golf tournament planned for next month, so traffic will probably be a nightmare for a couple of weeks."

He pushed a button on the visor to open a single-bay garage that the SUV barely fit in. The girls jumped out, and Kennedy put a leash on Milo to let him relieve himself before going into the apartment. While she walked the dog, Mason carried the bags and the rabbit cage inside.

Kennedy stood on the grass near the apartment, allowing Milo to sniff around. The cool evening air gave her chills. Maybe her circumstances with this fugitive child gave her the chills. Maybe the idea of staying with Mason gave her chills. Watching her pseudo-family entering the home, she wondered what her life could be spiraling into. And now, the fear of becoming emotionally vulnerable had joined forces with the fear of whatever enemy they were facing on Joy's behalf.

Milo tugged on the leash, so Kennedy followed him into the apartment. Mason met her just inside the door and shut the garage. The small entry area opened to a kitchen on the left and a short hallway to the right. Past the entry, a dining area and living room shared an open space. A sliding door to the left of the living room revealed a gorgeous view of the golf course in the soft light of the setting sun. Her assessment was cut short when Mason placed his hand on her back to guide her through the living room.

"You'll be staying in my room." He opened the door to the master bedroom where a blue and gray flannel comforter covered the king-sized bed. Nightstands flanked the bed. A dresser against the opposite wall was the only other furniture in the room. The walls, though... they were crowded with family portraits. Probably a few aunts and uncles, cousins, and other relatives. Gracie was featured in many of them, along with BB and Papaw. Others were black and white photos from older generations.

Again, her assessment was cut short when Mason opened a door to the right to finish giving her the tour. "The bathroom and closet are in here. You can just make yourself at home," he said as he grabbed a blanket off a shelf in the closet. "I'll camp out on the couch. Come on so I can show you Gracie's room."

The hallway off the entry led to a second bathroom and a spacious bedroom. A princess canopy with twinkling lights around the top covered Gracie's full-sized bed. Joy and Gracie didn't bother looking up from the toybox when the adults entered. Kennedy smiled to see the ornate wooden box with Gracie's name painted in calligraphy across the front. Joy definitely would need a toy box like that one of these days. "There's plenty of room for both girls to sleep in here. We need to try to wind down for the evening. I'm feeling overwrought, and I know you are too." He seemed to be talking out of nervousness, stringing sentences together to fill any would-be silence.

They sat on the couch and turned on the television just in case the news had any more breaking stories they needed to be aware of. Kennedy cuddled up in a throw blanket to counteract the chill that had seeped into her bones. Milo settled on the floor where he had a clear view out of the sliding glass door.

"You're being really quiet, are you okay?" Mason quietly asked.

"Oh, yea, sorry. I'm just processing everything."

"If the Cinderella blanket isn't warming you up, the Little

Mermaid blanket is heavier."

Kennedy noticed all the throw blankets featured princesses, but now, she also noticed the throw pillows and lamp also featured princesses. The photos on the walls showed Gracie dressed as various princesses.

"Or if you need more than a blanket, you could scoot over here and let me warm you," Mason said, extending his arm towards her.

Cuddling with a man on his couch. This had never happened before. Kennedy quickly kicked off her sneakers and nestled against Mason's warm body, sighing as his arm secured her tightly to his side. His hand settled on her hip, and she felt that tingling in her core again. Kennedy mentally chastised herself for allowing such a physical reaction during such a time of stress.

The lady on the seven o'clock news only spoke about the upcoming golf tournament while Kennedy zoned out. Was this what she had missed out on by not pursuing relationships? Relaxing nights, cuddling while the kids play in their room? She had no sooner decompressed than the girls rushed into the living room, wanting attention from the adults.

After coloring mermaids for an hour, it was time for bed. Kennedy put forth the effort to keep some sort of routine with Joy, and as of tonight, Gracie would be included. With teeth brushed, Kennedy sat in the middle of the bed with a six-year-old on each side of her and twinkling lights above them. The Dr. Seuss selection of the evening was *Oh, the Places You'll Go.* It seemed like she was reading the book for the first time, like Dr. Seuss must've written it with Kennedy on his mind.

She had a brain in her head.

She had feet in her shoes.

She could steer herself.

There was fun to be done.

Kennedy had been stuck in *The Waiting Place* for years, and despite the pain, she was ready to move mountains. Joy was ready to move mountains too. Gracie was already an expert at moving mountains regardless of the *Hang-ups* and *Bang-ups* in her life. She finished the book with a new appreciation for her circumstances, for the challenges that were forcing her out of *The Waiting Place*.

Mason came into the room to make sure the window was locked when she finished reading. Kennedy kissed each girl on the forehead. He took his turn giving each girl a hug before they turned out the light. Milo, being the traitor he was, wasted no time occupying the space between the girls that Kennedy had just vacated.

"I've checked all the doors and windows, and I have a shotgun under the couch even though I really don't think we're in any danger here. I have a pistol in the nightstand. Do you know how to shoot?"

Shoot a gun? Kennedy had never even touched a gun. "No, but if you have a baseball bat, I could do some damage with that."

"Maybe later, we can do a crash course on guns. But tonight, you need to get some sleep. I'm just gonna put on some pajamas, and then you can get comfortable."

Kennedy pulled back the comforter and ran her hands over the luxurious sheets. She wondered if she could rest peacefully knowing that a man was in such close proximity to protect her. A moment later, Mason exited the bathroom wearing a tank top and pajama bottoms, providing her first glimpse at his athletic physique, and she wasn't disappointed. When his toned arms wrapped around her, Kennedy caught her breath and soaked up the closeness of his perfect body. Then she was completely disappointed when he only offered a small goodnight kiss before leaving her alone in the room.

She put on her own pajamas and scrubbed her face in the masculine bathroom. An electric razor and aftershave sat next to a cup that held his toothbrush and toothpaste. She dropped her toothbrush in the same cup and considered the implications of it. Sitcoms always placed emphasis on the simple act of allowing toothbrushes to cohabitate, like it was the gateway to something serious. Was she entering a gateway to something serious with Mason? In reality, they were already knee deep in some serious business, but their personal relationship needed some definition. A speed needed to be agreed upon to move the relationship forward.

The coolness of the sheets and plushness of the bed brought instantaneous relaxation to Kennedy's tense body. Thoughts of bad guys and imminent danger subsided into blessedly peaceful sleep.

FRIDAY, FEBRUARY 18

The soft knock on the door woke Kennedy from her deep slumber. She sat up, questioning where she was for a split second before reality hit her.

"Come in," she hollered at the door.

Mason peeked his head into the dark room and spoke quietly. "Sorry to wake you. Is it okay if I take a quick shower before the girls get up?"

"I guess I should apologize to you since you had to knock on your own door and ask permission to take a shower in your own bathroom."

"Don't apologize," he said, turning on the bathroom light to partially illuminate the bedroom. "Seeing your beautiful face first thing in the morning is a treat for me."

As he bestowed the compliment, Kennedy swung her legs over the side of the bed and stood up, stretching. With her eyes closed mid-stretch, she didn't see Mason ease towards her to envelop her in a hug. She only wore a tank top and shorts, and the sensation of her bare arms touching his was invigorating. He kissed the top of her head and moved on to the bathroom.

She waited on the couch until he finished his morning routine, and then she took her own shower and brushed her teeth. Without knocking, Kennedy opened the door to the girls' bedroom so she could take Milo for a morning walk. Upon returning, Gracie and Joy both sat at the dining room table, ready to eat breakfast. They made quick work of Fruit Loops, then the girls took baths so they could get the day started.

The first stop of the morning was Kennedy's house. Mason helped her feed all the animals before she checked her phone, which still sat on the nightstand. One message from her boss, Ms. Sue, reminded her of the birthday party the next day at the Cordova Skating Center. Kennedy replied that they planned to be in attendance, but she still needed to tell Mason about it.

After the twenty minutes it took to feed all the pocket pets, they returned to Mason's vehicle to go to his parents' house. With the three kids in the backseat, Milo being the honorary kid, Kennedy sat in the shotgun seat, holding Mason's hand. Other than the couple of kisses and hugs, he wasn't offering much in the way of physical closeness. Kennedy was almost scared of how bad she wanted to be close to him, touching him. She wished he would share the bed with her, even if just to hold her throughout the night.

What if he didn't find her attractive? What if he knew he was only helping her for the short term and was already bored with her? These thoughts caused her chest to constrict. This might just be Mason's reflex action to help someone with a crisis. Then once the crisis was averted, he would return to his routine, leaving Kennedy alone.

"What's wrong with you? You're about to break my hand."

Kennedy inhaled, not realizing she had been holding her breath and tensing up. "I'm just anxious. There's too much we don't know right now. I can't make plans or get back to normal. I don't even know what *normal* is going to become for me. You don't even know when you can have your normal life back. Mason, I'm so sorry."

"I already told you not to apologize. Our new normal is something we'll figure out together."

His words momentarily soothed her. "A week ago, I was worried about my bell pepper plants not developing like I thought they should. Seems trivial now. Plus, my office manager invited us to her granddaughter's birthday party at the Cordova Skating Center tomorrow at two. I don't know if it's a good idea to take Joy given the current situation."

"Oooh, Daddy, can we go skating?" Gracie exclaimed from the backseat.

Kennedy didn't realize they were speaking where the girls could hear, but she also knew that kids hear everything. She would have to be more mindful of conversations that children didn't need to be privy to.

"Gracie, we're still figuring out the plans for tomorrow. I'll think about it."

"Yes, sir." The respectful response was ingrained in the little girl, and Kennedy appreciated how well-behaved Gracie was. A better influence for Joy couldn't have been hand-picked.

BB and Papaw greeted them on the front porch, exchanging hugs and kisses.

"I need some help cleaning the flower beds and garden, so I hope you girls are ready to work in the dirt today," Becky suggested to the girls, receiving silly snickering in response.

Ronnie scratched the spoiled Milo behind his ear and made his own suggestion. "I'm cleaning stalls today, so Milo can hang out with me while you two do whatever you need to do."

As if there had already been a discussion without Kennedy, everyone cleared out, leaving her alone in the kitchen with Mason. He grabbed two bottles of water from the refrigerator and motioned for her to join him in the living room with their notebook from yesterday.

"We need to see if we can find even a hint of where our threat is coming from. I agree with your suggestion from yesterday; we need to find out what these politicians have been doing since they stopped working in the mayor's office when the term ended four years ago." He flipped the television on, turning it to a national news station.

Kennedy sat next to him on the couch and noticed a laptop on the coffee table. "Is that your parents' computer?"

"They bought it last night from Walmart, along with a couple of burner phones. I don't know whether this is extreme behavior or not, but we're going to play it safe until we know what we're up against."

They booted up the computer and investigated the five names remaining on their list. Mason suggested they get an overview of each man to determine if further scrutiny would be necessary.

Person of interest number one, Beau McFarland, had thirty years of accounting and comptroller experience in the private sector before his appointment to the City of Memphis leadership team as the chief financial officer. He obtained his master's degree in accounting from Tulane, but he moved to Memphis early in his career to work for several medical institutions. After his four-year stint with the City of Memphis, McFarland retired from working altogether.

Mason found the retired CFO on Facebook with no problem. McFarland regularly posted pictures with his grandchildren... fishing, eating ice cream, camping... nothing suspicious so far.

"Ken, what do you think? Whoever Destiny wanted to blackmail would have something going on now, right? Something had to trigger her timing."

"Yea, it only makes sense that whoever she's blackmailing has some recent change in status. It might not be something in the news, though. What if this McFarland guy had a rich uncle who just died and left him a ton of money? Destiny might have known the potential back then and bided her time until Uncle Moneybags kicked the bucket."

"Hmmm. I think it's going to be something more public. Let's keep digging. We can circle back to McFarland if we need to."

Next on the list was Brett Jamison, chief of staff. Kennedy had to do some reading to know what a chief of staff even contributed to the leadership team. The position appeared to be a glorified secretarial role, but Jamison didn't look even remotely secretary-ish. He did, however, resemble Mr. Clean with his shiny bald head and gray eyebrows. In the past four years, he had taken a larger role in the Boys & Girls Club, devoting his time to helping underprivileged kids.

"I'm not getting any sinister vibes from this guy," Kennedy said.

"Okay, who's next on the list?"

Councilman Reid Kilgore was next. This one was easy. Kilgore was re-elected for his third term on the Memphis City Council, and he served as chairman for one of the super districts. Mason didn't find any social media presence for the councilman, but he was in the news quite a bit for other reasons. Kilgore served as a board member for the Memphis Police Foundation, as well as making weekly appearances on the news to address concerns in his district.

Mason looked up from the computer screen and rubbed his eyes. "I don't see anything suspicious here, but Kilgore is still active in the government. Maybe we should look at the last two appointees and come back to this guy if nothing else stands out."

Turning the page in her notebook, Kennedy shared the name of the information services director, and Mason immediately searched the internet for anything pertaining to Anthony Duncan. He had previously worked for a couple of local logistics companies, but nothing exciting showed up in his history before his political career began.

"I guess I should have recognized his name," Mason said. "I didn't follow the Memphis elections that closely, but Duncan ran for mayor a few months ago. He lost to the new mayor, Kevin O'Neal."

"Oh, that's right. I lose track of all the elections, and I'm just happy when all the stupid political ads are done playing on TV. All right, so given our situation, Destiny wouldn't bother blackmailing the loser of the election. If Duncan were her target, she would've been asking for some hush money during the election rather than waiting until the end of January after he lost."

"Okay, then who's last on the list?"

Turning the page again, Kennedy responded, "Levi Kellerman. He was the general services director."

Again, Mason pecked on the keyboard, seeking out anything interesting on their last potential person of interest. Kennedy flipped through the articles they had printed out, and her eyes were feeling gritty from so much reading.

"Kellerman is all over the internet because he started a real estate business when his appointment with the mayor ended. He sells houses now, and it looks like nothing else exciting is going on with him." Mason sighed as he said this, obviously frustrated from another seemingly dead end.

Kennedy showed him an article. "What about before he worked in the mayor's office? This report shows he had been named in a scandal with an underaged girl that eventually led to his resignation at the Board of Education."

They both skimmed the article, and the picture showed a middle-aged man who could easily play the part of a television preacher, the one who would tell people he could heal them if they sent enough money to his church. His fake smile, snake eyes, and receding hair line wasn't a good combination. She got the chills just looking at the picture, as if Kellerman gave her the evil eye through a printed picture.

Mason shook his head. "He gives me the creeps too, and I don't like his history. But these recent articles show that his business is failing. I don't think Destiny could be blackmailing him for anything."

Kennedy made a few more notes on the pages in front of her before BB brought the girls through the living room. "We're going to wash up and have some more sandwiches for lunch if you two want to join us." Becky didn't wait for a reply as she ushered the girls to a hall bathroom.

After the quick lunch of sandwiches, Kennedy helped clear the kitchen table. Gracie and Joy chatted about grubworms and other interesting things they saw in the garden. Then Gracie changed the conversation. "BB! Daddy might take us skating tomorrow!"

Becky's face showed an instant change from granny-mode to mom-mode. "Son, do you think that's a good idea with everything going on right now?"

"No, Mom. Joy was invited to a birthday party at the skating rink, and now Gracie is excited about going." He turned his head to his daughter. "And what did I tell you, young lady?"

Gracie offered a pout face before saying, "You said you'd think about it."

"So don't mention it again. I'm still thinking."

Kennedy could remember being stubborn as a child, pooching out her bottom lip when she didn't get her way. More often than not, her dad would give in and come through with whatever Kennedy wished for. Not her mom. Kennedy's mom was the enforcer of the two. She wondered about the dynamic with Mason and Gracie. Would he give in? As a single parent, he was forced to be the good guy and the bad guy. That must be difficult for him. If Joy didn't find some family soon, it would become difficult for Kennedy as well.

BB took her two gardening apprentices back outside. As per their new routine, Milo followed Papaw back to the barn. Kennedy and Mason settled on the couch again and tried to come up with a new angle to investigate.

The brainstorming started with Mason. "All the leaders and appointees in the mayor's office have junior chiefs and administrators. Maybe we can check to see if any of them are independently wealthy or recently in the news for anything else."

"Well, Autumn said Destiny met up with her about three weeks ago to give her a head's up about her plans. Did anything happen during January that this could coincide with?"

Mason shrugged his shoulders. "It was an election year, so all our newly elected officials took office. That's across the country, not just in Bartlett, Memphis, and Shelby County. It's still early for all the new officials to be appointing their leadership teams and cabinet members."

"Can we look at anyone recently elected and maybe backtrack to see where they were seven years ago?" Kennedy suggested.

They got on a path down a different rabbit hole with similar results. They searched leaders in all the nearby jurisdictions... clicking links... skimming articles... with nothing to show for it after several hours. Kennedy's eyes were tired, and her muscles protested the prolonged awkward posture. She got up to pace for a minute, stretching her legs and back. Mason set the laptop back on the coffee table and stretched from his seated position.

Noticing his lazy stretch, Kennedy took the opportunity to sit down and cozy up against his side. Mason put his arm around her where she laid her head against his shoulder. He made such a comfortable pillow. Kennedy felt so safe here. So secure.

"Ken, wake up," Mason said softly.

Her eyes popped open. Where was she? The family portraits and framed embroidery on the walls reminded Kennedy that she was still at BB and Papaw's house. She wiped the sleep from her eyes as she sat up, realizing she had dozed off against Mason.

"Thank goodness, my arm had fallen asleep," he said as he manipulated his arm to encourage blood flow. "You ready to head out? We can pick up some fast food for dinner on the way home."

Home? In her sleepy state, Kennedy couldn't even fathom why he would mention *home* as if it belonged to both of them. Joy was an orphan, so *home* was relative to where she was staying at the time. Mason and Gracie had a home. BB and Papaw had a home. Kennedy would go so far as to say Milo had a home. Kennedy had a house, but not really a home.

"Take a minute to wake up; we can get whatever you want for dinner," Mason said as he got up, leaving Kennedy alone on the couch.

She shook off the drowsiness and got up to stretch some more. Mason went through the dining room towards the kitchen. Kennedy followed in that direction a moment later. From the dining room, she overheard a conversation in the kitchen, so she quietly stopped to listen.

She heard Ronnie speak first. "Mason, you have to be careful with this woman. You don't know what you're getting into."

"I'm the one who brought her into this, Dad. I'm going to see it through."

"You might be putting your whole family in danger. Your daughter, Mason. Think about that."

"What about Joy? She didn't ask for this, and neither did Kennedy."

"Just the thought of you risking your life... You know your mom can't handle anything happening to her only remaining child."

"I'm not Seth, Dad. I'm..."

"Just hear me out, son. I don't like the idea of you abandoning Kennedy and Joy either, but maybe you can take them to Uncle Joe's farm down in Georgia. Get out of town until the police figure this out."

"We aren't going anywhere. We're going to lay low and figure this out."

Kennedy felt guilty for eavesdropping, so she announced her presence as she entered the kitchen. "Thanks for letting me take that nap. I didn't realize how tired I was."

Both men whipped their heads in her direction. "Mom is getting the girls washed up so we can go. Did you decide what you want to eat?"

"Why don't we let the girls decide," Kennedy answered softly. She had no appetite left after overhearing the private conversation. She really did put Mason's whole family in danger, and she didn't deserve his level of commitment.

Joy and Gracie came bounding into the kitchen with clean hands, but the rest of them needed to be hosed off. Garden soil and good old-fashioned dirt had caked into the clothes of both girls, but their bright white smiles proved that they had fun getting dirty.

"Daddy, can we get tacos?"

Gracie took it upon herself to explain the concept of tacos to Joy while they walked towards the door to leave.

Becky joined them in the kitchen, catching Kennedy before she exited. "I found this at the store yesterday. I thought Joy might want it for luck. But I figured I would run it by you first," she said, extending her hand towards Kennedy.

A blue, furry rabbit's foot sat in Becky's hand. The traditional lucky rabbit's foot with the keychain attached to it. Kennedy accepted it, kind of grossed out even though she knew it didn't really come from a rabbit. "I'll let her have it after she cleans up later. Thank you." Becky gave her a hug and let them get on their way.

The Little Mermaid blanket became the base for a picnic in Mason's living room. He didn't want the filthy girls on the furniture at all. After tacos were devoured, each adult took a kid for a major scrub-down. Kennedy helped Joy wash her hair and get the dirt out from behind her ears in the master bathroom, while Mason did his fatherly duty in Gracie's bathroom. They met in the living room after bath time, and Kennedy asked if they had a blow dryer.

Kennedy sat on the floor, brushing and drying Joy's hair while Gracie watched intently. When Joy finally got up, Gracie immediately claimed the spot in front of Kennedy, expecting her own turn under the dryer. Kennedy obliged, making sure both girls received equal attention. Mason helped Kennedy get off the floor and then turned on *Frozen* to give the girls a chance to wind down before bedtime.

Kennedy followed Mason out of the sliding door to sit on the back porch. Since his apartment was on the first floor, he actually had a porch with a gate. Mason had a seat where he could watch Kennedy taking Milo for a quick walk. When she came back, she settled in the chair next to the handsome fireman. The porch itself only measured about ten-by-six, and it couldn't contain much more than the two chairs, a small table, and a grill.

As she reached her hand over the table, compelling Mason to hold it, Kennedy said, "I accidentally overhead a little bit of your conversation earlier. Tell me about Seth."

Mason didn't look in her direction. His gaze seemed to be fixated on the fairway of the golf course beyond his porch rail. "Seth's been gone almost fifteen years now. He was the best big brother though. When he was eighteen, he'd just started college at the University of Memphis on a baseball scholarship. He had his whole life before him, and I was three years younger, thinking Seth was blazing a trail for me too. I wanted to be a pitcher just like him, and I dreamed of us playing on the same professional baseball team when we got older. But however good he was as a baseball player, he was even better as a brother and a person. Always willing to help anyone."

The pause made Kennedy scared to ask what happened next. Fortunately, he continued without her having to say anything. Mason turned his head to look at their intertwined hands.

"His girlfriend had a flat tire on the interstate. Seth didn't hesitate to help her because he didn't want her waiting on the side of the road by herself, said it wasn't safe for her. Her insurance company was supposed to be sending a mobile tire repair company, but it would take them about an hour to get there. Seth decided that was too long and opted to change the flat for her. Unfortunately, the flat tire was on the side closer to traffic, and as he sat on the ground, turning lug nuts, a distracted driver hit him."

He pulled his hand away from hers and crossed his arms over his chest, inhaling deeply. Mason leaned his head back, maybe looking to the heavens, but only seeing the balcony above him instead.

"Mason, that's such a tragedy. So, you were only fifteen?" The night air was chilly as a cold front moved in, but Kennedy knew the cold she felt now was from the memory of the day her parents died. A teenager dealing with death. The same way Mason had to deal with his brother's death.

"Yea, and my parents got the call from a friend who saw it all instead of getting a visit from the police. We immediately got in the car and headed to the scene of the accident. The firemen were so respectful, compassionate, and so strong in the face of tragedy. That's the day my plan for the future changed. I wanted to help people the same way they helped me."

Kennedy reached over to put her hand on his arm. "Seth would be so proud of who you've become, Mason."

"I know that. But my parents still get overly protective of me and Gracie. I hate it when they start doing the comparison thing with Seth, as if he would've done anything differently. The flat tire seems like a stupid reason to die, but he was helping someone he cared about. He'd do it again, and I'd do this all over again, no matter the outcome." He got up, letting her hand drop from where it rested on his arm.

She followed him into the apartment, and they found the girls already asleep on the couch. A minute later, they carried Joy and Gracie to the bedroom where both girls remained blissfully in dream land. Milo joined them on the bed, settling directly in the middle.

Kennedy followed Mason back to the living room and sat on the couch. Not against him this time, but on the other end. She felt like she was just following him around and not really important to his existence in this moment. Kennedy knew he had just shared a painful memory, but she wanted to be close to him instead of being forced to remain an arm's length away. The television switched from Elsa building an ice castle to the local news.

With the volume low, they listened to stories about the cold front coming through and other stories about the Memphis Tigers basketball playoff chances. Mason turned up the volume a little when the reporter covered the story of the missing girl,

Jillian Young, as the newscaster called her. No new information yet regarding the girl's whereabouts. That only led to another story they weren't expecting.

The serious face of the new anchor matched the seriousness of her story. "The police have recently released some new information regarding the mother of Jillian, who was found shot to death behind a gas station. Surveillance videos of nearby businesses show this SUV was likely the transport vehicle that dumped Destiny Young's body. You can see on your screen this newer model, dark Chevy Suburban. The license plate appeared to be purposely covered. It was captured by a nearby security camera close to eleven on the night of February thirteenth. If anyone has any information regarding this murder or regarding the location of her missing child, the Memphis Police is urging you to contact them on the number listed on the screen now."

Kennedy and Mason both stared at the television as the news program took a commercial break. She was startled when Mason broke the silence.

"That Suburban has police tint on it. It's gotta be a government vehicle."

"How could you tell? That was a still shot from a video."

He shook his head. "The picture caught the SUV directly under a streetlight. If the windows weren't tinted really dark, you would've seen at least a silhouette of the driver."

"So, whoever has that vehicle has government, police, or firefighter tags? That's what you're saying?"

"That's exactly what I'm saying. Which means that whoever is at the center of this really is still involved in the government. We have to be on the right track to figuring out who's behind it."

Not wanting to jump to any conclusions, Kennedy replied, "By that standard, if your Suburban was black, it could easily have been your vehicle in that picture. This doesn't necessarily point to any kind of government involvement."

Huffing in response, "Fine, let's stay on the track we're on though. Suburbans are the preferred government vehicles, so it still goes along with our theory. And only because I've always driven Suburbans, I can tell you that something about that one doesn't look like a stock model. It's gotta be a politician."

The news had resumed, and the lady sat at her desk with some footage of the US president behind her. President Crawford stepped out of Air Force One and waved at the unseen crowd, while the anchor started talking. "President Crawford is continuing his Reuniting America Tour today with a stop in his hometown of Atlanta, Georgia. The City of Memphis is expecting a visit from the president in one week…"

"I'm drained." Mason clicked off the television. "Hopefully, we can get some rest tonight. We just need to feed the animals at your house tomorrow and figure out a different angle to research."

"Saturday is my cleaning day. All the animals get new bedding and baths. Plus, I have to feed the snakes. It'll take a little longer than it did this morning."

"Okay, I'll go change into pajamas and get out of your way. We'll plan on leaving here by nine in the morning."

As Kennedy lay in the warm bed on the soft sheets, restlessness became her unwilling bed partner. She wanted to believe that the earlier nap interfered with her sleep, but she knew it was more than that. Mason barely gave her a hug before he made camp in the living room. She forced him to open up about a painful subject this afternoon, and she feared it had created a wedge between them.

The idea of being in a relationship was so new to her, so the idea of problems in a relationship was inexplicable. Was

Mason mad at her? Or was he just feeling raw from exposing his emotions? Kennedy stared at the shadows on the ceiling created by a small gap in the curtains. The curtains over her heart had been closed for the past eight years. The tiny amount of light could symbolize hope... or it could hinder attempts to sleep depending on the perspective.

In the wake of her grief as a teenager, Kennedy had purposely stayed out of her head. She gave all her attention to rescuing animals, planting a garden, working as a vet tech, and learning everything she could about veterinary medicine. Now, she found herself not only all the way inside her head, but in the bed of a man. And the man had no interest in joining her. Mason barely looked like he was tolerating her tonight. Did his father's advice make him reconsider the commitment he made to her and Joy?

The doubt and fear bounced around in Kennedy's head until she fell into a disturbed sleep. Tossing, turning, tossing again. By the time Mason knocked on the bedroom door, Kennedy didn't feel like she had rested at all.

SATURDAY, FEBRUARY 19

Mason eased into the room and took care of his morning routine without speaking. The light under the bathroom door was the only thing letting Kennedy know she didn't dream him coming through the room. When he finished and opened the door, the smell of steamy men's shampoo tickled her nose. He whispered that the bathroom was all hers as he exited the bedroom.

Kennedy's chest tightened. She wanted so much more from him, but her imagination created a relationship where none existed. Her brain tried to rewind a week, to a time when she kept her emotions safely under lock and key. Her own shower was brief, and fear gripped her heart as she turned the doorknob to exit the bedroom.

Maybe she should recommend that Mason leave her at her house this morning, let her handle the business with Joy on her own. Not that Kennedy knew how to handle it, but Mason seemed to be creating distance between them. If there were distance, it needed to be miles, not mere feet.

Taking a deep breath, Kennedy opened the door and entered the living area. Both girls were already active, and Mason set the table for breakfast. Another gourmet breakfast of Fruit Loops and orange juice. As they crunched on the cereal, Milo crunched on the last couple of morsels of his dog food.

"I'll take him for a walk," Mason said, getting up to

put Milo on a leash, obviously trying to vacate the awkward situation.

Gracie broke the silence. "Ken, can I dry your hair when we finish eating?"

Joy didn't say anything, but she nodded like that was a great idea.

Kennedy's long hair usually air dried, and the thought of two girls tackling her head with a brush and dryer sounded downright painful. She pasted a fake smile on her face to answer. "Of course, I would appreciate that very much."

A minute later, Kennedy sat on the floor with both girls standing over her, brushing and drying. In reality, it was more like yanking and burning. When Mason came back into the apartment, he stopped to take in the scene of giggling girls making a mess of Kennedy's hair. By nine, her hair looked like it belonged to an alpaca, but she gathered it into a ponytail so they could get on the road.

Once at home, Kennedy got four plastic totes out of her garage to fill up with warm water. The three snakes and one lizard all bathed in their individual totes while she thawed out frozen mice to feed the snakes. The hamster and rat both got new bedding in their cages and water bottles were refilled. As her newest animal, she didn't know the best plan for long-term care of the tarantula. She stopped short of replacing his coconut-fiber bedding. Instead, she sprayed down his tank with water, watching the mist collect on his funnel of webbing. More research into how to take care of Rimshot needed to be done.

Cleo the scorpion had a regal terrarium filled with live ferns, bromeliads, and moss. Kennedy's mind wandered as she misted the lush terrarium. She actually hiked into the woods and personally collected the moss, taking great care to give Cleo a home fitting for a queen. She wondered if Joy might like to set up an aquarium or a fish tank for her own animal. Or maybe decorate Medusa's tank differently. During her childhood years, Kennedy's parents let her have a Betta fish, a frog, and all kinds of creatures. For her tenth birthday, Kennedy received a habitat kit so she could witness Painted Lady caterpillars transform into butterflies.

As she replaced the substrate for her snakes, Kennedy's mind wandered all over the place. She went from childhood experiences to wondering why she expected Mason to hold her hand on the drive over here. Her mom told her as a teenager, "If you never expect anything, you'll never be disappointed." Maybe that was the key to contentment. Kennedy just had to find that place again.

Getting back into her comfort zone of caring for animals provided a few minutes of peace though. She peeked out the window to see Joy playing with Milo in the backyard. The weather had cooled down a little, but the sun still remained bright. This was the first time in forty-eight hours that Kennedy had been apart from Mason. He decided they might need to make an appearance at the birthday party later, so he took Gracie to the store to pick out a gift suitable for a girl they had never met.

Within a few hours, she had returned all the critters back to their tanks and condos. Her Jeep sat in the garage, next to the rows of shelves where she kept her animal and gardening supplies. Kennedy contemplated taking her Jeep instead of riding with Mason later. A means of escape might be best for her sanity. With the clean totes back in their place on the shelf, Kennedy rounded up Joy and Milo to come inside to warm up.

Joy was in the middle of modeling pink Play-Doh into a snake when Mason and Gracie returned. Gracie immediately joined Joy at the coffee table, choosing her own color of clay to create something. While the girls played, Mason pulled Kennedy back to her bedroom to speak in private. They stood just inside the doorway where Mason spoke quietly.

"I'm thinking that if you don't show up to this party today, your boss might become suspicious. There's going to be so many kids there, I doubt anyone will be focused on Joy. She doesn't really look like that fuzzy picture they put on the news anyway. But I do foresee one problem we need to avoid."

"What's that?" Kennedy asked, already predicting what he would say.

"I think if Gracie and I go with you, that will invite your boss and other friends to ask you a bunch of personal questions, and we need to avoid that as much as we can."

"Mason, that's fine. Just go home, and I'll take Joy to the party. I'll come get Ginger later so you won't have to fool with us anymore." The words sounded confident, but inside, Kennedy felt the cold fingers of dread spreading through her torso, wrapping tightly around her heart. She tried to keep her breathing normal even though her heart rate started accelerating.

The surprise on his face surprised her. "What? You don't want me to stick around? You don't want to stay with me?" He shook his head in disbelief.

"You're already pulling away from us. And you just said you didn't want to be seen with us. You've already helped plenty, but I can't expect you to fight my battles for me."

The hug she desperately needed yesterday almost smothered her in that instant. Mason's arms grabbed her in a bear hug. Kennedy tried to hold onto her fortitude, refusing to yield to the embrace. After she held her ground for a full minute, Mason guided her back to have a seat on the bed, but he remained standing in front of her.

"Ken, you didn't let me finish. I wanted us to go into the skating rink a few minutes apart so I could still be close by in case you need me. Then we would leave a few minutes apart. There's no way I'd let you go without me."

"You haven't acted like you wanted me around since yesterday afternoon, Mason. I think you realized that I'm just baggage you don't need in your life."

"Look, I haven't talked about Seth in years, and I felt like I was punched in the gut when my dad compared our situations. Then, when you were drying Gracie's hair last night, I thought about her mom and how she abandoned her daughter. Gracie deserves to have someone sharing moments like that, just simple quality time, and she's missing out." He paused to have a seat next to her on the foot of the bed, staring at the floor in front of them. "I told you that I'm having trouble coming to terms with this anger I have for Bethany, but I'm really working on it. Then this morning, when Gracie was drying your hair, I could've punched a hole in the wall. Instead of being happy at the fun Gracie was having, I was mad that Bethany wasn't woman enough to spend that time with her. Seeing you with Gracie is causing me to deal with anger I had pushed to the back burner for the past two years."

"And now you've added another reason you don't need me around. You have my permission to go. No hard feelings, Mason."

"I'm not going anywhere," he said, sounding offended.

Kennedy kept her gaze on the floor, refusing to look at him. She didn't expect him to reach a hand to her face, gently forcing her to make eye contact with him. No words were spoken as he leaned in to tenderly press his lips to hers. She tried to pull back, but he had already moved his hand to the back of her head, keeping her face close to his. He deepened the kiss, and Kennedy's fortitude melted away. She had never felt intimacy like this before, and she gave into the moment.

When he relinquished the kiss, he moved his mouth to her cheek, and then her neck, and then her ear. Just butterfly kisses, but they shook her world like an earthquake. He stayed near her ear to whisper, "I promise, Kennedy. I'm not going anywhere."

The tender moment was interrupted when two squealing

girls ran into the room to scare the adults with their Play-Doh snakes. Mason and Kennedy jumped up, acting frightened by the silly girls. Kennedy ushered everyone back to the kitchen where she made sandwiches for an early lunch. Still reeling from the emotions of the day so far, Kennedy turned on the news to fill the quiet after they finished lunch, and the girls resumed playing with the colorful dough.

The midday news covered sports... upcoming golf tournaments, the Memphis Grizzlies home schedule, and the University of Memphis Tigers' chances for a conference title. Kennedy cared nothing for the sports, but she appreciated the next story as the anchor took over speaking from the sports guy. She turned up the volume to hear.

"The FBI has confirmed that Miley Sullivan has been found alive, and she is safe with her parents today. She was originally reported missing on January 30th from a marina in South Carolina, and authorities presumed her to be held captive by the Marina Marauder. While we don't have all the details yet, we can all breathe easier knowing this young lady has been reunited with her family. As more details are released, you can trust Channel Four News to keep you informed..."

"Mason, they found that girl alive. I hate to be cynical, but I sure didn't have any hope for her."

"Good things still happen every day. In fact, I'm holding out for a happy ending for Joy in all this."

Kennedy's phone dinged, notifying her of a text message. "Ms. Sue is making sure I'm bringing Joy today."

"I guess we should get going then. Just bring your phone with you to the party, and we'll drop it back off here when we pick up Milo."

Mason turned off the congested Germantown Parkway

onto a side street where the skating rink was nestled off the busy thoroughfare. In the same area, the YMCA and the Cordova Bowling Lanes attracted more Saturday traffic. Still harboring some anxiety about this party, Kennedy jumped when her phone rang.

"Hey, Ms. Sue," she said quietly into the phone.

"We're set up in a party room now. Are you here yet? Do you want me to come outside and get you?"

"Oh no, that's not necessary."

"It's crowded in here. Let me come get you. Are you in your Jeep?" Sue insisted.

"Um…" As she considered her answer, Kennedy felt something under her foot. She leaned down to find the blue rabbit's foot where it must've fallen on the floorboard last night. While she leaned over, Mason put his hand on her back, urging her to stay down. Kennedy craned her neck to see that he was giving her a look of warning. "Um… Ms. Sue, the lady from Child Protective Services found some closer family for Joy, so we're headed out of town this afternoon. I hope y'all have a wonderful party though. Thanks for inviting us."

After a couple of minutes with Kennedy staying in the crouched position, Mason removed his hand from her back to let her up. "What happened?" she asked.

"We'll talk later, but we aren't going to that party."

"But Daddy, I want to go skating!" Gracie hollered from the backseat.

"Not now, Gracie."

Ten minutes later, they loaded Milo into the SUV and left.

Behind the locked doors of Mason's apartment, the girls were finally placated when Mason spread out a disposable plastic tablecloth on the kitchen floor and got out finger-painting supplies. With Gracie and Joy thoroughly occupied with making a colorful mess, Kennedy joined Mason in his bedroom so they could talk without six-year-old eavesdroppers.

"When I pulled around the side of the skating center to find a parking place, a black Suburban with dark tint was idling. I know I'm borderline paranoid right now, but that's a chance I wasn't willing to take. We're just lucky you leaned down when you did, or they would've seen you."

"I guess your mother's rabbit foot is lucky after all," Kennedy said as she thought about the sequence of events. "Ms. Sue had just asked if I was in my Jeep so she could come get me. Do you think she was trying to set me up?"

"We don't have the luxury of thinking anyone is on our side right now."

Then a knock on the front door startled them both, causing Milo to bark.

"Get Joy and hide in my closet."

Fortunately, there was no clear view from Mason's front door into the apartment. Kennedy hurried to scoop up the paint-covered Joy and ducked back into the bedroom. "Joy, we're going to hide for a few minutes, but I'm staying with you. We're going to be very quiet."

Joy nodded silently as they settled in the back of Mason's closet, underneath jackets and behind a suitcase. She could hear a man's muffled voice talking in the living room.

"We're following up on a tip regarding a missing child. You were reported to be in the Dollar General store in Bartlett with a girl fitting the description of the missing Jillian Young. And your vehicle fits the description of the SUV connected with the death of her mother."

"I was in the store earlier, but my daughter was with me. I'm going to put my dog on the back porch, so I don't have to keep holding him by the collar. Gracie, say hello to the nice officers."

The discussion with Gracie wasn't as audible, but Kennedy knew the girl would entertain a conversation with a head of cabbage. Hopefully, she wouldn't mention anything about her new playmate.

Again, Kennedy heard the officer addressing Mason, "You understand we need to be thorough with this visit. Do you mind if we take a look around?"

"The apartment is nine-hundred square feet so that won't take long at all. Here, let's start with my vehicle in the garage. It's red, so it doesn't actually match…"

The voices faded, and Kennedy knew that only gave them a split second to vacate the apartment while the officers were in the garage. Snatching up Joy, she ran towards the bedroom window, thankful that it opened easily and quietly. Setting Joy on the ground outside, Kennedy climbed out and lowered the window behind them. Apartments on golf courses were lavishly landscaped, so they managed to stay behind the evergreen Juniper bushes as they headed towards the breezeway between the buildings.

Kennedy peeked around the corner of the breezeway, and not finding any potential danger, she pulled Joy to the next building where they ducked behind another group of thick bushes. They sat under the cover of the heavy brush for what seemed like an eternity, but Joy was a pro at hiding and staying silent. The cold mulch didn't provide a comfortable seat for Kennedy, and the extra forty pounds of Joy in her lap didn't help either. Her legs tingled from the cramped position while cold dread seeped into her body.

Despite her feeling of impending doom, Kennedy soothed the child as much as she could without making noise, stroking her hair and patting her back. The fingerpaints that Joy had been playing with left smears and streaks on both of them now. A smudge of red paint was now drying in Joy's hair.

Throughout their time in the bushes, questions raced through her head. Would the officers leave without finding Joy? Were the officers legitimate to begin with? Was Ms. Sue setting her up at the party? Was Ms. Sue involved with the officers checking Mason's apartment now?

No one even knew she was hanging out with Mason except for his fellow firefighters, and she seriously doubted they would betray the trust of each other. Mason's parents, however worried, would never involve the authorities. The four of them had eaten in restaurants on two occasions and visited the zoo, but that was before Joy's picture had been plastered all over the news.

The panicked pulsating in her ears almost caused Kennedy to miss the sound of Mason's voice. She adjusted to peer over the bushes to see Mason searching for her, and she slowly stood, feeling the blood rush back into her legs. He beckoned them back to the apartment.

A half hour later, Kennedy hunkered under a blanket in the cargo area of Mason's SUV with Joy cuddled next to her, choosing to stay out of sight. Milo sat in the backseat, and Ginger travelled in a box with holes poked in it. Kennedy felt the vehicle slow down, speed up, and turn occasionally. Maybe twenty minutes into the ride, they came to a stop.

"Come on, we weren't followed," Mason said as he opened the hatchback of the SUV.

When Kennedy and Joy emerged from underneath the blanket, she found herself in the parking lot of Mason's fire station. They moved their overnight bags into the back hatch of a smaller SUV parked in the adjacent space. Next, the booster seats were moved into the backseat of what Kennedy finally recognized as a white Nissan Murano. While they buckled the girls in, Chief Rice came outside to trade keys with Mason. At the last second, Kennedy reached back into the Suburban to grab the lucky rabbit's foot from the console. She clipped it to a belt loop on her jeans to keep it close by.

"I'll park your Suburban in the garage at home and drive my wife's car the rest of the week." The two men shared a brief hug before the foursome loaded into the Nissan and pulled out of the parking lot.

Once Kennedy occupied the shotgun seat of the vehicle and stretched out her legs out, she tried to wrap her head around what was happening. "Mason, what's going on? How did anyone get a lead on us?"

"I was thinking about that too, but it's more likely that no one has connected me to you. I think your boss suspected that Joy might be the missing girl, and she notified the authorities. Which means they'll be checking your house, so we need to figure out how to feed your animals in the meantime. Those guys who checked on me at that apartment were probably only following up on an anonymous tip. He said they're getting a bunch of tips every time someone sees a young blond girl near an SUV."

"So, you don't think they'll check on you again? No one at my work knows I'm hanging out with you. My neighbor is my only other friend, and Pennie's out of town." Kennedy continued to work it out in her head.

"I don't think anyone is looking for me to find you, but since I'm not leaving you alone through this, people might find me while looking for you."

"That sounds reasonable, I guess. What's the plan? Where're we going now?"

Mason hesitated before speaking. "I think we need to let the girls stay with my parents, and then we can try to figure this out without carting them around with us. It's better if we separate them from what we're doing."

Feeling defensive, Kennedy bristled, "Do what? Let them stay with your parents? Did you intend to ask my input about this?"

"How long will we stay with BB and Papaw?" Gracie asked from the back seat.

"Just a couple of days, Gracie." Leaning towards Kennedy, he said, "Why don't we talk about this privately when we get to my parents' house?"

For the remaining ten minutes of the drive, Kennedy fumed in her seat with her arms crossed. Up until today, she didn't recognize the potential for real danger even if she admitted things seemed a little dicey for Joy. Now, she was fleeing her home like a refugee. In the course of today, she felt more intimate with a man than she had ever experienced in her life. Then, within two hours, she felt more scared for her life than she had ever experienced.

The roller coaster of emotions left her almost dizzy. Her heart rate had still not returned to normal and now, Mason had exerted control of the situation. In her adult life, Kennedy had never relinquished control of her decisions to someone else. Not even once. That required trust, and she simply wasn't capable of trusting. Or was she? Did she have a better plan?

"I can hear you grinding your teeth, Ken. That can't be good. Plus, your RBF is back."

Realizing her teeth and jaws were hurting, Kennedy made a conscious effort to relax them before responding. "This isn't funny, Mason."

"I know, I guess I just wanted to make you smile."

"Maybe tomorrow," Kennedy replied as they pulled into the driveway of his parents' home.

With Milo wedged between Gracie and Joy on the couch, they watched *101 Dalmatians*. Ginger had been moved into a larger cage. The adults gathered to talk in the kitchen.

"I knew this would happen," Becky said as she loaded groceries into bags.

"Mom, what are you doing?"

She paused while putting a loaf of bread into a paper sack and slowly turned her head towards Mason. "Y'all are going to hide somewhere, and you're gonna need food."

Kennedy almost did laugh then. Between being a grandmother and a Southerner, Becky treated food as the solution to all problems. Every occasion between birth and death deserved a casserole or other nourishment.

"Look, son," Ronnie stepped in, leaving his wife to her self-assigned chore, "I know you're going to find somewhere to hide, but you aren't planning to sit back and do nothing. Please just let us know if you get into any danger, if we can help at all."

Mason shook his head. "We have burner phones, and we have each other's numbers. I'll let you know if there's any way you can back us up, but while we're digging into this, it's best that we don't call any attention to the girls. Their safety is most important right now. If any authorities connect us to Joy, and they show up here, Joy knows how to hide. Show her our favorite hide-n-seek spots tonight so she can go unnoticed during any visit and tell them you don't know anything else. As far as you're concerned, I went camping, so my cell phone has no signal."

Kennedy didn't contribute to the conversation, and she followed Mason's lead when he went to the den to tell his daughter goodbye.

"Babydoll, you be good for BB and Papaw. I'll be back in a few days." Gracie wrapped her small arms around Mason's neck, and he stood, picking her up with him to offer an encompassing hug in return. "I love you, punkin."

Kennedy sat next to Joy, but she still had reservations about physically expressing herself. To her surprise, Joy climbed in her lap and hugged first. Kennedy squeezed her back. "I promise, I'm coming back for you, sweetie. BB and Papaw will take good care of you, okay?"

Joy leaned back to look Kennedy in the eye and spoke softly, "Okay, Ken. I love you."

Her throat had already tightened, and now tears filled her eyes. "Love you too, sweet girl."

The tears flowed when Gracie joined Joy in Kennedy's lap, turning it into a group hug. Mason plucked Joy up and held her for a minute. "You be good, kiddo." He kissed her on the cheek as he sat her back on the couch.

"Well, I don't know where we're going, but it looks like your mom packed us a week's worth of groceries."

"Chief Rice has a hunting cabin in Eads. It's only about twenty minutes up Highway 64, then another fifteen minutes to the cabin. I don't think he stocks it with much food, so it's probably a good thing Mom sent us with supplies."

"Does he have any neighbors nearby?"

"No, he owns over a hundred acres. The cabin does have basic plumbing and electricity, but not much else."

"So, what's the plan when we get there?"

Mason tightened his lips in frustration. "We keep digging. I can't come up with anything more definitive to start with, but I brought the laptop. We can use the burner phone to create a hotspot for the internet and just keep investigating. Following leads, looking for anything that helps."

Kennedy huffed and looked away from Mason, sensing a

dead end in their near future.

"We don't have a lot of options right now, Ken, but we know they're actively looking for Joy. Someone is on alert and hunting for her. They don't know we're hunting too, and I'm hoping we catch them unaware because, frankly, that's the only chance we've got to get Joy out of this alive."

Keeping her face turned away, she let a few more tears fall. What was happening? In the matter of a week, she went from a perfectly quiet existence to all hell breaking loose. Trying to mask her crying, Kennedy spoke slowly while still facing away from Mason, "Is there no one we can trust? This is too big for the two of us."

"We're already using the people we can trust. My parents and Chief Rice. Marla isn't sure who she can trust, so her hands are tied. It's just me and you, Kennedy."

She let that sink in. A week ago, her mentality was *me against the world*. At least now, her manpower had doubled. The last few minutes of the drive allowed her to get her mind straight and put a stop to any more tears. She made an intentional effort to get off the roller coaster of emotions so she could set her sights on a resolution to this dire situation.

The cabin had a rustic charm to it despite the cold temperature and stale smell. The large porch probably contained as much square footage as the A-frame structure itself. Even though the exterior wood was painted dark brown, the mismatched wood on the interior displayed a variety of natural warm shades and grains. Outdated wooden paneling made the open area of the downstairs seem smaller than it was, while knotty pine planks covered the low ceiling. The laminate floor imitated hardwood with a gray tinge, and the flooring continued through the downstairs until it met up with the knotty pine staircase that led to the only bedroom upstairs.

Every inch of the space under the staircase was used to construct a bathroom. The room barely held a shower stall, pedestal sink, and toilet. No cabinets. Just a few wall-mounted shelves that displayed towels. A wire caddy hung from the showerhead to store soap or shampoo and not much else.

Mason had set their bags on the floor next to the worn-out, L-shaped couch. Kennedy brought as many grocery sacks as she could carry to the kitchen area. They worked as a team to finish bringing in the case of water and groceries, and it only took about ten minutes to stow the sandwich supplies and snacks away. She was eternally grateful that Becky sent a container of Folgers coffee.

With that much done, Kennedy observed the rest of her new temporary home. Aside from the threadbare couch, a battered table with mismatched chairs sat in the corner of the kitchen. A collection of antlers hung on the wall, flanked by a selection of fishing poles. The flannel curtains had faded over the years, but they managed to cover the windows completely. All the furniture and decoration items were probably discarded from someone's home over the years to find a second life in this cabin in the woods.

"Let me carry your bag upstairs, and I'll sleep on the couch tonight," Mason said as he picked up her canvas tote bearing the Whole Foods logo. A minute later, he came back downstairs carrying a pillow and a blanket.

Kennedy sat on the couch now, noticing the old black and white office clock on the wall. Five o'clock. Exhaustion and the cold encroached even though it was barely dinnertime.

Mason sat on the other end of the couch where he had better access to his own bag. He wasted no time setting up the laptop, but Kennedy couldn't mentally focus on any research right now. She stared at her hands, still smudged with the primary colors of the fingerpaint from earlier that afternoon.

"Does this cabin have hot water? I need a hot shower

before I can think straight."

Mason looked up from the laptop, "Sure, go ahead. I'll try to figure out how turn on the heat since it's just going to get colder tonight."

Kennedy always felt tall for a woman, but nothing made her feel taller than a short shower. In her haste to pack, she didn't grab any of her bathroom supplies, so she stood in front of the chest-height showerhead using Old Spice body wash as her shampoo, face soap, and body wash. It was probably a product of her mental fatigue, but Kennedy almost giggled thinking about the Old Spice commercials from years ago. She pictured the handsome black guy delivering his monologues in a deep baritone, standing in a bathroom, wearing only a towel, and saying, "Look at me, the man your man could smell like." The Old Spice bottle was labeled Pure Sport, so she guessed that's what men should smell like. For this particular night, Kennedy would smell like Pure Sport as well.

Even though luxurious towels were never a necessity for Kennedy, she felt gross drying off on the worn-out towels found in this bathroom. In fact, Milo used better towels than these after his baths. The cold floor with no bathmat was borderline unacceptable, making it obvious to Kennedy that women never stayed in this cabin. Instead of being unappreciative, she gave herself a mental peptalk about the safe place to stay with all the basic amenities. Hopefully, Mason found some heat.

After donning her fuzzy pajamas, Kennedy stepped out into the living room to find Mason on the couch, watching the news. She detected a burning smell, and she hoped they weren't at risk of fire with or without the assistance of arsonists.

"What's the smell?" she asked, checking the kitchen for burned toast or something of that nature.

Mason called out from the couch, "I got the furnace

turned on, but the dust has to burn off. It should warm up pretty quickly in here." He joined her in the half of the downstairs dedicated to the kitchen to grab a bottle of water.

"I'm going to make a sandwich for dinner if you want one too. I know it's also what we had for lunch, but sandwiches are my go-to meal at home anyway."

He got the sliced turkey out of the fridge and helped assemble dinner while he asked, "Why is that your go-to meal? Is it your favorite food?"

Shaking her head, she didn't look up from her task of smearing mayo when she answered, "No, but it's the easiest thing to make for one person with the least amount of mess. When my garden produces this spring, I'll have fresh tomatoes, cucumbers, lettuces, and other sandwich fixings. I'll also have a variety of vegetables, and I prefer things that are home grown. I can get a package of organic chicken and cook one piece at a time for salads or whatever. I guess I'm just a minimalist, and the only restaurant I splurge on is Chick-fil-A."

"It's just me and Gracie at home, so we do a lot of simple things too. Homemade pizzas are her favorite, and they're easy to make. That's why we go to my mom's house so often. Mom loves to cook, and we love to eat." He managed a chuckle as they carried their food to the table.

Eating hardly took ten minutes before they moved back to the living room where the evening news played in the background. Mason set up a mobile hotspot with the burner phone and booted up the laptop. Kennedy sat ready to write with the notebook and pencil. She perused some of the notes and articles from their previous research and hoped that something would jump off the page at her. They needed some kind of direction to help with this investigation.

Mason revisited some of the pages he had bookmarked on the internet and tried to find more information about every pertinent staffer in the mayor's office from seven years ago. They started over with their list and added all eight members of the mayor's leadership team, all thirteen council members, and all eight appointed offices. This time, the race and gender didn't matter. Kennedy added notes for the two men who had died and the one who was in jail. Including the mayor, that added up to twenty-seven names left to investigate.

By this time, the hour hand on the clock had barely reached eight, and Kennedy could no longer process a coherent thought. "Mason, I need to tap out for the night. I think the extra stress of today has mentally and physically exhausted me."

"I'm with you on that. We can hopefully shed some new light on this in the morning with fresh eyes and strong coffee." He leaned over to kiss her forehead before getting up to check the locks on all the windows and doors.

Feeling dismissed, Kennedy moved upstairs. She only had a glimpse of the bedroom earlier when she came up to retrieve her pajamas and toothbrush. The theme of natural wood continued upstairs on the trim and angled ceiling, but the walls were painted sheetrock, and the floor had been carpeted. She pulled back the quilt on the queen-sized bed and ran her fingers over the sheets. They felt like a jersey material, warm and soft. With her level of exhaustion, Kennedy hardly remembered lying down before succumbing to a dead sleep.

SUNDAY,
FEBRUARY 20

The sun hadn't risen yet, but Kennedy's internal alarm let her know it was time to wake up. Sitting up in bed, it took a minute to get her bearings... Just like it did the last several times she had woken up, both in Mason's bed and on his parents' couch. She got out of bed as quietly as she could and peeked downstairs to find Mason still asleep on the couch. After she changed into jeans and a sweatshirt, she prayed that the stairs wouldn't creak as she crept down to the bathroom to brush her teeth and hair.

Kennedy noticed it was almost six. She had slept for almost ten hours! On the bright side, she felt refreshed. She silently started a pot of coffee, waiting for the aroma to wake Mason. While listening to the coffee drip, she had a seat on the opposite leg of the couch and watched him in the tiny amount of illumination coming from the nightlight by the staircase. Even in the dark, he sure was handsome. But what was he thinking? Did he think that Kennedy and Joy were just people who needed his help? Or did he want to help because he cared about them?

As much as she wanted to believe Mason cared about her, and as much as she felt vulnerable around him, Kennedy had no idea what their life would entail when this ordeal ended. The experience so far had been a massive eye opener for her, forcing her to rely on a man and develop a companionship of sorts. But the hand holding? The kisses? The words of affirmation? Those might be insignificant things for Mason to offer, but they were mind blowing in the realm of Kennedy's solitary existence.

If he wanted reciprocity, what could Kennedy even offer? Other than a couple of high school kisses, she had absolutely zero experience with men. Nothing deeper than the surface, and nothing that could lead to a long-term relationship. Certainly, nothing that ever came close to love.

Love? Where did that word even come from?

Kennedy's brain went haywire. Love was a feeling reserved for her parents. More recently, Kennedy would admit that she loved Joy like a daughter. She loved her job and her dog. But a man? That's a different kind of love altogether, and she might not be capable of giving or receiving emotions of that caliber. While her brain tried to make sense of the emotions, Mason stirred on his leg of the couch.

"Hey, I'm making some coffee," she whispered as Mason sat up.

He rubbed his eyes, then stood up to stretch. They both shared a breakfast of frosted cherry Pop Tarts and coffee before Mason showered and got ready for the day. After a short discussion regarding Kennedy's animals at home, they decided all the critters had enough food to last for today, but she would have to find a way to feed them tomorrow.

The sun peeked into the curtains by the time they turned on the laptop. Mason also switched on the television to keep the news playing. They had no idea what developments might impact their situation, so they kept tabs on the news stories while researching the expanded list of names of local politicians from the time of Joy's conception seven years ago.

Starting with the mayor, they dug into his past and his current whereabouts. Mason clicked on various articles, and Kennedy didn't bother picking up a pen this time. She sat close and perused whatever he clicked on, making suggestions as they went. If they found anything pertinent, she would write it down then. For the time being, the notebook only held a list of names that would either be crossed off or not depending on the current research.

Russ Wigginton only served one term as the mayor even though he had thrown his name in the hat for the past two election periods. He currently served on an advisory board for the City of Memphis but held no official position. Throughout the articles on the former mayor, they discovered nothing evil in his history, and nothing about his present-day routine seemed out of the ordinary. Even though no recent events could put Wigginton on the short list for blackmail candidates, Kennedy didn't scratch his name off the list.

Moving on, they searched through all the men first. It took two pots of coffee, three pee breaks, and four hours to get through the remaining fifteen men. A message from Becky let them know the girls enjoyed playing hide-n-seek all morning, which sounded way better than the morning Kennedy and Mason were having.

"Can we take a break for a minute? Maybe walk around, get some fresh air, and eat a sandwich?" Mason said, already rising to his feet.

Kennedy answered by putting on her sneakers, then rolling her head around to loosen her neck. When she attempted to stand, she realized how far she had sunken into the cushion of the couch, and she gladly accepted Mason's outstretched hand to help her up.

"Let's go for a short walk," he suggested as he pulled her into a hug.

The hug was brief, but Kennedy was happy for the small amount of affection. Maybe that was how pound puppies felt... after being abandoned and ignored for so long, any attention was appreciated on a deeper level. They moved outside into the refreshingly crisp air and followed a trail that took them deeper into the woods. It wasn't quite cold enough to see her breath, but Kennedy was slightly concerned that she didn't bring a jacket. Hopefully, the field trip would get them back to the cabin before her teeth started chattering.

The pine trees provided a little green coverage, but the branches of the oaks and elms remained bare in the winter. She estimated that they walked about a hundred yards when she noticed a clearing in the trees up ahead. Eventually, they approached a small lake, not an open field as Kennedy had expected.

"The only times I've been to Chief's cabin were to bring Gracie fishing here. It's a honey hole, and she loves catching crappie even though we release them."

Kennedy walked up to a tree that grew close to the edge of the water, and she leaned her back against it, taking in the serene environment. It reminded her of Lyles Lake in Shelby Forest where her own father took her fishing once as a kid. As an eight-year-old, sitting still to fish simply didn't happen. Her dad never lost patience, but he did eventually give her a small shovel and assigned her to dig up worms to fish with. It never occurred to her at the time that they bought worms on the way to the lake. She smiled at the recollection.

A splotch of bright red in her peripheral disrupted her trip down memory lane, and her gaze quickly found a cardinal perched on a nearby branch. With the slightly overcast sky, this cardinal appeared dazzling as the only real splash of color in the wintery woods.

"You really are beautiful when you smile like that." The compliment was spoken quietly from a few feet away, as if Mason didn't want to spoil Kennedy's peaceful moment.

The cardinal took flight at that time, passing behind Mason as the bird disappeared deeper into the trees. This left Kennedy's gaze now fixed on the gorgeous fireman, but she couldn't read the expression on his face. She had no idea how to accept a compliment, so keeping her mouth shut was the only way she could avoid spoiling his own peaceful moment.

He walked towards her, where she still leaned against the tree, and he wrapped his arms around her waist. She returned the embrace, feeling him kiss the top of her head. Kennedy tilted back her head, inviting him to kiss something else besides her Old Spice-scented hair. His lips found her forehead, leaving her still wanting more. After a few feather-soft kisses to her face, he finally found her mouth.

The kiss remained gentle, again leaving Kennedy wanting more. Not knowing how to truly initiate anything, she squeezed his body tightly against hers, welcoming him to amplify the moment. He moved his right hand to her face and caressed her cheek with his thumb, but he backed his own face away enough to look in her eyes. Attempting to hold his eye contact without flinching, she tilted her head back against the tree. Even though she couldn't see her own expression, it must've communicated exactly what she was feeling because the next kiss could in no way be classified as gentle.

Kennedy found herself trapped between the tree and Mason's body, and she relished the physical attention. The way his lips felt... the way his mouth tasted... the way his right hand tangled into her hair... the way his left arm held her body tightly against his... This encounter was unlike anything she had ever known. After only a few minutes of bliss, Mason backed away, leaving Kennedy breathless.

He silently took her by the hand, leading her back to the cabin without a word. Her head spun from the intensity of the previous few minutes, so she watched her steps closely to avoid falling head over heels physically since she had already fallen emotionally. As they climbed onto the porch, Mason stopped and pulled Kennedy into another embrace.

He resumed kisses on top of her head and spoke softly

into her hair, "Ken, I don't want my feelings for you to distract me from what's going on with Joy. Let's stay focused on helping her, okay?"

What could she do? She nodded and held onto the hug as long as he was willing to offer it. They moved into the cabin and made sandwiches for lunch before doing any more research.

The passionate events of the last half hour were stored away in Kennedy's brain, safely behind a door, so she could effectively help scrutinize the potential bad guys on the list. She sank down into the raggedy couch and picked up her notebook.

Mason took his seat beside her and said, "What do we know after all the digging this morning?"

Scanning the names, Kennedy huffed before answering. "Not much, I guess. I'm learning a lot more about politics than I ever wanted. Of the eighteen men, four are dead, and two are too old to be viable suspects. One is in jail, which surprises me."

"You didn't expect a politician to go to jail?"

"I'm surprised it's only one," she replied, shaking her head. "Then there's two who are retired, leading uninteresting lives. Then seven who assumed other political roles like court clerk or committee director of some sort, which would all be lateral moves. Then the three who moved on to other careers including selling houses, teaching, and starting a law firm."

"The ones who are still involved in politics seem to be holding positions that are lateral to what they held seven years ago. No one is making more money or holding a position of high esteem compared to seven years ago. I'm still thinking that whoever Destiny wanted to blackmail had an elevation in status in the last month. That's the only thing that would bring her out of hiding. She wouldn't risk it if the reward weren't worth it."

Kennedy glanced at the names of twelve women on

the notebook before she spoke. "Well, we have two different directions to choose from. We can either look into these women who worked in the mayor's office with Destiny, or we can look into the recent election winners and work backwards to see if any of them crossed paths with the mayor's office seven years ago."

Scratching his head, Mason looked at the television and seemed to contemplate the best direction to take. The midday news centered on the happy story of Miley Sullivan being reunited with her family after almost three weeks of captivity in South Carolina. Kennedy smiled when they reported that the Marina Marauder died during the rescue of his young hostage. But back to the business at hand, she turned to Mason.

He finally answered, "I still contend that whoever killed Destiny has to be Joy's father. He's going to be a white guy who has something to lose right now. If Marla could use all of her resources without garnering any attention, she could use a cheek swab from Joy to find a potential paternal match through a DNA database. The problem is that if she were to find a match, it would be broadcast through every government agency. It won't be for only us to know. The next problem is that the authorities don't have any DNA samples from Joy since the house burned down. If Marla got a cheek swab or hair sample, everyone could easily deduce that she knows where Joy is. We can't create that kind of trail."

Kennedy's mind raced now. "What if they scour the debris and find some kind of DNA? They're already looking for evidence of arson, who's to say they won't find a hairbrush or something?"

"Are you asking because you're scared or hopeful?"

"Yes to both," Kennedy exclaimed. "If it's immediately publicized who the father is, then someone will have to intervene and have him arrested. He won't be able to hurt Joy."

"No, he'll step up and take custody of Joy, reuniting with

his long-lost daughter. He'll do everything he can to save face in the public eye, and he'll never be accused of murdering Destiny."

"There's just no winning." Kennedy hung her head, wondering what all would have to play out before Joy could find some stability and peace.

"The only way that Joy wins is if we can prove he's a murderer before he finds out where Joy is. And the only way we can prove he's a murderer is to figure out who he is to begin with."

Mason's burner phone notified him of a new message. "They're playing Sardines with Gracie and Joy now," he said with a snicker.

"What kind of game is that?"

"It's like hide-n-seek, but only one person hides, and everyone else seeks. As they find the person hiding, they join them in the hiding spot until everyone's packed in like sardines. The last person to find them is the loser. We used to play that with my cousins when we were kids. My parents' house has been renovated so many times, it has some great hiding places."

"I guess my childhood was really lonely compared to everyone else's. I never felt like I was missing out, and now, being alone is all I know."

"Ken, think of it this way... Joy's been isolated too, and she needed someone like you to make that connection with. Everything in your life has prepared you for this day, and you're doing a superb job." He followed that statement with a quick peck on her lips and then picked up the laptop to get back to work.

"That being said, let's start with recent election winners and work backwards. We can screen them for white guys and go from there."

Working through the recent elections, they both felt inundated with information. Bartlett was part of the Memphis metropolitan area, so local elections included everything from the State of Tennessee to Shelby County, to all the outlying towns and municipalities. The citizens in this area alone had to vote for the US president along with casting ballots for multiple senators, house representatives, aldermen, school board members, and mayors for each municipality. In total, forty-seven winners were elected in this corner of Tennessee.

Applying their theory that the baby-daddy had to be the culprit, Kennedy only wrote down the names of the men. That only culled out eleven names, leaving thirty-six to dig into. Mason started by pulling up pictures of the men so Kennedy could scratch the names of anyone who wasn't white. After removing the non-Caucasians from the list, they were left with twenty-one names. Kennedy got out a blank page to write notes on these guys, knowing her hand would be cramping by the time the night was over.

A new segment of news started, and Mason turned up the volume. Since this was the national news, most of the stories had nothing to do with their current situation, but this particular headline made *Jillian Young's* potential abduction a nationwide concern. The same blurry picture of Joy holding Ginger was displayed for all to see. Kennedy feared at some point that her own picture might appear as the person of interest, so she watched the news coverage while holding her breath.

The reporter sat stoically at her desk, acting worried about a child she never met, sharing the same details they had previously heard on the local news. She recounted the heartbreaking tale of Destiny being murdered and wove the tale of *Jillian* being abducted in the process. A tip line and reward were set up for anyone with information.

"I'm actually glad they don't have anything new to report, because that would probably lead to me and you," Mason said as he picked up the controller to turn the TV back down.

Kennedy hadn't taken her eyes off the screen yet, and she

watched the digital indicator on the screen, moving down in sync with the volume. If only she could make her heart rate go back down to normal that easily. The reporter lady moved to the next story before Kennedy looked away, and the US president's face filled the screen.

Mason continued talking as he set the controller down. "I guess President Crawford plans to spend his whole term travelling to reunite America instead of choosing his cabinet and getting to work."

The footage switched to another clip of the president stepping off his plane, waving to the crowd. Kennedy wondered if they replayed the same footage or if they got current videos of him exiting the plane every time.

"Who're all the people getting off the plane with him if he hasn't chosen a cabinet yet?"

Mason immediately turned the television back up so they could hear. "The blonde there is his wife Paulina. I'm assuming the suits are the secret service agents assigned to protect him. I don't know the three other people, but the president will always bring in some trusted advisors from day one even if they don't have an official position, like a transition team or something."

The news lady spoke about the president's Reuniting America Tour, laying out the stops. The POTUS planned to stay in Atlanta, his hometown, for two more days before travelling to his next stop in Nashville. After two days in Tennessee's capital city, Crawford would head west to Memphis. His tour would continue west of the Mississippi River after his rendezvous in Memphis.

The reporter finally elaborated on the president's entourage who joined him on this leg of the tour. Crawford brought along three advisors to Atlanta, none of whom would hold official cabinet positions or require Senate confirmation. His senior advisor, Jordan Atwood, walked closely with the group to the waiting limousine. The entourage also included

Director of Office of Legislative Affairs Jenn Fitzpatrick. Rounding out the trio of advisors, Director of the Office of Public Engagement Pamela Anderson.

A condescending laugh escaped Kennedy's mouth before she could stop it.

"What was that about? You don't have any confidence in his advisors?"

"Oh, I don't know anything about his advisors, and I've never given politics as much attention as I should have. After this, I promise I'll be the most informed voter on the face of the earth though. I only scoffed because of that woman's name. Pamela Anderson. At least she didn't choose to go by Pam Anderson like that chick from Memphis. I think of *Baywatch* every time I see her name."

Mason didn't respond, but he immediately pecked on the computer again. "Ken, you won't believe this."

"What?" she asked, scooting closer to see the computer screen.

"Pamela Anderson is the one from Memphis. She's the same one who served with Mayor Wigginton seven years ago."

"No way! How did she get from Memphis to the White House?"

Mason gave her an incredulous look. "I don't know, but I guarantee we need to find out."

The next two hours were spent dissecting the life of Pam Anderson, the politician and not the *Baywatch* actress. Anderson was born in Memphis forty-four years ago, and she graduated from a public high school with honors. Her college path took her to Georgia State University, where she majored in journalism. Upon graduation, Anderson worked for a local Atlanta news station, hosting a segment as an investigative reporter on behalf of consumers. The reporter created a minor scandal, claiming sexual harassment in the workplace, but when the claims went unsubstantiated, Anderson left Atlanta to come home to Memphis.

In her mid-twenties, Anderson found a new career in marketing for a couple of local logistics companies in the Memphis area. Her investigative instincts never went away, and she quickly uncovered corporate policies that favored men in the logistics industry as a whole. Her outspoken criticism of the discriminatory hiring and promotions practices thrust her into the political arena where she served as an advisor to various political figures in Memphis before becoming the chief communications officer for Mayor Wigginton eight years ago.

When Wigginton lost his bid for re-election four years ago, Anderson stayed on as an advisor to the new mayor. Her timeline got more interesting a couple of months ago when President-Elect Robert Crawford called on her to become one of his presidential advisors.

They took a dinner break, but Kennedy decided to mix things up by making grilled cheese sandwiches rather than serving them cold. Sitting at the table with warm sandwiches, they bounced ideas off each other about their new lead.

"How likely do you think it is for Anderson to be central to Destiny's murder?" Mason asked, washing down a bite of sandwich with a drink from his bottle of water.

"I'd say she has to be central. She would've worked alongside Destiny every day during her stint in the mayor's office. I don't know how she wound up working in the White House, but something about her history is screwy."

Puffing up his cheeks and exhaling, Mason stayed lost in thought for a minute. "Well, she definitely has two factors we were looking for. First, she worked with Destiny. Second, she had a recent change in events that makes her blackmail worthy. The big problem with Anderson as our suspect is that there's no way she could be Joy's father."

"What if her husband is the dad? That would put Anderson in the same position because it's her career on the line."

"We didn't see anything about her husband or personal life yet. I guess that's the next level of research we need to do. Blackmail would definitely make perfect sense if her husband was Joy's father."

Without wasting any time, Mason and Kennedy delved back into the life of Pam Anderson. While trying to find specific results of the native Memphian, they found that Pam Anderson was a fairly common name. Aside from articles about the actress, they found several other politicians from other states who share the same name.

They quickly ruled out Tommy Lee and Kid Rock as the husbands they were seeking. The personal life of their specific Pam Anderson wasn't highly publicized. Eventually, they found an article from eight years ago that gave a brief overview of her life when she became part of the mayor's leadership team. At that time, she had never been married. Further digging finally revealed that Anderson tied the knot five years ago but untied it after only two years of marriage.

"Mason, we've been sitting on this couch all day. I need to give my eyes a rest."

"It's after nine, so I'd say now is a good time to quit for the day. You wanna go for a quick walk before we hit the hay?"

Under the pitch-black sky, the cold weather fully settled in. The overcast sky prevented their view of any stars, but Kennedy hoped the gusty wind would push the clouds out before sunrise. She could use a few rays of sunshine to improve her outlook. During the course of the day, she knew they made progress on the investigation and felt confident that Anderson had to be the key to figuring out the puzzle that surrounded Joy.

The frigid wind funneled through their path, forcing Kennedy to pull her hands up into the sleeves of her sweatshirt and cross her arms across her chest to brace against the cold. Mason extended his right arm around her shoulders and pulled her close. Walking slowly and not speaking. Feeling the warmth of his body along her left side, Kennedy's mind wandered to earlier in the day. She wanted to feel his warmth for more than just this short walk. She wanted to taste his kiss for more than a fleeting moment.

"It's too cold to stay out here long; let's head back and get ready for bed."

As they entered the cabin, Kennedy tried to be subtle about her wishes when she said, "I don't know if I can shake these chills." She kept her fingers crossed, hoping Mason would offer some prolonged physical contact.

"Why don't you take another shower to warm up?" he replied as he sat on the couch and removed his shoes.

Another Old Spice shower with threadbare towels. Not quite what she had in mind for warmth.

She retrieved her pajamas and committed to staying under the hot water as long as it took to get the feeling back in her frozen toes. While lathering Old Spice into her hair, she wondered why Mason wasn't picking up on her hint. Maybe he simply wasn't into her. Did she misunderstand him earlier when he said he had feelings for her? Maybe the feelings weren't deep. Maybe it was like the feeling he might want to take her on a normal date one of these days. Not a feeling like he wanted to join her for more intimate activities.

Kennedy laughed at herself. Mason probably slept with women without it being intimate. He probably knew that sleeping with her would be life changing for her. Being the gentleman that he was, Mason likely wanted to prevent her from being brokenhearted. Her insane level of attachment to him had to be one-sided. Taking a few deep breaths of Pure Sport-scented air, Kennedy calmed herself. She had to allow the relationship to develop at a pace he was comfortable with, and she had to keep quiet about her extraordinary affection for him.

MONDAY, FEBRUARY 21

This time, Mason woke before her and had coffee ready by the time Kennedy got dressed and joined him downstairs. Another Pop Tart breakfast was half-eaten by the time they started any real conversation.

"You know I need to feed my animals today."

Mason set down his pastry and looked at her, refusing to speak until she returned his eye contact. "I've been thinking about that, and I'm trying to figure out how to get you home without actually going through your front door. I'm really concerned someone might be watching your house."

"I have Pennie's garage code next door. Maybe we can pull into her garage, and I'll climb over the fence from her backyard to mine and go in through my back door."

"I don't have a better solution, so I guess that's better than nothing. We should get your animals fed before we research Pam Anderson any more this morning."

They finished breakfast while watching the sunlight filter through the curtains. Birds chirped outside. Kennedy considered her current state. She enjoyed coffee and breakfast with a handsome man on a beautiful Monday morning. She made a conscious decision to keep a clear head until the mystery surrounding Joy was resolved. No pulling Mason into the quagmire of emotions she was currently sinking in.

Kennedy rode shotgun in the Nissan, allowing Mason to

hold her hand on the console. This made her quagmire even thicker, but she wouldn't pass up the simple physical contact. The time spent in the car was spent telling Mason about her neighbor. Pennie moved next door a couple of years ago after her husband died, and she had recently started dating again even though she spent most of her time with her golden retriever. As they approached her neighborhood, Kennedy fought the urge to duck down in her seat. She and Mason both wore camo ballcaps from the cabin to obscure their identity, but she still felt completely exposed.

No strange vehicles seemed to be parked on her street or in neighboring driveways. Nothing looked amiss. Kennedy nodded to Mason that it appeared safe to stop.

As they pulled into the driveway, Mason eased next to the F150. He jumped out and punched in the numbers on the keypad to open the garage. There was just enough room inside the garage to pull the small SUV in before Mason jumped out again to shut the garage.

"Are you sure your neighbor is okay with us coming through her house like this?" Mason said as he opened the door into the house.

"Yea, she's probably the most..."

Her words fell short as she stared down the barrel of a gun.

"You scared the crap out of me, Kennedy," the animated redhead spouted off as she set her pistol on the kitchen counter. "I texted you last night to tell you I got home."

"I'm so sorry, Pennie. My phone is at the house, and I didn't stay there last night. It's kind of a long story."

"Does it start with why my bunk room has been ransacked? It seemed odd that a thief would come in to steal kids clothing, so I figured I'd talk to you before reporting it to the police."

"Pennie, again, I'm so sorry," Kennedy said earnestly, realizing she had pushed the boundaries of their friendship further than she should have.

Mason joined in at that time, "Can I just go out the back door and take care of our business? Ken, you can explain it however you need to, but we don't need to stay here long."

After he stepped outside, Pennie gave Kennedy the most unexpected hug, then pulled her to the couch to have a seat. "Honey, I don't know what you're going through, but you know I'll help if you need me. I've always respected your privacy, so you don't have to explain anything. Just tell me what to do."

"Why are you being so understanding?" Kennedy couldn't grasp the absolute support her neighbor was offering.

Pennie smiled. "You're my friend, Ken, and you're a good person. Whatever's going on right now, I'm on your side."

Kennedy felt a surge of emotion, different from the emotion Mason evoked. Maybe this was a sisterly attachment. Pennie had always been generous and unreserved in her offers of unconditional friendship. Knowing they had to be rushed, Kennedy chose to share the severity of her situation with very few details.

"Okay, let me be quick. The police are looking for a little girl whose mother was murdered. The girl's life might be in danger, so I'm helping keep her whereabouts secret for now. You'll see the story on the news if you haven't already, but no one knows I have her. My friend Mason is feeding my animals as we speak since I'm not staying at home. We're being super cautious about things, so we decided to jump the fence into my backyard, so no one sees us go through the front door."

Pennie's eyes widened with the information. "I can feed your animals every morning and put the hens up at night like I did when you went out of town last year. If someone might be watching your house, you need to stay away. Do you need me to do anything else?"

"I guess the only other problem I have, I'll have to figure out on my own," Kennedy said, turning her head to stare at the back door that Mason exited a minute ago.

"Oh honey, you mean the studmuffin? What's the problem?"

"Pennie, I don't know anything about relationships. Now I've got this kid and this guy. I don't know what to do with these crazy feelings."

"Does he know how you feel?"

That was a good question, and Kennedy didn't know how to respond. "He knows we like each other, but I don't think he realizes how much I've fallen for him."

"I can tell time is of the essence here, so let me be frank. Tell him exactly how you feel. I'm sitting here alone right now because I can't seem to tell Chip exactly what I'm thinking. It's not over for us, but it's not heading the direction I want either. I keep letting our moment pass us by, that moment where we could become so much more than we are right now. So learn from my mistakes. Love will pass you by if you aren't bold enough to act when the moment is right."

Kennedy's jaw dropped at the brazen advice. "Really? Just tell him?"

"I wouldn't lie to you, sweetheart. Now, do you have a gun or any way to protect yourself?"

"I've never shot a gun before." She slowly shook her head as she answered.

Pennie stood to remove a piece of art off the wall and retrieve a small gun from a hidden compartment behind the frame. Setting the gun on the coffee table, Pennie ducked into a bedroom and came back a moment later with some stretchy-looking material.

"This is a Glock 26. It's compact and easy to use. 9mm with ten rounds. No safety, just point and shoot." Pennie reached down to pull up Kennedy's pant leg and strapped a holster snugly around her ankle. "It has a bullet in the chamber, and it's not a toy. If you pull that trigger, you better intend to kill your target. Now stand up."

Kennedy stood, kind of in shock at what was taking place. Pennie instructed Kennedy to hold up her sweatshirt and proceeded to wrap a black band around her waist. Then she took the pistol that had been sitting on the kitchen counter and slid it into the compartment against Kennedy's stomach. "I hope that rabbit's foot wasn't your only line of defense." She laughed at the fuzzy blue good-luck charm dangling from the belt loop before she continued, "Now, this belly band is a great way to conceal a pistol. This one's a Glock 23. It's a 40-caliber, so it's bigger, and it holds thirteen rounds. Again, there's no safety, and it's hot. Keep your finger off the trigger unless you intend to pull it and only pull the trigger if you mean it."

Kennedy pulled down her sweatshirt and marveled at how well she had concealed two guns. "Is there anything else I need to know?"

"Yep, anything worth shooting is worth shooting twice. And you'll know when the time is right to tell Mr. Hot Stuff how you feel." Pennie added the last statement a split second before Mason came back through the door.

Mason stood still for a second, looking back and forth between the women. He must have picked up the vibe that some serious woman talk just took place. "Are you ready, Ken?"

"Yes." Before she turned to go, Kennedy turned back to give Pennie the kind of hug sisters must share. She felt the tears stinging the back of her eyes, but she took a deep breath and kept her composure.

"Y'all get out of here," Pennie said, shooing them towards

the garage. "I'll shut the garage behind you."

⁂

"You said your neighbor was a widow with a dog. That's not what I expected."

Kennedy almost laughed from the passenger seat. "You didn't expect a gorgeous gun-wielding redhead?"

"That would be a big fat NO."

"Pennie didn't ask for any details, but she's going to feed my critters until I'm able to move back home. She's been my neighbor for a couple of years now, and I trust her completely." She paused a minute, thinking about what she really knew about Pennie. "You know, not long after she moved in next door, she convinced me to go to a Krav Maga class with her."

Mason squinted his eyes, "You mean a fighting class?"

"Yep, I didn't know what to expect when I showed up. Pennie just said it was self-defense. But don't let her pretty smile, blue eyes, and *Jesus Loves Y'all* shirt fool you... She'll rip your arm off and beat you with it if she has to."

She sat back in the seat and contemplated things. Pennie had been dealt a bad hand when she lost her husband in a workplace accident, but that never stopped her from living life to the fullest. Pennie took chances and invited people into her life without ever exhibiting a single ounce of regret for decisions, good or bad. Kennedy might need to heed the advice of the feisty redhead.

A ringing phone broke her train of thought. "Hello," she heard Mason say.

Continuing to listen to a one-sided conversation, she knew he was talking to his daughter.

"Hey punkin... I miss you too... No, you'll just need to stay with BB a couple more days... love you too... okay..."

He handed the phone to Kennedy. "Gracie wants to talk to you."

"Hey, Gracie, are you having fun with BB and Papaw?"

"Hey, Ken. We're having macaroni and cheese for lunch, and that's my favorite."

"That sounds great. Are you keeping an eye on Milo and Joy for me?"

"Yes, ma'am. Joy says she loves you."

"Tell her I love her too, please, Gracie."

"Okay, bye."

Kennedy stared at the disconnected phone for a second. Kids were so unpredictable and so resilient. They completely depended on the adults to protect them from the evil in the world, and now, Kennedy was one of those adults who needed to offer protection.

From the driver's seat, Mason said, "Let's get back to the cabin and see what we can figure out. I'm ready to get this situation behind us so I can get back home to my daughter."

The first thing Kennedy did when they got to the cabin was to go upstairs and remove the belly band and pistol. She felt self-conscious about it, and she wondered if Mason would insist that she relinquish the gun to him if he found out she had it. The truth was that she felt empowered after the pep talk from Pennie, along with knowing she had two guns at her disposal. After tucking the larger of the two guns under the bed, Kennedy thought twice about it before leaving the smaller gun under the bed too. She would need to put them back on before leaving the cabin again, but she felt better knowing the guns were nearby.

By the time they settled on the couch to resume their research, the clock on the wall revealed it was after ten. Mason pulled up the recent internet searches and tried to find a new rabbit hole to enter.

He spoke as he clicked different websites, "We know that Anderson's husband isn't a direct factor because they didn't meet until well after Joy was born. Since they divorced after such a short marriage, I doubt he could be involved."

"Then why are you looking him up now?"

"We can't find much information on Anderson herself, but her ex has a Facebook page, and it's not set to private."

He scrolled through the social media of Kevin Leonard, looking at his friends list and then his friends of friends. "His timeline goes back a number of years, but his posts were minimal. Leonard occasionally sent birthday wishes to friends, but he never updated his status or shared any personal information. His bio showed that he worked for a local mortgage company and nothing else interesting."

"The ex is a bust," Kennedy said, trying to come up with another angle. "How did Pam Anderson even get a job working with the president?"

"Let's see if we can find anything about her political contributions over the last eight years."

"I mean, the president looks like a perv, but I don't think he hired her over the phone thinking she was the *Baywatch* babe." The words were more sardonic than she intended, but she still meant what she said.

Mason tilted his head back and laughed. "You sure aren't placing much confidence in the leader of our great nation!"

"Well, what kind of vibes are you getting from him?"

"Just being honest, I don't like his political platform. His ideas on universal healthcare are absurd, and he doesn't have any clear plan for economic reform or foreign relations. I don't have confidence in him based on his lack of capacity to serve our country. You don't like him because he has *perv vibes*."

Kennedy rarely engaged in deep conversations, choosing to observe rather than speak in most situations. But this conversation had her feeling defensive. Taking the opportunity to be honest and stand firm on her perceptions, she narrowed her eyes and shared exactly what was on her mind. "That *Baywatch* reference was a joke, Mason, but you should know that I've done more listening than talking in my lifetime. I compare what people say to what they do, and I've become adept at interpreting what people really mean when they talk. Even through the TV, I can tell that our president is nothing more than a manipulative blow-hard, and I'd bet that sexual promiscuity would be the least of his transgressions."

"Damn, Ken. Remind me never to get on your bad side!" Mason laughed, while Kennedy seethed. "Never mind about Crawford anyway; we're digging into Anderson. So, unless you think she got her position in the White House by sleeping with Crawford, his promiscuity isn't a factor here."

"Fine, let's get back to her political resume for the past eight years," she replied, glad to get back on task.

Mason performed a variety of searches including keywords of Pam Anderson, Pamela Anderson, politician, Memphis, Georgia State University, Office of Public Engagement, Chief Communications Officer, investigative reporter... Some articles pertained to the correct woman, others didn't. All they could do was click on links, read the information available, and decide if it mattered.

By noon, sandwiches and another walk became necessary. As they strolled down another trail through the trees, Kennedy commented, "I don't think I'll ever eat a sandwich again after this week."

"I'll take care of dinner tonight, and I promise to serve you something other than a sandwich."

Kennedy glanced at him with an appreciative smile. He seemed so genuine. Was there any way possible that he felt as deeply for her as she felt for him? The only way to find out was to ask. Was it the right time? Her brain was in overdrive, but she couldn't come up with words to express herself. Plus, Pennie told her to wait for the right time, and now didn't quite seem like it. She had to trust herself to identify the *moment*.

Mason kept his hands tucked into the front pocket of his hoodie, which seemed smart except that Kennedy wanted his arm around her. Should she tell him that? Why was her brain so crazy around him?!

"Maybe after this is all over, we can bring Gracie and Joy here for a weekend and let them fish together? Chief would let us stay here, and I bet Joy's never been fishing," Mason said as he looked around to see if anything interesting showed up.

"How do you see things playing out? You think Joy will stay with me forever?"

Mason glanced at her before keeping an eye on the uneven trail they were traversing. "Well, I don't really know how it'll play out. I do know that Joy probably doesn't have any family left, and when she's officially declared an orphan, one of two things will happen. Either you will file to adopt her, or I will."

"That sounds like a hard row to hoe, Mason. A single dad with two six-year-old girls."

"It's not about what's hard or easy. It's about what's right."

The path they travelled on made a loop, bringing them back to the cabin. Kennedy tried to hide her disappointment that Mason never held her hand or anything during the walk. She also hid her disappointment that he mentioned a potential future with two girls, but he didn't voluntarily include her in that potential future, even after her "single dad" comment.

Despite the sunshine of the afternoon, the temperatures reminded them that winter still had a hold on the area.

Kennedy's nose, fingers, and toes were freezing, and the warmth of the cabin welcomed her inside. Sitting on the couch, she rubbed her hands together between her thighs to generate some extra heat. Mason grabbed an afghan off the back of the couch and sat close to her, wrapping the blanket around both of them.

"I'm wishing we had some aspirin here. All this internet searching is giving me a raging headache," Mason said as he adjusted his position to pull Kennedy into some kind of upright cuddling position on the couch.

She felt her disappointment dissipate as she closed her eyes and leaned her head against his shoulder. The tension in her muscles left her body, and she relaxed as the coldness also left her body.

"Ken, wake up."

She raised her head, unaware of where she was for a split second. Then she saw Mason's face so close to hers. They must have fallen asleep. She found herself lying on his chest. At some point during their slumber, they sprawled out on the couch. A glance at the clock only showed half past two, so they hadn't been asleep very long.

She sat up, awkwardly placing her hands on Mason's chest to push herself up. Their legs untangled as he righted himself, but the close physical contact made Kennedy's core tingle.

"That was an amazing power nap, and my head doesn't even hurt anymore. You want me to grab you a water while I'm up?" Mason asked.

"Sure, thanks. I guess we can get back to this research, see if we find a clue we can do something with." Kennedy accepted the bottle as Mason reclaimed the seat next to her. She tried to ignore the tingling to focus on their assignment.

The computer resumed its position in Mason's lap so

he could immediately dive back into the articles about Pam Anderson. After clicking and reading articles over the next two hours, they put together a rough timeline of Anderson's existence. A lot of "where she was" but not a lot of "what she was doing" to help them figure out her qualifications.

They found no important legislature that she assisted with, no committees she chaired, no movements she started. Her biggest political influence happened before she ever became a politician, back when she spoke out against discriminatory hiring practices. Ever since then, she held the role of advisor and nothing more.

Kennedy leaned back, stretching and scratching her head. "Where would President Crawford even hear about her to make her an advisor right off the bat?"

"Maybe we need to check out Crawford since his history will be more accessible. We might find where their paths have crossed along the way. But first, dinner."

While Mason busied himself in the kitchen, Kennedy kept poking around the internet. Even without the comparison of the sparse information available on Anderson, the wealth of details on President Crawford was staggering. To get the process started, Kennedy wrote down the demographic and timeline information on Robert Crawford. During his forty-eight years, Crawford had been all over the place.

Kennedy had barely scratched the surface of details on the president by the time Mason announced that dinner was ready. Whatever he just removed from the oven already had her mouth watering, so she hastily abandoned the laptop to have a seat at the table.

"Our menu is severely limited, but at least it's not sandwiches," he said with a smile, placing three slices of a frozen supreme pizza in front of her.

"I do live alone, so heat-em-and-eat-em pizza is kind of a food group for me." She snickered as the steam rose off the melted cheese, warning her not to dig into it recklessly. Hot cheese was the worst enemy for the roof of her mouth.

"Don't fill up too much, though. I found some frozen cookie dough, I guess from some kid's fundraiser, so I have dessert in the oven too."

While taking a tiny bite, testing the food for scald-ability, Kennedy nodded and set the pizza back down to cool for another minute.

"You got dinner ready so fast, the only things I've learned about Crawford's history is that he graduated from a public school in Atlanta, but he moved to Miami for college. After he finished his undergrad work, he went straight into Miami Law to get a degree in constitutional law. He returned to Atlanta a couple of years later to start his political career, serving on the Fulton County Board of Commissioners. That's as far as I got, but it looks like he never had a real job other than being a public servant."

Mason, showing more bravery, had already eaten a whole slice of pie before responding. "We're really just trying to see where his timeline overlaps Anderson's, so we can figure out how she got the position she's in now."

Shaking her head and taking her first real bite of dinner, Kenny responded, "Well, I just wonder what Anderson has to do with anything. What kind of blackmail angle could Destiny have on her? And are we really wrong about Joy being central to this conspiracy?"

"We do know that Anderson tried to stir up some crap in Atlanta when she worked for the news station, claiming sexual harassment. That was all unsubstantiated, and I guess her only option was to leave the job, but she left the city and the state too. Maybe she tried to stir up some problems in the mayor's office, and Destiny was part of it."

Considering that Anderson might have a propensity for drama, Kennedy tried to develop any theory that would work. Coming up short, she shook her head. "I don't know. I can't think of anything that wouldn't have made the news, but also that would've forced Destiny to quit working and hide for seven years. That's extreme for some kind of possible workplace drama."

"I tend to agree, so we need to keep digging. Pam Anderson did work directly with Destiny, and now, she has a lot to lose by working directly with the president. The only thing that doesn't fit with our original theory is that she couldn't be Joy's dad. Now, she did live in Atlanta for college and those few years after graduation, but we don't know if she would have ever come into contact with Crawford while she was there. I've lived here my whole life without ever coming into contact with the mayor of Bartlett, so living in the same city doesn't mean much."

"Okay, so we'll narrow down where Crawford was during the period that Anderson was in Atlanta."

A few minutes and two satisfied bellies later, they returned to the couch with a plate of warm cookies. Setting up a side-by-side timeline for Pam Anderson and Robert Crawford, Kennedy filled in an overview of where their lives took them as Mason shared details from his research. It took an hour and a plate of cookies to construct the data for comparison before they could sit back to analyze their handiwork.

Pointing out her chicken scratch writing, Kennedy explained, "So, our timeline starts when Anderson went to Atlanta for college. During her college years, Crawford was in Miami in law school. He finished law school during her final year of college, but he started working as a junior attorney for a firm in Florida that advocates for the rights of immigrants. By that time, Anderson was still in Atlanta, working for the news station. During her last year in Atlanta, Crawford must have moved back to the city because he started working for the Fulton

County Board of Commissioners."

Mason interjected, "Which means their timelines in Atlanta only overlapped for about one year?"

"Yes, because she moved back to Memphis when she was twenty-five, and she worked in the logistics industry for about a decade until she started some momentum against the industry's hiring practices. Anderson had only been back in Memphis for about four years when Crawford went on to become a US Senator, when he moved to McLean, Virginia. That's where he's been ever since as far as we can tell."

Mason squinted his eyes as if that would bring something into focus. "Crawford was serving his second term as a senator by the time Anderson started working for the mayor's office. That was back when Crawford was a democrat and not an independent."

"Hmmm, I guess any campaigning Crawford did to become a senator was contained to the state of Georgia. Can we see if he did guest appearances in Memphis at seminars or guest speaking events?"

A little more digging uncovered a multitude of guest appearances by Crawford around the Mid-South, and Mason had to keep narrowing the results to find anything that interested them.

"Oh, I didn't expect this."

"What?" Kennedy asked as she peeked at the laptop screen.

"Crawford helped Wigginton become the Memphis mayor eight years ago. He actually came here and campaigned for him."

"So, he probably would've met Pam Anderson during the campaign. She must've made quite an impression for Crawford to remember her eight years later."

Mason closed the laptop and sat back again. "Okay, so we

assume that Pam Anderson is a likely blackmail target because she worked with Destiny seven years ago, and she moved on to a high-profile career. We assume that Anderson got her career through some contact with Crawford during the mayoral election eight years ago. I'm getting stir crazy in this cabin though. How about another walk before bed?"

For this evening walk, Kennedy saw her breath condense and dissipate in the freezing air. She thoroughly appreciated the opportunity to stretch her legs as they followed yet another trail around the cabin. As a vet tech, Kennedy was accustomed to being on her feet all day for ten-hour shifts. She couldn't even imagine how people work in offices, sit at desks, or stare at computers for a living. The dynamic workplace and constant change of pace suited Kennedy perfectly.

This past week certainly offered a change of pace she didn't expect. Being thrust into the role of mother was strange enough, but then– cue the romantic music– she *caught feelings* for Mason, as Becky would say. Now, he walked next to her, appearing lost in his own thoughts. Could he be thinking about her? Or thinking about their future together?

"We really need to figure out what Destiny could have over Anderson. By implying that Anderson is involved, we're implying that she's also a murderer." His statement answered the question she didn't ask aloud.

His current thought process still focused on their case. Not Kennedy. Not their future. Maybe Pennie was wrong. Maybe she wasn't waiting for the right moment. Maybe she needed to create the right moment. If Kennedy wanted something to happen, she needed to put it into motion. Where could she find the gumption to make something happen?

"What do you think, Ken?"

Trying to get her mind back on track, Kennedy asked, "Is

there some way to look at the meeting transcripts or anything that Destiny and Anderson would have both attended? Were there any controversial projects during the year they worked in the office together?"

"That sounds like a good place to start. It's not like Destiny would've had any influence over projects, but she would've witnessed everything. I'm guessing she witnessed some drama or got dragged into some drama."

"Yea, but drama probably wouldn't force Destiny to hide for seven years, and drama wouldn't lead to murder. It's going to be a step up from drama. Something major happened seven years ago, and we thought *Joy* was what happened. At this point, we've got to entertain alternate theories."

The scurry of a nocturnal animal nearby caused Kennedy to jump, and it was a good thing Mason was there to steady her footing. "Calm down, it's probably just a racoon," he said, laughing under his breath as he tucked his hands back in his hoodie pocket.

"Are there trail cams or anything here that we can use to see if it's more than a racoon?" Even though it probably was a racoon or coyote, Kennedy wished she still had a gun on her. She made a mental note to herself: *Carry a gun at all times.*

"I'm sure there's trail cams all over the place, but we'd have to find them and pull the memory card to take a look. It's not like a security camera with a live feed we can follow."

"As much as I needed to walk around, Mason, this cold air is getting to me. Can we please head back to the cabin?"

The warmth returned to her feet and hands as Kennedy stood in the shower. She lathered the Old Spice into her hair as she contemplated all the mysteries in her life. Joy. Motherhood. Mason. Emotions. Murder. Conspiracy. Until these issues reached a resolution, she couldn't take a break at all. Mentally, Kennedy felt stretched thin. Ducking far enough to let the stream of water rinse the suds from her hair, she wondered if she could do some kind of compartmentalized compartmentalization.

Joy and motherhood were currently being handled by BB and Papaw. Murder and conspiracy would be researched further in the morning. Mason and emotions were tied together and could be addressed tonight if she could find the gumption. Just a direct conversation. Just a hint of what the future might hold. If she could put her mind at ease that Mason wanted something long term, if she just had a glimmer of hope past the madness of their current situation, Kennedy might find some clarity for her muddled mind.

She took a few extra minutes to shave her pits and legs with the men's Bic razor that had probably been in the shower caddy for over a year. Nothing about this situation was ideal, but Kennedy chose to use whatever she had at her fingertips to make the best of it. After drying off and wearing the same pajamas from the night before, she stepped out of the steamy bathroom.

"Did you save me some hot water?" Mason laughed, holding his own pajamas in his hands. "I need to fight off the frostbite myself."

"It's all yours," Kennedy said as she moved to the couch.

She settled back on the lumpy couch, staring at the wooden decking that covered the ceiling. Gumption. That was what she needed. Her life would be forever changed by the events of the past week. Even if Joy found a family somewhere, and Mason moved on, Kennedy was done with being alone. If she wanted to take a chance with anyone, be vulnerable to anyone, Mason would be the man. She got distracted trying to figure out where the word *gumption* even came from... was there some Latin root word like *gump* or what?

Her mind was brought back to the present when Mason

stepped out of the bathroom wearing nothing but boxers. The crazy tingling in her abdomen returned with a vengeance. His chest was toned without being bulky, and she had never seen anyone so stunning in her life.

"Sorry, Ken, I thought you'd already be upstairs," he said as he ducked back into the bathroom to grab a t-shirt. He pulled it over his head, effectively covering his pectoral crossed-axes tattoo, as he came back into the living area.

"I wouldn't go upstairs without telling you good night," she responded with a surprisingly even voice given the excited state of her hormones. "You know, this couch is terribly uncomfortable. I don't know how you sleep on it." She sat up, waiting for him to respond.

He came over to sit on the opposite leg of the sofa and said, "You took a nap on it earlier too, so you know it's not so bad."

"I think I took a nap on you, while you took a nap on the couch." She thought about gumption for another second before speaking again, "There's plenty of room in the bed upstairs if you want to stretch out tonight."

Mason shook his head and shifted his gaze towards the opposite wall. "I need to stay down here, Ken. I can see the front and back doors from here, and I'll be able to defend us if I hear someone trying to break in."

"I'd feel safer if you were upstairs with me." Kennedy felt the gumption now. Maybe it was a level up from that. Ultra-gumption. That might not be a real word, but it was her frame of mind. "Come on, Mason. Let's go to bed." She stood and walked right past him without looking back.

Her confidence waned when she realized he didn't follow her upstairs. Kennedy turned out the light and got into bed, fully prepared to not sleep that night. She rolled onto her left side, facing away from the door. Pouting. Kicking herself for letting her stupid gumption embarrass her like that.

Until a minute later...

Mason entered the room without saying a word. Kennedy refused to roll over to face him when she felt the bed shift along with the comforter as he joined her. Every nerve ending in Kennedy's body anticipated what would happen next, and she almost forgot to breathe when Mason's arm reached over her, pulling her against himself. She marveled at how well they fit together, her backside molded perfectly against his front side. His strong arm draped over her, lightly touching her arm with his fingertips. Spooning. It felt magical.

Even though no one else could hear, he whispered in her ear, "Ken, you're scaring me."

"What do you mean?" she whispered back, still not facing him.

Mason lifted his right hand, reaching over her to switch on a lamp on the nightstand, shining the light directly in her face. "Look at me."

She shifted to lie on her back, pleased that Mason stayed against her. The soft kisses started immediately, and she relished the feel of his mouth on hers and how his right hand cradled her face. She was disappointed when he backed his face away from hers a minute later. At least he continued caressing her face with his thumb. When she dared to open her eyes, Mason wore a smoldering expression, appearing to look right through her.

"Kennedy, I can tell you don't have a lot of experience with things like this, so I'm trying not to move too fast with you."

"I'm the one who invited you to join me up here. This isn't about you moving too fast."

"Yea, but I don't think you know what you're asking for,

Ken."

Kennedy sighed before answering. She maintained eye contact and said, "Maybe for the first time in my life, I know exactly what I want, and I don't mind asking for it."

With a slight shake of his head, Mason responded, "Tell me then... What exactly do you want?"

The tingling in her core had escalated to an overwhelming physical and emotional overtaking of her entire body. Her chest tightened, and her words caught in her throat. After reminding herself to breathe again, she forced back tears that threatened to form. Now was her moment to be honest, more honest than she had ever chosen to be with a man. "Mason, I want to know what it feels like to be loved."

His smile was unexpected, almost like he had to stifle a laugh. Her heart pounded so loud, she was scared she wouldn't hear his response over the pulsating in her ears.

"Well, Kennedy, how do you feel right now?"

The smile remained on his face, but Kennedy couldn't determine what it meant. Was this a joke to him? Would her heart literally explode in her chest?

"What? Why are you asking me that?" She barely squeaked out the question.

"You said you want to know how it feels to be loved. You are loved, right now. I'm pretty sure I loved you the first night we met. So tell me, how do you feel right now, Kennedy? Knowing that you're loved?"

The tears escaped before she could do anything about them. She searched his eyes. Even though she had no frame of reference for this feeling, she knew he was telling the truth. She knew without a doubt that he meant every word. How could she even answer his question? How could she describe the indescribable? Her heart flooded with hope and elation, emotions that were dead a week ago. Her mouth opened, but nothing came out.

"Speechless? Is that how you feel?"

Kennedy nodded. Mason reached back over to turn off the lamp. No words were necessary for the rest of the night.

TUESDAY, FEBRUARY 22

The ringing of a phone woke them. Kennedy rubbed her eyes, trying to wake up. She listened Mason answer, and again, she was privy to a one-sided conversation.

"Hello... Hey punkin... I guess y'all have to play inside then... Okay... Hey, Joy... Are you having fun at BB's house... Oh, okay... Okay, hang on..."

Mason handed the phone to Kennedy, "Joy wants to talk to you."

"Good morning, Joy."

"It's raining outside." Her pronunciation made it sound like *waining* instead of raining.

"Does that mess up your plans to play outside?"

"No. BB says you have my lucky rabbit's foot."

Kennedy smiled. If all Joy had to worry about was a rabbit's foot, things would be so much simpler. "I do have it because I needed some luck, honey. Do you have Ginger with you?"

"Yes, she's eating lettuce."

"Well, as long as you have Ginger, you have four lucky rabbit's feet. So, you're four times luckier than me right now."

"Okay. Love you."

The phone hung up before Kennedy could respond. She

stared at the screen. It was almost nine o'clock. She had never slept this late in her life, but the comfy bed in conjunction with her warm bed partner didn't spur her to give up her position. The raindrops spattering on the metal roof didn't help the situation either. If they weren't knee deep in this conspiracy, Kennedy would turn off the phone and stay in bed with Mason all day.

She glanced over at the handsome fireman who sat up and stretched. His perfect muscles provided an ideal vision to start the day. After he finished stretching, he looked over his shoulder at her. "Good morning, beautiful. You ready to get started?"

The ringing phone interrupted breakfast. Mason put the call on speaker to see who the unrecognized number might be.

"Hello..."

"Hey, Mason? This is James Walker. You okay?"

"I'm okay, how'd you get this number?"

"Your dad shared it with me. I spoke to Marla this morning though. Man, I gotta tell you, I think whatever you and Kennedy are involved in is fixing to hit the fan."

Mason and Kennedy made eye contact before he responded, "What do you know, James?"

"It didn't take much effort for me to figure out that you're helping Kennedy with that missing girl. When I talked to my sister this morning, she said Kennedy went out of town for a few days. You should know Pennie isn't a good liar, but she didn't tell me any details, assuming she knows anything worth sharing."

"So, why are you calling me? Do you want to help?"

"I'm just letting you know I've got your back. I suggest you stay hidden, and I'm going to keep an eye on your parents' house. Keep Kennedy and that little girl safe. Don't you have a daughter?"

"Yes, and I'm taking all the precautions I can to keep everyone safe. What did Marla say this morning?"

Officer Walker sighed through the phone. "She's going to run a DNA test. The police found a toothbrush at the fire scene, and they compelled her to do the test to see if the father could be found. My gut tells me this bastard doesn't want to be identified. A pandora's box is fixing to be opened."

"I'd certainly appreciate you doing a drive by of my parents' home. I might ask them to go stay with some family out of town for a while until this blows over."

"Okay, man. I'll keep an eye on their house but sending them out of the area might be wise."

They hung up the phone and finished the last two packs of frosted cherry Pop Tarts before getting started on any research. Even though they were apprehensive about any DNA test, they welcomed some kind of action to crack the case wide open. Instead of discussing the phone call with Officer Walker any further, they decided to keep on doing their own research for the time being. Mason tuned into the news station as their usual background noise, and they dove right into the notes and articles about Pam Anderson.

"It looks like Mayor Wigginton posted weekly updates and remarks on activity in his office." Mason pointed out all the articles listed as links on the government website. "We're really only interested in the articles from the first sixteen months he held office. Destiny stopped working there in April, so we might need to focus on the articles from April and work our way back."

Kennedy nodded. She was only reading with him, not taking notes right now, so she leaned on his shoulder to see the screen. He provided such a sturdy resting place for her. The idea of trusting a man enough to lean on him was still so new to her, but she welcomed all the feelings that blossomed these days.

"It looks like mostly budget stuff so far. Recruiting more police officers... streetlights... economic growth... proposed legislation about taxes." He shook his head at the wealth of information that proved useless to them.

"What about minutes reports from all the council meetings?" Kennedy asked.

Mason clicked on a few links to find the City Council *Meeting Agenda and Documents*. They started with the minutes from the month of Destiny's departure from her job. Twenty pages into the first document, Kennedy's brain threatened to stop working. Twenty pages of *Ordinance to amend the ordinance, Resolution pursuant to, Unified development code,* and other legal-sounding phrases that probably didn't mean anything special.

They clicked the next document to find more of the same. Then the next. More of the same.

"Mason, we're not finding anything dramatic or otherwise. We haven't even seen a single agenda item that's worth digging into further."

"We've only looked at six documents, Ken. Patience isn't your specialty yet but wait till you've been a mom for more than a week. You'll learn about patience."

Resting her head against the back of the couch and closing her eyes, Kennedy inhaled, hoping to restore some endurance. With an audible exhale, she sat back up and saw the same story being covered on the news. President Crawford was speaking at an event in Atlanta, pounding his fist on the podium to emphasize his message, his faithful entourage standing behind him on the stage.

She turned the volume up to see if he had anything new to share during this news snippet, but she didn't turn it up in time to hear what the president had to say. The anchor took over speaking from her desk in the broadcast studio. Kennedy and Mason both froze as they listened to the newscaster.

"As the president wraps up his visit to Atlanta, the state of Tennessee is preparing to host him in both Nashville and Memphis in the next week. In light of recent events in Memphis, the president's own director of the office of public engagement, Pamela Anderson, took the microphone to share her thoughts."

The TV screen replaced the news lady with a close-up of Anderson at the podium. Her shoulder-length brown hair, dark eyes, and heavy glasses gave her the appearance of that teacher in elementary school who struck fear into the hearts of all the kids. With a stern expression, Anderson spoke into the microphone, "As a native Memphian, and as a proponent of women across the country, I am seeking justice for Destiny Young. Furthermore, I am seeking justice for her daughter Jillian. If anyone knows the whereabouts of this innocent little girl, please help us locate her. A reward is being offered to find Jillian and to find the murderer of her mother."

The news anchor took back over, discussing Crawford's upcoming meeting with the governor of Tennessee in Nashville. Kennedy turned the volume back down.

"What do you think, Mason? Did she orchestrate Destiny's murder and now, she's offering a reward to find Joy? To what end? What will she do if she finds Joy?" The plethora of questions without answers kept coming.

"Don't get carried away, Ken. This doesn't change anything for us right now. We're pretty sure that Anderson is in this up to her neck, but we still need to focus on what the angle is. Maybe she's really on Destiny's side, and she's trying to help. I don't think that's the case, but we've got to keep an open mind about it all."

"Then let's discuss other angles. We originally suspected that Joy's dad was at the center of this, and blackmail was

Destiny's end game. Instead of going on our assumptions, let's talk about the facts. What do we actually know?"

Mason leaned his head back against the couch. He stared at the ceiling in contemplation for a spell before answering. "Just facts. For starters, Destiny is dead, and the hunt is on for Joy. That's why any of this matters to us. The next fact... Destiny lived off the grid in fear. In hindsight, we can see her fear was very well founded. Another fact... Destiny worked for in the Memphis mayor's office for three years, only quitting when she found out about her pregnancy. Those are the facts."

"Those being the facts, what are the possible scenarios? Joy is in danger. How do these facts help us determine the source of her danger?"

"The most likely scenario is that Destiny was sleeping with a politician. Maybe she slept with more than one, who knows. I'd bet money on her pregnancy being the direct result of an affair, and she recently sent out some kind of blackmail letter that got her killed."

Kennedy knew that was their supposition all along, but some of the twists and turns weren't consistent. "Our research shows Pamela Anderson as the most likely candidate for blackmail based on her elevation in status, along with her working in the office with Destiny. These scenarios don't go together since Anderson can't be Joy's dad. Can we come up with any alternate theories that involve Anderson?"

"We'd have to consider theories that place her on the good and the bad side of things. What do you think?" Mason asked.

"Hmmm. Maybe she really was Destiny's friend. She could have witnessed other politicians taking advantage of Destiny, and she knew about the pregnancy. Now that Destiny is dead, maybe Anderson really wants to help."

"Do you really think that's the case?"

"I don't know what I think. Given Anderson's history,

she's been an advocate for women. But she also started some drama at the news station in Atlanta. What could she have done to make her a target of blackmail?"

"If Anderson is on the 'bad guy' side of this equation, then maybe she knows who Joy's father is, and she's trying to protect his identity. We couldn't find any boyfriend or husband of hers who could be the potential father."

Kennedy's mind raced, trying to put together something, anything, that made sense. "Maybe..." The sentence trailed as she came up short. Then an idea struck her. "Maybe we could look back to that period of time when Wigginton was elected as the mayor eight years ago. You easily found that President Crawford was here campaigning for Wigginton. We deduce that Anderson met Crawford during that time. But what other politicians were here to help him campaign? Who came back to help him set up his administration?"

Nodding in agreement, Mason jumped on Kennedy's train of thought. "Joy was born in the first week of November, so her conception would have been around the first week of February. Wigginton won his election three months earlier. That means whoever helped him campaign in October or November isn't really suspect right now. But he would have taken office in January. If we could figure out if any big wheels rolled into town to help the new mayor set up his administration, that would be the pivotal timeframe."

"How can we find out who Wigginton's key advisors were during his early days in office?"

"I guess we put our noses back into the computer. We do more specific searches. Maybe look at news stories from January of that year to see if they covered any major politicians visiting the city."

Kennedy repositioned on the couch as Mason picked the laptop back up. "I guess we don't need to fixate on Anderson unless we find something that actually links her to something specific."

Mason resumed his posture with the computer in his lap. Pecking away, he found articles on mayoral processes in general. Even more articles about recent campaign efforts. Kennedy watched him enter dates and years to narrow down results. After an hour of searching, they finally found an article specific to Wigginton's key appointments.

"It looks like he had all his appointments picked out before he ever took office in January. I'm not seeing anything special that happened at the end of January or beginning of February at all. Let's take a break for lunch and come up with a different angle to investigate."

Over their lunch of toast and fried eggs, Mason and Kennedy went in circles around what little they knew versus the whole lot they didn't know. After eating, they resumed searching on local Memphis news sites during the timeframe of Joy's conception.

"Here's something interesting," Mason said as he clicked on an article. "You know our senators are elected every six years on a staggered schedule, so only a third of the senate is replaced every two years. Eight years ago in January, a group of senators started a bi-partisan movement to create some unity between the democrats and republicans. These were all senators who had maintained their seat, not ones who had recently campaigned to be elected. This group of senators included our new President Robert Crawford, along with two of his new advisors: Jenn Fitzpatrick and Jordan Atwood. Somewhere along the way, they picked up Pamela Anderson even though she was never a senator."

Wanting to know more about this group, Kennedy asked, "Did their movement include travelling to Tennessee? Who else was part of the group?"

He scrolled too fast for her to read the article, so she patiently waited for him to share the pertinent information. "It looks like the group included eight senators: Crawford, Atwood, Fitzpatrick, and five others. They did make a stop in Memphis at the end of January. They only stayed for one day from what I can tell since they were in Nashville the day before and Little Rock the day after."

"Then let's focus on this group. One of them might be Joy's father," Kennedy said as he got out her notebook.

"Only four of them were men. We already have Robert Crawford listed if you want to believe the president is at the center of this. Jordan Atwood, Mike Bird, and Ted Hatton were the other three guys."

"I believe Crawford is pervy enough to be at the center of it all, but I believe he's too smart to let a one-night stand ruin his chances of becoming the future president. Let's see what these other guys are about."

"Mike Bird sounds familiar even though I don't follow politics closely. Maybe I'm thinking of a basketball player or something," Kennedy said, trying to recall where she had heard the name before.

A quick search revealed that Mike Bird represented the state of Mississippi. "He's from Southaven. These days, if I didn't see the 'Welcome to Mississippi' sign, I wouldn't realize I left Memphis and entered Southaven."

"Oh yea, I remember seeing some of his political ads on TV, something about 'birds of a feather,' but his opponents compared him to a vulture."

Mason kept clicking on articles until he found something useful. "It says here he retired from the senate two years ago. This article talks about how he pushed funding for a rural highway in Mississippi to increase the value of some land he eventually sold for millions."

"That's corrupt. What else is in his history?" Kennedy

asked, wondering if they might've just stumbled on their blackmail-worthy suspect.

"Did you know that senators are exempt from the Freedom of Information Act? We can't dig into his personal life too much. Any scandals that happen within the senate are settled through the Office of Compliance. I never realized the senators get so many perks."

"Mason, I don't care about the perks of being a senator. I'm asking about Bird in particular. What information is available about him?" Her frustration showed more than she meant it to, but Mason seemed to share her mentality.

"I'm looking, Ken. He's fifty-five years old. He married his high school sweetheart, and he has one adult son. Oh, maybe he's not our guy." Mason scrolled further down Bird's bio page to reveal a personal tidbit neither of them expected.

Pointing at the screen, Kennedy asked, "Does that say he lost both his balls to cancer twenty years ago?"

She noticed Mason instinctively wriggle in his seat, as if he needed to protect his own testicles from an article on the computer. "Yea, his wife was heartbroken that they couldn't have any more kids. His shady politics and crapload of money make him viable as a blackmail candidate, but there's no way he's Joy's father."

"Fine, let's move on to Jordan Atwood." He clicked a few more links to find recent history on the senator. "He represented Alaska as a democrat. This picture makes him look like American-Asian descent, so I don't know how likely it is that he fathered Joy. Atwood is mostly known as a pork barrel politician. He worked as a senator for the past twenty years before he took this position as the president's senior advisor. This elevation in status alone puts him on our short list if we can't rule him out for any other reasons."

Glancing back at the notebook, Kennedy inquired about the last name listed. "What about Ted Hatton? Why was he part of the movement back then but not part of the president's selections now?"

"Because he's dead." Mason didn't have to dig much to find that fact. "He killed himself a few years ago after he was indicted on child pornography charges."

Kennedy vowed to learn more about politics from this day forward. She knew this was a narrow view of a few questionable politicians, but she would make sure her vote mattered in every election henceforth. Huffing slightly at their investigation so far, she said, "That leaves us the option of President Crawford or Jordan Atwood for Joy's potential sperm donor from this group."

"It's eight, and we haven't eaten dinner. Let's find something to snack on and take a quick walk since the rain's moved out. I want to be back by the time the local news starts at nine."

The subfreezing temperatures made their venture outdoors quick. Ten minutes into the brisk walk, they turned around to head back to the cabin. Kennedy's teeth chattered almost immediately, but she felt restless after being on the couch all day. Maybe this would be the most appropriate time to describe her state of mind as *cabin fever*. Some kind of physical stimulation would be greatly appreciated about now. The kissing and cuddling Mason offered the night before were unlike anything she had ever experienced, but she still wanted more.

Knowing the depth of the conspiracy they found themselves in, Kennedy knew any potential displays of affection would be on the back burner. The rest of the day had passed without hearing from BB, Papaw, or the girls again. Kennedy intensely hoped they were on the verge of a breakthrough to bring this situation to a close. Not only to continue building a relationship with Mason, but to offer some kind of normalcy for Joy without danger lurking around every corner.

As the warmth of the cabin welcomed them inside, Kennedy hurried to take a shower before the news came on. Again, she shaved with the rusty Bic razor. Again, she lathered her hair in Old Spice body wash. The entire set of circumstances surrounding them was less than ideal. Cooped up in a cabin in the woods, surrounded by invisible threats wouldn't nurture a new relationship, nor would it assist in their investigation. For a moment, Kennedy considered exposing herself to the media just to spur some kind of action. Would that benefit them or hurt them in the long run?

She wrapped up the shower. This particular towel wasn't any cleaner since she used it yesterday. Her pajamas weren't in much better shape since this was the fourth time she'd worn them to bed. Maybe some cuddle time with Mason on the couch would improve Kennedy's disposition.

After Mason's quick shower, they settled into the lumpy couch to watch the local news. Anticipating stories about upcoming golf tournaments, basketball, and the presidential visit to Memphis, Kennedy didn't anticipate the breaking story that kicked off the news.

The ever-serious anchor made eye contact with the camera, pleading with the viewers to help. "We have an update on the disappearance of the little girl, Jillian Olive Young. This woman you see on your screen, Kennedy Hughes, is reported to have the child in her possession. We don't know the relationship between Ms. Hughes and Jillian, but our investigative team is working hard to uncover anything we can tonight to discover the whereabouts of the missing child..."

The anchor gave a brief history of Kennedy's life while the picture swiped from the staff photos on her veterinary website hovered on the screen. Tunnel vision prevented her from hearing the next minute of talking, but she was snapped back to awareness when a picture of Joy holding eggs from her chicken coop covered the screen.

Her voice sounded hollow and breathless when she finally spoke, "Mason, I sent that picture to Marla. Did they get into my house and take my phone? How did they unlock it? Can they really get into my message history to get pictures I sent? They'll know I've been talking to you, and they'll find your parents and the girls." She felt on the verge of hysterics. Mason wrapped his arms tightly around Kennedy. He didn't speak; he just held her while the news continued.

"Another breaking story tonight is being reported live from East Memphis. Ernie, what details can you tell us about the harrowing scene behind you..."

"Yes, Sarah, you can see the carnage on the other side of the police tape behind me. The police have been trying to sort out the events that transpired only two hours ago when gunfire ripped through a coffee shop in this otherwise quiet neighborhood of East Memphis. We have been informed of three deaths in the wake of this senseless violence. Since next of kin has already been notified, we have been cleared to share the victims' names with the public tonight. Marla Jamison, who worked tirelessly with the Child Protective Services for over twenty years succumbed to her injuries as well as another government worker, Autumn Gibson. We've been told that Gibson has worked faithfully in the mayor's office for over a decade. The last victim, Erika Shelton, was the barista on duty tonight. She was only eighteen, working here part time and attending college full time."

The reporter swiveled to let the camera focus on the glass front of the coffee shop that had been riddled with bullets. Ernie continued, "Police have been hesitant to release any official statement on any potential suspects or motive in this violent incident, but we're being told they suspect it's related to gang activity. The tragic events of tonight have left our community stunned, to say the least. I will remain on the scene to report any updates as they happen throughout the night. Sarah, back to you in the studio."

"Thank you, Ernie. In lighter news, let's talk about our Memphis Tigers. They are on a winning streak..."

Feeling her heartrate accelerating, Kennedy tried to concentrate on her breathing. Anxiety took ahold of every fiber of her being in that moment. Strong hands gently encouraged her to lower her head down between her knees. Mason's voice sounded miles away.

"Kennedy, breathe. Listen to me. Inhale... Exhale..."

They remained this way for several minutes until the dizziness passed, and Kennedy felt her awareness return. Barely a whisper escaped her lips when she was able to talk again. "Mason, they're killing everyone. They're gonna kill us too."

"No, we're going to be diligent. Our eyes are wide open. Mom and Dad are keeping the girls safe, and we're all prepared for any surprises."

"How did they find out Marla was helping? What about Autumn? This..."

A ringing phone interrupted her, almost causing Kennedy to jump out of her skin.

"Hey, Dad, we saw the news," Mason spoke into the phone. After only a couple of one-word responses, he hung up.

"He wanted to make sure we saw the story. Come on. We need to get some rest tonight. I have a feeling tomorrow's going to be a long day."

Kennedy allowed Mason to lead her upstairs, where he continued to hold her closely. Her thoughts were no longer consumed by lingering desires to be intimate. Only the security of strong arms around her would quell the shock of the last half hour. Eventually, her breathing evened out, and she passed out more than she fell asleep in the aftermath of her anxiety attack.

WEDNESDAY, FEBRUARY 23

The sun hadn't risen by the time the phone rang. Mason didn't bother sitting up in bed to answer the phone, but he did put the call on speaker so Kennedy could hear.

"Mason, this is Chief Rice. I thought you might want to know a lady came by the fire station this morning looking for the crew who responded to the fire that night. The lady's name is Pam Anderson, but I gotta tell you, she probably hasn't ever been a lifeguard, much less played one on TV."

"What did you tell her?"

"Your name inadvertently came up in the conversation since you were part of the crew that night. When this Anderson lady asked how to talk to you, one of the guys mentioned you took vacation. I could tell she did the mental math to deduce you might be the one who found that girl."

"That means she's going to talk to my parents when she doesn't find me at home."

"Mason, I'm here if you need anything. Just call me."

"Thanks, Chief. Someone else is beeping in now. I'll holler at you later."

Mason pushed the button to end one call and accept the unidentified number calling in.

"Hello."

"Mason, this is James Walker. Are you still safe?"

"Yea, I'm safe for now."

"I've been trying to dig into Destiny Young's murder investigation and arson as best I can. I guarantee you that DNA test is what got Marla killed. This is bad news, man."

"Did she find the dad? Do we know who it is?" Mason asked.

"I don't know what she found, but it put a target on her back. I've already told your dad to get ready for trouble. There's a major storm brewing."

Yet again, another call beeped in. "James, let me get this other line. Thanks for the head's up."

Kennedy wanted the calls to cease so she could talk to Mason, but she knew he needed to answer.

"Hey, Dad. I just got off the phone with Officer Walker."

"Okay, what all do I need to know?"

Mason rubbed his hand over his eyes, seemingly contemplating how to communicate the lurking danger. "A woman named Pam Anderson might come visit. I don't know whether she's on our side or not. We still don't know who Joy's dad is, but I'm sure he's the catalyst for this killing spree."

"We're prepared, son. I'll let you know if anything happens."

With the calls out of the way, Kennedy ate some toast for breakfast without really tasting anything.

When Mason sipped his coffee, he said, "Ken, this coffee is strong enough to wake the neighbors. Did you need an extra jolt of caffeine today?"

She eyed her cup. It was half gone without her noticing how strong it was. "I guess I wasn't paying attention. What are we doing today, Mason? How can we protect the girls and get to the bottom of this?"

"I still trust my parents to shield the girls from whatever's coming their way. We have no way of knowing whether or not Pam Anderson is trying to help. When we left off our research last night, either Jordan Atwood, senior advisor to the president, or the president himself could be Joy's potential father."

Kennedy stood up in exasperation. "If you're proposing more research today, I don't think that's a good plan, Mason. Marla did a DNA test. Joy's dad, whoever he is, is obviously aware that Joy exists, and your parents will be the next clue to finding her location. That scares the hell out of me because that's exactly where our girls are right now. We're hiding in a cabin, while our girls and your parents are sitting ducks. Researching on the computer won't cut it today."

"I wasn't proposing any research, Ken. Hear me out. I'm just as agitated as you are, and I'm trying to break down the facts. We know that some high-ranking government official is behind this. They have the Secret Service or some other agency protecting them, and I don't think they'll stop until Joy is dead, so all this can be covered up. Which also means they intend to kill anyone who gets in the way."

Slamming her hand on the table, Kennedy found herself yelling at Mason, "Thanks for the grim synopsis of our situation! It's time for action, Mason! What are we gonna do? I'm not sitting in this cabin today, while Joy sits as easy prey for this prick!"

When Mason stood, the anger in his eyes caused Kennedy's to flush. He stood a few inches taller than her and looked down to hold her gaze. He answered through gritted teeth, "My daughter is in danger too, so don't talk to me like I don't care. We can't rush in, and I'm trying to come up with a plan to gauge the scene without making our presence known. Our only chance at survival is to catch them unaware, and that's what I plan to do."

Knowing an argument would be futile, Kennedy stomped out of the kitchen, hollering over her shoulder, "I'm going to get ready for the day! Just let me know when it's time to go!"

Rifling through the upstairs closet, Kennedy found a selection of camouflage clothing items. After she donned some camo pants that were just a little loose, she strapped the bellyband snugly around her waist. The gun was perfectly concealed behind the band and the high waist of the pants. It almost wasn't noticeable even with just the pants and t-shirt she wore. As she checked the concealment in the mirror, a splotch of blue in the background caused a second glance behind her. She thought twice but went ahead and hooked the lucky rabbit's foot onto a belt loop on the front of the pants.

She covered her t-shirt with a button-down camo shirt that hung down long enough to cover the rabbit's foot anyway. The ankle holster and smaller gun were quickly concealed under the pant leg. She was glad the only pair of sneakers she brought were gray. Kennedy owned a variety of sneakers to match all her different scrub colors, but the gray ones were best for her plans to blend in today. A brown-knit beanie covered her head. Kennedy was ready for action.

After she descended the stairs, Kennedy put all her effort into keeping her tone even. She knew they were equally unnerved by this terrifying situation. The next twenty-four hours could easily mean life or death for anyone involved. Kennedy had still not processed the death of Marla or Autumn, and the grave reality of their situation weighed heavily on her.

"There's a variety of camo in the closet upstairs if you want to wear something aside from a black hoodie and jeans." She didn't try to make eye contact as she plopped on the opposite end of the couch. Mason stopped after tying one shoe to look up.

"You look like you're going hunting," he said quietly.

"Maybe I am going hunting. I'm hunting bad guys."

He sighed and leaned back on the couch. "We'd do better hunting as a team."

"Mason, you know I've never worked as a team. This is all so new and so scary. But I'm ready to try if you are. Our girls... your parents... they need us today." Her voice trembled a little, both from fear and fury. "It's time to get them out of the city if we can. If no one has shown up at their house yet, if no one is watching, we need to get them out of here."

"I know. I didn't think anyone would find us so quickly. I guess, in a way, I was hoping the police would solve the murder and unravel the conspiracy, while we were all safely tucked away. Obviously, that's not going to happen, and the crap's going to hit the fan before this is all resolved."

Kennedy sat up more erectly, pleased at least that they were talking about an actual plan. "Okay, so where do we take them if we can get them out of the area? We need to get some cash or something to live off of without being detected."

"I'm sure my parents have some cash stowed around the house to get them by for a few days. We have family all over Georgia with a few hunting cabins and one lake house. We can talk it over with my parents to see where they will feel safest in the meantime. They might rather stay at a friend's house that's further removed from the situation, but they can help decide who they trust for this. Any of our family or friends would meet us with some cash if we needed it."

Her head reeled at his statements. A whole network of people to depend on? Multiple places to stay? How had she been on an island for so long? A mere two weeks ago, Kennedy was proud of her independence. She was practically smug to all her coworkers and acquaintances who needed to be in relationships. But now... Now, she could never go back to her lonely island. Whatever Mason had... confidence and trust in his family and friends... Kennedy needed it in her own life.

She stared at the handsome firefighter on the couch. Kennedy knew for a fact she wanted to wake up to his beautiful face every day. She wanted to read bedtime stories to their girls every night. She wanted to take naps on the couch, cuddled up with Mason. Wanted? No, she needed this. Her life had become a complete void. A vacuum. A black hole ready to suck in the love and passion and feelings of belonging that surrounded her.

"What are you thinking, Ken? Do you have a better suggestion?"

"Nope. I'm ready to follow your lead."

Within fifteen minutes, Mason drove the Nissan towards Bartlett, wearing his own camouflage outfit. Kennedy could tell he was playing a game of chess inside his head. His lips would move without saying anything. He would nod and squint his eyes, showing deep contemplation for whatever obstacles they might encounter. Since they had no idea what they were up against, she couldn't fathom how he planned to stay one move ahead of the competition.

Finally, he did speak, "My parents' house sits on fifteen acres. I think we can feel safe knowing they don't know what vehicle to watch for, so I'd like to drive around the area of the property as best we can to see if any suspicious vehicles are lingering. We can approach the house from several angles that don't include parking in the driveway."

The ringing phone startled them both. Again, Mason put it on speaker so Kennedy could hear.

"Hey, Dad. What's going on?"

"Mason, I'm standing here with a lady who came to the house this morning, thinking you might know the whereabouts of that little girl who's missing."

Mason and Kennedy shared a wide-eyed glance before

Mason had to refocus on the highway. She saw that Mason and his dad were both playing stupid for the sake of Pamela Anderson.

"That's crazy, Dad. If I knew where that girl was, I'd call the police immediately."

"That's what I thought, son. The lady is also suggesting you know a young lady named Kennedy Hughes who might be involved. If you know anything that can help, you need to let us know now."

A rustling over the phone line preceded a lady's voice coming through the speaker. "Mason, my name is Pamela Anderson, and I'm an advisor to the president of the United States. I used to work with Destiny Young, and I want to help bring justice for her surviving daughter. Your friends say you took vacation without notice after the house fire ten days ago. I think you know something, and I'd like to talk to you about it. When can we meet?"

"If you're at my parents' house now, I can head that way. I've been camping, but I'll do anything I can to help out."

Mason hung up the phone and looked over at Kennedy. "I don't know if they can trace the call that quickly, but I don't want to take any unnecessary risks. Here, write down the few numbers we saved in this phone in case we need them again later."

Locating a napkin and pen in the console, Kennedy wrote down the saved numbers for his dad, her neighbor Pennie, Officer James Walker, and Chief Rice. She didn't bother writing down the number for Marla Jamison. After she pushed the button to turn the phone off, Mason stopped to place the phone on the ground where he could run over it. Then they continued on without looking back.

The clock on the dash showed 7:06 a.m., and the night sky was relenting to the rising sun. Kennedy couldn't come up with anything appropriate to say. It only took a moment of silence for

Mason to speak again.

"We're still going to do a check around the house to see what defense Anderson might have brought with her. Then we can park somewhere else to approach the house cautiously."

"Do you think Anderson might be trying to help?"

"If she's there alone, she might be genuinely trying to help. If we find a dozen SUVs surrounding the house, then we might conclude she's one of the bad guys."

"When your dad called, do you suppose he would have hinted if Anderson had an entourage with her?"

"I'm sure he would have. We simply don't know if she's there alone."

"Where are the girls? Will they be able to stay hidden while she's there?"

"Don't worry your pretty little head about that. You know they were playing sardines, so she knows the hiding places. I'm confident they're well-hidden."

Again, with the *pretty little head* comment. It wasn't amusing this time, but she knew he meant it to be comforting. Instead of responding, she closed her eyes and leaned back against the headrest. Her brain swirled with possible outcomes. None of the outcomes were favorable. All the variables seemed to be stacked against them.

"Kennedy, I can't hear myself think over you grinding your teeth. I'm feeling the same turmoil, and I don't know what's fixing to play out. I do know that when we get there, I'll probably go into the house to talk to Anderson. I don't want her to know you're with me, but I don't like the idea of leaving you outside alone. Tell me your thoughts since we only have another ten minutes to make our plan."

"I can't come up with anything better. How will I know if you're okay in the house or if something is wrong?"

"That satchel in the backseat has some walkie talkies in

it. I'm going to leave one in my pocket with the talk button locked. You can listen from outside, just keep the volume low so you don't attract any attention to yourself. We'll find you a good hiding place with a view of the house. Hopefully, this Anderson lady is just trying to help, and she'll move on when I tell her I don't know anything. Then we can all hit the road to a better hiding place until this all resolves on its own."

"Wasn't Anderson supposed to be in Nashville with the president today? I wonder why she came to Memphis first."

"Clearly, the business with Joy is much more pressing than a speaking engagement with the president. Or maybe she truly was Destiny's friend, and this is her opportunity to be involved in the investigation."

As they approached the rural area of Bartlett where BB and Papaw live, Mason repositioned his hands on the wheel and took in the surrounding area with diligence. Kennedy mimicked his attentive posture, observing the details of everything around them. In her state of mind, every car in every driveway seemed suspicious. The gray-haired man rolling his garbage can to the curb appeared sinister. Her eyes noticed every movement and calculated how it might be a threat against them.

Mason turned down a two-lane street that would take them around the east side of the property, but not close enough to get a view of the house. They found no dark-tinted SUVs, and traffic remained sparse in the early morning hours. He turned again onto a street that wound around the back side of the property. A small community park with a soccer field occupied this street.

"This park is adjacent to my parents' land. After we finish scoping things out, I think we can leave the car here and walk to the house. The path comes out behind the barn, so we can get you into a good hiding place before I go back and park around front. I'll go in through the front door, so it won't look suspicious to Anderson."

As the Nissan ventured onto the street the house faced, Mason stopped well before they reached the driveway. Kennedy saw one black Suburban with dark-tinted windows in the driveway. Trees still obscured the view of the house itself, but they would assume that Anderson wasn't alone. He turned around and headed back to the park.

The cold air nipped at Kennedy's nose as they followed a trail through the woods. She wished the trees offered more coverage, but the bare branches wouldn't sprout leaves in response to her mental demands. After about twenty minutes of walking, they came upon the back of the barn. From where they stood, the barn completely obscured the view of the house.

Sticking close to the side of the barn, they eased around a corner to find a view of the back porch. Kennedy stood back after taking a peek, trusting Mason to assess the situation. Kennedy observed everything around her. They were on the edge of a pasture area where the horses could graze, and a split-rail fence divided the pasture into several areas. A grove of dormant fruit trees and bushes occupied an area of the farm about twenty yards away from them. She knew from her previous visit that a pond sat on the other side of the barn.

Mason pulled his head back around and faced Kennedy to speak in a hushed tone. "I don't see anyone. Do you have the walkie talkie in your pocket?"

Kennedy abhorred stupid questions, but she assumed he was just trying to be conscientious of the details. "Yes, Mason. It's still here in my pocket where we put it twenty minutes ago."

"Once we get you into a hiding place, it'll take less than thirty minutes for me to get back to the car and drive back around to the front of the house. I'll do a quick check from the car to make sure you can hear me. After you answer me that one time, I won't expect you to do any more talking. Unless you hear me speak to you directly on the radio, I want you to stay hidden and stay quiet. If you see anyone walking in the vicinity, turn the volume down so you don't give away your position. Hopefully, nothing transpires that forces you to make any moves on your own."

"I won't go anywhere unless you tell me to, Mason."

With unwavering eye contact for a moment, Mason nodded and turned away. He reached his hand back for Kennedy to grab. Her cold fingers lightly held his as Mason ducked below the split-rail fence to start their journey towards the house. The fence only offered partial concealment, but Kennedy remained low and kept the steady pace towards a cluster of cedar trees near the house.

Their hands released to make a fast beeline to the trees. Even though the trek to their hiding spot was short, and not all too strenuous, Kennedy's heart raced like she had just completed a marathon. They sat on the cold dirt amid the bushy branches of the trees while she tried to force her breathing to remain somewhat normal. In through her nose, out through her mouth. Her sinuses complained about the cold air, but they would just have to suffer. Nothing about their circumstances was ideal, and cold air was the least of her problems.

Mason finished checking their surroundings again before turning back to Kennedy. He gently placed his hand on her cheek and guided her face towards his. The soft kiss was far too brief, but she knew this wasn't the time or the place for intimacy. Just the fleeting reprieve from their dire situation renewed Kennedy's outlook. She had something worth fighting for.

With barely a whisper, Mason said, "Ken, I love you. Leaving you hiding here is probably the hardest thing I'll ever do."

"I... " Her voice caught in her throat. She had never said this to a man. She tried again. "Mason, I love you too. Don't let this part be difficult, just come back for me. Please."

With only a nod, Mason backtracked towards the barn. Isolation crept in along with the frosty temperatures as Kennedy remained under the branches of the cedar trees.

Sitting on the cold, hard ground under the cover of shrubbery for the second time in a week left Kennedy feeling a bit lost. Hiding with no idea what would happen next. The difference this time was that she just told a man she loved him. The frightening part was that she meant it. Kennedy also loved two little girls more than life itself. That was the next level up from frightening. Joy didn't ask for this situation, and Gracie certainly didn't deserve to be thrust into the middle of this danger.

Whatever isolation Kennedy used to feel was slowly being replaced by a feeling of belonging. Mason, along with his parents, stood ready to fight on her behalf. They were all ready to fight for the safety of Gracie and Joy. Teamwork. Family. As terrifying as that sounded, Kennedy needed it more than she ever realized.

The aroma of the cedar trees evoked some holiday memories... Hunting for a live Christmas tree with her parents as a child, and even as a teenager... Making colorful Christmas countdown chains... Cutting out cookie dough into bells and stars and adding red and green sugar sprinkles... It had been six years since Kennedy put up any decorations for any holiday. Her life had truly become stagnant. Maybe Kennedy needed to be rescued just as much as Joy.

Daydreams of hiding Easter eggs for Joy and Gracie were disrupted by the chirp of the radio in her pocket.

"I'm in the car, Ken. Can you hear me?"

She pushed the button to answer. "Yes, I can hear you clearly."

"Okay, stay low and quiet. I will do one more quick check when I pull into the driveway."

"Okay."

As she waited in anticipation, Kennedy tried to examine her surroundings. From where she hid in the cluster of trees, she might be about forty feet from the back porch of the house. The fence that formed the perimeter of the horse pasture ran behind her, leading to the barn and around the field. She couldn't see the street that ran in front of the house, so she would have no way of knowing when Mason pulled into the driveway. The grove of fruit trees off to the east side of the house were still visible, but she couldn't see the pond or anything on the west side of the house or barn aside from more pasture area. If she were forced to leave this hiding place, her only option would be to retreat towards the barn.

Her mind wandered to other hiding places. Where were the girls now? Anderson wouldn't have called Mason if the girls were in plain sight. How could they be hiding this long? Was Gracie hiding along with Joy? She had no doubt that Joy was an expert at laying low, but they had no idea how long this ordeal would last.

The radio chirped again, breaking her train of thought. "Ken, I'm pulling into the driveway now. After you answer me, I'm locking the talk button so you can hear everything."

"I hear you. Good luck in there."

Kennedy heard the rustle of the radio against his pocket before she heard his car door close with a *thunk*. Her eyes continued to scan the area while she listened to the radio and hoped all the conversation would be discernable. With the volume down low, Kennedy's trembling hand held the radio close to her ear. A minute more of rustling and undistinguishable sounds was all she heard before the communication started.

Through the radio, she heard Mason greeting his parents

and being introduced to Pamela Anderson. Then Mason made observations and asked questions to keep Kennedy informed.

"Who are these two guys?" he asked.

It must have been Anderson answering, "Now that I work for the president, I have to travel with bodyguards. They're only here for my protection. Thank you for meeting with us this morning, Mason. We're desperately seeking the whereabouts of Jillian Young."

Kennedy was surprised by how clear the conversation came through the little walkie talkie. The people in the house exchanged a few pleasantries. Being a good hostess, Becky offered coffee for her son and the guests. At least Kennedy now knew that Anderson had two men in the house with her. Once everyone seemed settled, the conversation became more to the point.

Mason asked, "Why do you think I have information about this girl?"

The female voice replied, "I know you responded to the fire at Destiny Young's house that night. We assumed the girl, Jillian, was there, but her presence was never reported. Of course, we know now that her mother was murdered that same night. In retrospect, we don't know whether Jillian was at the house or with her mother elsewhere, but either way, we're concerned the girl is in grave danger."

"I'm just as concerned as you are. I've seen the story on the news," Mason responded without giving anything away.

Then Becky joined in with a grandmotherly point of view. "That poor child, she must be so scared."

After clearing her throat, Anderson attempted a more direct approach. "Mason, I've been told that you took off work quickly after the fire that night. I'm wondering if you brought Jillian home with you. In fact, I saw that the police responded to your apartment Saturday because you were seen with a girl matching Jillian's description."

"They did search my home, and they found my daughter, who's the same age and general description as the missing girl."

"And where is your daughter now?"

Kennedy wished she could tell more of the tone and see the facial expressions, but the audible conversation would have to do.

"My daughter is staying with one of her friends for a few days while I've been camping."

"You look like you've been hunting. Do you normally wear camo when you camp?"

Even through the radio, she heard Anderson's condescending attitude that time.

"No, but I was actually clearing trails and doing maintenance on my deer stands and duck blinds. It's not any active hunting season, so this is when I do all my prep work."

"Let's talk about Jillian, please. Her mother, Destiny, was a friend of mine, and it's become my personal goal to get her daughter to safety. Let me tell you what I know... A girl fitting Jillian's description was reported to be in the custody of Kennedy Hughes. Do you know Ms. Hughes?"

"Yes, we've been on a couple of dates but nothing serious. She doesn't have any kids."

"Well now, she's missing too. She hasn't been home in a couple of days, and we think she has Jillian with her. Can you tell me where to find Ms. Hughes?"

"No, I haven't talked to her in a few days, and she knew I'd be in the woods. If she's missing too, how do you even know we're dating? I haven't introduced her to anyone."

Kennedy held her breath, waiting for this answer. The depth of information Anderson had might let them know if she was here to help Joy or to harm Joy. If only she could see

Anderson's face when the question was aimed at her.

Anderson answered directly with no hint of deceit. "I spoke to a mutual friend of mine and Destiny who said she saw you with Ms. Hughes at the scene of the fire. You told her you were one of the first responders who put out the fire. Why would you go back to the scene?"

"Kennedy's keeping the bunny that used to live there. I guess the bunny belonged to the little girl, and we just stopped to see if there was any cage or food in the shed. I first met her the night of the fire when I took the bunny to her, and I've never seen her with a kid at all."

"For right now, we'd like to be thorough. Do you mind if my guys take a look around the house?" Anderson asked, probably trying to gauge the reaction of Mason and his parents.

A distant voice, probably Ronnie's, answered, "Go ahead, we've got nothing to hide."

Kennedy listened to some rustling for a few moments before Anderson instructed her men to check every nook and cranny in the house. She apologized to Mason and his parents for the inconvenience but thanked them for their cooperation. Small talk ensued for the next few minutes, until Mason redirected the discussion.

"Have you had any luck finding this girl's father or other family? She might already be with someone she trusts."

"There was no father listed on her birth certificate, and authorities haven't found any living relatives nearby."

Mason continued asking questions, "What will you do with the girl when you find her?"

"We'll put her into a foster situation. We take endangered children very seriously, and we need to make sure Jillian is safe. If this Kennedy Hughes lady kidnapped the child, there's a good chance she was also involved in the murder of Jillian's mother. Our secondary goal is to bring a murderer into custody."

With that statement, Kennedy knew her life was truly in danger. Anyone who could potentially know the truth had a target on their back. Whether or not Anderson was the bad guy, the outcome would be the same if Kennedy's whereabouts were discovered. She'd end up full of bullet holes just like Marla Jamison, Autumn Gibson, and Destiny Young.

The paralyzing thought brought a wave of dizziness over Kennedy. Then a few other questions plagued her. Where was Milo? Where was Ginger the bunny? If the guys found the animals in the house, they would know Ronnie and Becky were helping hide Kennedy and Joy. What if the men searched outside next? Were the girls in the barn? Would they find her too?

Before her imagination could finish creating the worst possible scenario, Kennedy caught some movement in the peripheral of her vision field. Two suit-wearing men were walking stealthily from around the front of the house. Kennedy made herself as small as possible within the branches of the cedars as the men passed within twenty feet of where she hid. She craned her head to watch them move towards the barn. After they were out of sight, Kennedy shifted just slightly so she could see when they came back out.

Watching the barn entrance intently, she didn't anticipate that the chatter on the radio would pick up back when it did. An unrecognizable male voice informed Anderson that the house was clear. If the two men were in the barn, who was in the house? Kennedy realized there must be at least four bodyguards here, and Mason only knew about two of them. Did Anderson purposely keep them in the dark about the number of men she travelled with? If Mason knew about the other two men, he surely would have made mention so Kennedy would be aware.

The people inside the house seemed to be making plans

to stay in touch in case they heard from Kennedy or found out where the missing girl might be. It appeared the visit might be coming to a close, but Mason would have no way of knowing a couple of the bodyguards might be left behind to keep an eye on things.

Since Mason had his talk button locked on the radio, it wasn't like Kennedy could give him any head's up about the extra manpower. Ideas bounced around her head of ways she could help, but she couldn't settle on any one clear plan. The best she could hope for was that the girls weren't discovered, and Anderson would move along, taking all her bodyguards with her. At that point, Kennedy and Mason would load up the girls and get out of town as quickly as humanly possible.

Living on the run should sound scary, but surprisingly, Kennedy was excited about the idea of running away with a family. That sounded better than being stable at home alone. With a family, they could accomplish anything. Alone, she could grow old and die without anyone caring. From this point forward, Kennedy was done with being alone. She would cling to Mason and his family, and she would live to protect Joy and Gracie. Simply having a purpose made Kennedy feel alive. As if her whole existence had been resurrected.

"Come out with your hands where I can see them."

The command from behind almost caused Kennedy to black out. The men never came from the barn, and other two men appeared to still be inside the house. That meant Kennedy was receiving orders from yet two more men. She dropped the radio where it was and extended her hands in front of her as she slowly and awkwardly moved through the branches that failed to hide her completely. She focused on her breathing, trying to conquer the urge to scream or run.

These two men also wore black suits. Probably

government agents of some sort. They could easily join Will Smith and Tommy Lee Jones in defending the world from evil aliens. Kennedy tried to take in any details. The guys both stood in a defensive posture. One man aimed a gun at Kennedy, while the other spoke quietly into his own radio.

Once they decided that Kennedy didn't appear threatening, the one agent holstered his gun and instructed her to walk in front of them towards the back porch. Thankfully, they didn't actually search her for weapons. When they entered the den where Mason sat with his parents, she made eye contact with him. His eyes seemed to silently apologize for bringing her into this mess, but Kennedy slightly shook her head, letting him know she was here of her own accord. She signed up for whatever happened on her own.

Without any conversation, two agents followed Anderson to another room to talk privately, leaving the original two agents in the den with Mason, Kennedy, Becky, and Ronnie. One agent stood at the door that led into the dining area. The other agent remained near the door that led to the sitting room adjacent to the back porch.

Kennedy took a seat next to Mason, and she tried to develop a little more fortitude. Two weeks ago, it was Kennedy against the world. One week ago, it became Mason and Kennedy against the world. As of today, her forces had doubled again with Becky and Ronnie on their team. Feeling bold, like there was nothing to lose, Kennedy tried to make eye contact with one of the agents.

"How many of you suits are hanging around here? I've noticed at least six of you."

Only silence answered her.

Mason reached over, putting his hand on Kennedy's leg. She placed her own hand on top of his, feeling the solidarity.

Anderson returned to the room without the original two agents. She coolly took a seat in the chair to face Mason and

Kennedy.

"I need answers, and I need them now. Mr. Dean, I asked you and your parents to be straightforward, and now, it's clear you've been blatantly lying to me. You could be charged with obstruction of justice at this point." Anderson stopped to take a calming breath before continuing, "As it is, I'm more interested in finding little Jillian than sending any of you to jail. So, why don't we start over?"

Anderson paused to make eye contact with each of the four members of her captive audience. Kennedy could still not determine if this woman were legitimate. Could a woman ever be on the bad side, willing to kill a little girl to protect a powerful politician? Kennedy still wasn't sure if the president or his advisor was the father, or if another person altogether donated the sperm that brought Joy into this world. If they answered truthfully to Anderson's questions, there were equal chances of Joy being taken to safety versus Joy being taken to her death.

Even a one-percent chance was too much for Kennedy. She had to stick to the only people she knew she could trust, and Anderson wasn't inside that circle.

Since no one volunteered any information, Anderson started with questions.

"Ms. Hughes, please tell me why you were hiding outside?"

"I feel like my life is in danger. I saw on the news that Marla Jamison was killed, and she's the one who brought me the girl that night. I feel like anyone close to this situation is at risk, and I was scared."

"Do you have any idea where Jillian is now?"

Kennedy had to remember not to refer to the child as Joy in front of these people. Any anonymity would only serve to protect Joy further. "No. I've been helping Mason at the hunting grounds, clearing trails and stuff."

"Please don't try to bluff me, Ms. Hughes. I've seen the details in Ms. Jamison's phone, and I know you had the girl in your custody. We've learned a lot in the last twelve hours. It's time for you to come clean and tell me where the child is?"

"I wish I could. A few days ago, I asked Marla to take her back. I felt like we were both in danger, and Jillian needed to be with someone who could protect her. Like I said, I got scared. Marla mentioned that she might've found the father, so I assumed that's where she was taking her. I haven't heard from her since, and now Marla's dead."

Of course, that conversation with Marla never happened, but Kennedy wanted to see how Anderson might respond to any mention of Joy's father. With a true poker face, Anderson didn't even remotely flinch.

"So, you've just been hiding out until this is resolved? That's your story?" Anderson inquired, disbelief obvious in her tone.

"That's my story."

"And when did you relinquish custody back to Marla Jamison?"

Kennedy looked to the side and puffed her cheeks like she was contemplating. "It was a week ago, last Thursday night. I saw that picture of Jillian on the news, and I called Marla immediately. I really freaked out. Marla came and got her that night." Any mention of Ginger the bunny would have to be avoided if she could help it. As it was, Kennedy had no way of knowing if Ginger was in the house in plain sight for the suits to see, and she didn't want to risk any contradiction of information with her fabricated details.

With a huff, Anderson continued with her distrustful line of questioning. "Why didn't you contact the hotline they posted on the news story?"

"Marla specifically asked me not to communicate with

anyone but her."

"Did you consider that Marla Jamison might be the suspicious one here? You didn't think to contact the police?"

Shaking her head, Kennedy knew Marla wasn't even remotely the suspicious one. "No, ma'am. Marla seemed genuine to me, and now that she's dead, I'm thinking we should all be scared. I'm terrified out of my mind right now. I truly hope that Jillian is with someone she can trust."

"Ms. Hughes, I sense that you're playing games with me. Maybe I should've introduced myself to you. I'm Pamela Anderson. I work directly for the president of the United States of America. I am here today representing the White House. The news of this missing girl bothers me personally because I used to work with her mother. It bothers me politically because the news has cast a shadow over what President Crawford is trying to accomplish in his first few months in office. Also, from a political viewpoint, returning this girl to safety will reflect positively on the president and his efforts to reunite this country. So, you see, my only goal from this point forward, personally and professionally, is to find Jillian. If I feel like for even one second that you're withholding information, I will escalate things, and you won't like the consequences." Pam adjusted the glasses on her face. Her eyes turned to slits. She seemed to morph into a snake right before their eyes before she hissed, "Now, Ms. Hughes, tell me what you know."

Kennedy, empowered by the small squeeze of Mason's hand on her leg, stuck to her story without hesitation. "Ms. Anderson, I respect your position with the White House, and I want Jillian to be safe as much as you do. I really don't have anything else to tell."

"If you want to play hardball, I'm just getting warmed up." Anderson stormed out of the room towards the kitchen, leaving the two suits standing guard.

With the foursome sitting in the den, Kennedy could practically see the tension in the atmosphere. A can of worms was being opened, and she had no way to communicate with her team to come up with a plan. To her surprise, Ronnie made the first move.

He stood with a flourish and walked towards the door leading to the back of the house.

"Have a seat, old man," the suit barked without moving one extra muscle.

"I have to use the little boys room. This stress is causing my IBS to flare up. Plus, this is my house, so I'll do what I please." Ronnie stayed the course, and the agent chose to follow him rather than argue.

While he was out of the room, Anderson re-entered with her original two agents in her wake, bringing the agent total to three in the room, with one manning the bathroom door, and two more still outside somewhere. "Where'd the father go?"

The original agent answered, "He was about to shit his pants. Riley escorted him to the restroom."

Shaking her head, Anderson resumed a seat on the chair. "I've called in some help so we can get to the bottom of this. We're not leaving here until someone tells me where to find Jillian."

Becky sat up from her spot on the couch and spoke defensively, "You can't hold us here like hostages. This is a free country, this is my home, and we aren't under arrest. I'd be in my right mind to call the police on you, I don't care who you work for."

Before she could finish her tirade, the agent standing closest to Anderson took a step forward. "Ma'am, you need to shut up. You're withholding vital information to our investigation, and you're being detained. If you would rather, we can transport all of you to the local field office. If not, keep seated and keep your mouth shut."

Kennedy wanted to defuse the situation, knowing that any pertinent information wouldn't be learned by posturing against the agents. "Guys, we're just really nervous. Can Becky and I get some coffee from the kitchen? We're happy to cooperate with whoever is on the way."

Taking Becky by the hand, Kennedy didn't wait for permission to leave the room. One of the agents followed them through the dining room into the kitchen. Coffee was poured, and Becky remembered her Southern manners, offering some refreshments to the suit. He politely declined. From the kitchen window, the ladies saw an agent standing on the front porch. Kennedy deduced that the second agent remaining outside must be guarding the back porch.

Becky took a few extra minutes to search in the pantry for some more sweetener. "Where did I put that fake sugar? I know it'll probably give me cancer, but I just love the way it tastes."

"Come on, ma'am. Quit wasting time," the agent spurted with impatience.

"There it is on the top shelf. Kennedy, come get this down for me."

Kennedy moved to the pantry to reach the baby-blue box on the top shelf. Then she realized Becky was sending a text from a phone she had hidden in the pantry. Kennedy positioned herself in a way to block any view of the phone while she grabbed the sweetener. Then both ladies backed away from the pantry to resume their coffee preparation.

The group moved back to the den without much delay. Ronnie had already returned to his seat, bringing the fourth agent back to man his post at the door. Kennedy wondered how long they would have to wait for someone else to show up. She mostly feared what tactics they would use to extract information from them. The anticipation only lasted another five minutes before the front door slammed shut.

"Dammit, Pam, we've got to be in Nashville for our meeting at four. Can't you handle anything on your own?"

Jordan Atwood charged into the room with a palpable mood of annoyance. Kennedy recognized his face from the online articles. He had a slim build and short stature. The angry brown eyes appeared larger thanks to his bushy eyebrows and bald head. Anderson didn't reply to him, and Atwood refused to have a seat. He snarled and glared at the four hostages sitting in the room. "Who do we have here?"

"I'm Mason Dean. These are my parents, Becky and Ronnie. And this is my friend Kennedy Hughes. We want to help find the missing girl, so ask your questions, and let's get this over with."

With an insincere smile, Atwood looked to Anderson. "Tell me how these people are involved?"

Keeping it concise, Anderson swiftly explained, "Mason was the fireman on the scene when Jillian went missing. Kennedy took custody of the girl, but she claims to have relinquished custody back to CPS. The elder Deans were the only way we could get in contact with anyone since Mason and Kennedy have been hiding."

"Okay, guys, my name is Jordan Atwood. I'm the senior advisor to the president of the United States. You can appreciate that my time is very valuable, so it would behoove you to tell me what you know." This menacing stare gave Kennedy the chills, but she tried not to show any fear. If this situation weren't dire, she would almost be amused by his Napoleon complex.

"Sir, we signed up to help the little girl initially, but I got scared when I realized her mom was murdered. Marla Jamison with CPS took her back last week. I think she found the girl's father." Kennedy said all this knowing full well she may be speaking to Joy's father right now. He didn't falter or flinch at her words, but he was likely skilled at masking any response to illicit dealings over the years.

"What do you have to say?" Atwood aimed this question at Mason.

"Other than the night of the fire, I haven't seen the girl."

"And you two?" Atwood alternated his gaze from one parent to the next.

Ronnie answered, "We don't know anything. Your men have searched our house. We don't have any child here, and we don't have a clue where you can find her."

Atwood rolled his head so they could hear his neck pop. He was making an obvious attempt to intimidate his captives, and it worked just a little from where Kennedy sat. "Let's do this the hard way, then." His glare shifted to the two agents standing over Anderson. "You two join the other two outside and make a perimeter of the house."

Once the two suits split up and left the room, only two more suits remained posted at each door to the room. After a moment, they heard the back door and front door opening and closing with the exit of each agent. Kennedy wasn't sure if it benefited their situation, but four guards were outside, leaving only two on the inside.

"I've gotta run to the bathroom again!" Ronnie exclaimed as he jumped from his seat.

The agent at the back of the room rushed to stay with Ronnie as he went towards the restroom.

Atwood shook his head in disbelief before setting his sights back on the remaining three captives. "I know one of you three can tell us where the girl is. Just tell me where to find her, and we can be on our way."

Kennedy knew it would never end that peacefully, not

that she even knew where to find Joy right now anyway. "I'm telling you the truth. Ms. Jamison took her back days ago. We don't know where she is. Maybe if you hadn't killed Ms. Jamison, she could tell you." She hoped the accusation would provoke some kind of response from Atwood, but he only snapped his head in her direction to face his accuser.

"I just got into Memphis thirty minutes ago, and I don't have the patience for your insolence. Since you're quick to deflect the blame here, that lets me know you're hiding something. Wait here."

Atwood's face transformed into a leery expression. His eyes took in Kennedy while he slowly backed out of the room towards the kitchen. Kennedy had the feeling he was undressing her in his mind, and she had no idea where he was going or what he had planned. A hornet's nest had just been poked. Mason must have felt Kennedy's trepidation because he moved his hand from her knee to wrap his arm around her shoulders.

"You'll wish you had just been honest by the time he gets done with you," Anderson spat from her chair.

A crash from the back of the house caused everyone to jump. While all three captives on the couch jolted, the one remaining agent in the room told them to stay seated. The agent rushed past them. Everyone heard the conversation from the next room.

"What happened, old man?"

"I tripped coming out of the bathroom, I don't know. I landed on him, and I guess I knocked him out."

The voices got louder as Ronnie and the agent came back into the den. The agent shoved Ronnie back down onto the couch before speaking into a microphone that must be attached to his earpiece. He barked out a few orders for someone to take the incapacitated agent outside and for someone else to resume his post in the house. While the changing of the guards took place, the agent drew his gun and aimed it at Ronnie.

A minute of rustling and opening doors from the back of the house was all they heard as Atwood reentered the room from the front of the house. Atwood addressed the agent first, "Put the gun away. We need the location on the girl before anyone dies."

"Okay, where were we?" Atwood appeared to be playing a game of eeny-meeny-miny-moe among the foursome. "You." His pointing finger landed on Becky. "Come here." His finger now pointed to the floor directly in front of himself, only six feet away from where they sat.

Becky turned her face towards Ronnie, desperately hoping he could shield her from whatever torture might ensue.

"Don't be scared, woman. Come here, now." He snapped his fingers as he spoke to her like a dog.

Hesitantly, she raised herself from the couch and walked the few paces towards Atwood. When she was within his reach, Atwood backhanded her hard across the face. The crack of his hand meeting her cheek caused everyone to gasp, including Pamela Anderson. Ronnie rushed over to where his wife crumpled into a heap on the floor. The agent who had just entered the room grabbed Ronnie by the collar and forced him back to the couch.

Mason had instinctively jumped up to defend his mother, but the second agent instantly moved to block any rescue attempts by the distraught son.

"Maybe I have your attention now," Atwood snarled as the two agents resumed their posts by each door. Becky crawled back to the couch, sobbing lightly while allowing Ronnie to help her up to her seat.

Through her tears, the defiant grandmother snapped, "We aren't telling you bastards anything."

Atwood's sinister laugh made Kennedy's skin crawl, but the level of respect she had for Becky just jumped up a notch. She could certainly take a lesson in gumption from the spunky grandmother.

"I was hoping you would say that," Atwood growled. He turned his attention to his dinging phone. After reading the message, he glared at Kennedy. "My favorite form of *encouragement* is next."

Atwood took two strides towards the couch and grabbed Kennedy's arm, pulling her up. Mason and Ronnie both stood, but the agents quickly restrained the men, adding flex cuffs to further impede their ability to help. Kennedy tried to struggle, but Atwood never let go, his fingers biting into her arm. She stumbled along as she was pulled towards the back of the house. Before they exited the den, Atwood turned his face back towards the men.

"If either of you gentlemen feel encouraged to share some details on the whereabouts of the little girl, let Pamela know. That's the only way to stop what's going to happen to your girlfriend here."

Kennedy wanted to fight, maybe stand toe to toe with Atwood once they got to the base of the staircase in the back of the house, but another agent had come inside to follow them up the stairs. Even if there was a chance she could best Atwood in a physical fight, there was no way she could fight off two men. Atwood led the way up the stairs, while the agent followed behind her. By the time she made it to the top, Kennedy's chest had completely constricted. Panic was setting in. Her vision blurred.

Through the fog that had entered her brain, Kennedy thought she might lose consciousness. Maybe that was best. Maybe she could just pass out for whatever might happen next.

Her legs turned to rubber when Atwood forced her into a bedroom. She fell to the floor, but she managed to sit up. Looking around, she realized she was probably in Gracie's bedroom. The princess pillows on the pink bedspread reminded Kennedy what she was fighting for– Joy and Gracie. She was also fighting for herself now that she had a reason to live. Now that she had a future.

The slamming door made Kennedy turn her head back. Even though the agent must have taken up post on the other side of the door, she found herself in the company of two men on this side. Not just Atwood stood in the small room, but another man joined him. Robert Crawford, president of the United States, towered over her. The cold stare of his blue eyes and evil smile made Kennedy want to vomit. He didn't don his usual suit and tie as seen on TV. Instead, he wore jeans and a dark-green sweater.

"Who do we have here?" Crawford calmly asked, leaning down to assist Kennedy in standing. Instead of helping her completely stand, he only got her far enough on her feet to shove her back onto the princess bed. "I don't have time for games. My presence is expected in Nashville after lunch, so it's time to come clean. Now talk to me, young lady. Where's the girl?" His voice still resonated as if he were giving a speech to the American people instead of making direct threats.

"She only stayed with me a few days, but I haven't seen her in almost a week. I really don't know where she is."

Atwood stood next to the president in the small bedroom. Both of them glared at Kennedy. "I really don't know," she squeaked out again.

The creepy smile returned to Atwood's face as he took a seat in the rocking chair. "How do you think your boyfriend feels right now? Knowing you're up here with at least one man?"

She swallowed hard. Mason had to be ready to explode.

"Do you think he wants to rush up here and rescue you?"

Atwood asked smugly.

Again, Kennedy remained silent.

"He doesn't care about you or the girl. I bet he's going to protect his parents, though. He'll know we're serious when they hear you screaming, but I'm sure they won't give up any information until we take our turn with his mother."

Atwood and Crawford both laughed. The president spoke directly to Atwood as if Kennedy weren't in the room, "You can have this one. These days, I prefer women who are too old to get pregnant. Plus, I had a look at the mom. She'll get my motor running without a problem."

"Pregnancy won't matter. They might all die in another house fire... Maybe some faulty gas pipes will cause this house to explode along with everyone in it," Atwood suggested.

A commotion downstairs interrupted their vile conversation. It sounded like a lamp crashed to the floor, but Kennedy had no way to be sure. Atwood left the room in a hurry to follow the agent down the stairs, leaving her alone with the president.

"You folks are on my last nerve. I'll give you one last chance to fess up. Where is the girl? If you tell me now, I'll make sure all of you live to see tomorrow."

She couldn't fathom how the president of the United States could speak so calmly about his potential involvement in rape and mass murder. Kennedy could only deduce that Crawford was Joy's father, and he was desperate enough to go to any lengths to keep it a secret. As she stared into his icy-blue eyes, she couldn't find one shred of human compassion.

"Answer me, young lady!" His voice boomed and echoed in the small room.

Kennedy shuddered. Her mouth went dry. She tried to respond, but no sound came out.

The slap across her face abruptly brought Kennedy out

of the trance. Her knit cap flew across the room. She followed its path with her eyes and stopped when she saw herself in the mirror on the opposite wall. The fire in her eyes made her almost unrecognizable, even to herself. The gumption was spilling over now. It was time to fight.

With a raspy voice, Kennedy managed to blurt out, "Screw you."

Crawford responded with a menacing laugh. "No, ma'am. That's what I'm going to do to you."

Before Kennedy could wrap her head around the predicament she found herself in, Atwood barged into the room wearing a scowl. He slammed the door shut behind him. "Damn gramps down there just knocked out another agent on the way to the bathroom. He's trying to be a hero, taking our agents one at a time. Next time, he can crap his pants for all I care."

"You've gotta be kidding me?" Crawford asked incredulously.

"That only leaves us four agents. Do you want me to call in some back up?"

"No, these are the only men I trust, the only ones who've been involved from the beginning. Let's get the show on the road, here. These four people are the only ones left who can tell us where to find the brat. Let's get our information and get out of here."

Kennedy smiled internally, knowing that Ronnie had single-handedly knocked out two agents. They underestimated him. The gray hair and gentle demeanor had them fooled for a minute but not anymore. She figured they had two agents posted outside and two posted inside. It appeared that no one followed Atwood back upstairs.

Turning to Kennedy, the president asked, "You ready to

talk yet?"

"I don't know where she is."

"What the hell?!" Atwood yelled as two gunshots rang out downstairs. "I didn't bring a pistol. Do you have one?" he asked Crawford.

The president pulled up the hem of his shirt and removed a small gun from a holster inside his waistband. Atwood accepted the firearm and stealthily moved out of the room.

Despite the fact Kennedy's heart just skipped a beat with the sound of gunshots, Crawford nonchalantly pulled the rocking chair closer to the bed. He threw the mermaid pillow on the floor so he could lean all the way back and slowly rock. His stare stayed fixated on Kennedy as he reached over to grab her thigh. She cringed and tried to back away, but his big paw locked down on her leg, keeping her in place.

"You don't have any chances left. Just so you know what you have to look forward to, we're both going to have a turn with you."

Atwood came back into the room. He huffed and set the gun on the dresser next to the door. "Your boyfriend tried to be cute, thought he could take down our guy. Instead, he has a bullet in his leg. Now, he knows we're not here to play. Do you understand that as well? No more games."

Unbuckling his belt, Atwood dropped his pants. "Get all the way on the bed!" he barked at Kennedy. She remained in place, sitting on the edge of the bed. No sense making things easy for them. Crawford decided to help by moving his hands to her ankles. He forced her legs onto the bed, but as he did, he felt something he didn't like.

"What's this?" Crawford said, as he eased up her pant leg to reveal her gun. He removed it from the ankle holster and aimed it at Kennedy's face. "What were you planning to do with this little pea shooter?"

Kennedy could see down the short barrel of the gun that hovered just inches from her nose. She held her breath, hoping he would aim the weapon elsewhere. Maybe she would be better off being shot now instead of being raped. Her mouth opened slightly, trying to get oxygen to her brain. She needed coherent thought right now.

Atwood let out a laugh, sounding much like a hyena. He took the gun out of Crawford's hand and set it on the dresser next to the other gun. "This works out better than I expected. Now, we can use her gun to kill the family, turning it into a murder/suicide. I think Pamela needs to be a victim too. She's nothing but dead weight."

He unbuttoned and shed his shirt, revealing a white tank top underneath. Atwood kept talking while standing in his undergarments. "If Pamela would've made sure that whore had an abortion when she was supposed to, we wouldn't be in this quandary right now."

Rather than acknowledge what his partner just said, Crawford responded with, "Just take your turn with this one. Make sure she screams loud enough to make her boyfriend talk."

Crawford scooched the rocking chair back away from the bed where Atwood had room to get to his prey. Atwood wasted no time straddling Kennedy on the bed. He ripped the buttons completely off her camouflage shirt as he tore the first item of clothing from her body. He flung the shirt across the room and then noticed the rabbit's foot hanging from her belt loop. He snatched the lucky charm, breaking the keychain in the process.

With another hyena laugh, he dismounted and turned around to show the president. "Look at this... she brought a pea shooter and lucky rabbit's foot to defend herself." Crawford joined in the laughing.

From the bed, Atwood had his back to her, and he stood

between her and Crawford. Kennedy only had a split second, and she chose not to waste it. In the blink of an eye, she pulled the bigger gun from the belly band under her t-shirt. Simultaneously, Kennedy said a prayer of gratitude that the blue rabbit's foot distracted them from finding her second gun and squeezed the trigger. And squeezed it again. And again.

She had no idea how many times she shot the gun. Kennedy wasn't even sure she heard the gunshots, but she definitely saw both of her captors lying on the floor by the time she finished shooting. The president and his advisor were no longer a threat to her. No one burst through the door, so the agent must have stayed downstairs rather than guard the upstairs.

Easing the door open, Kennedy kept the gun aimed in front of her. Imitating a spy in a movie, she crept out of the room, peeked around the corner, and faked some confidence. She heard the agent coming up the stairs before she saw him. A couple of bullets were sent in his direction. Kennedy didn't know if she hit him, but the tumble down the stairs seemed to have incapacitated him. That meant at least three more agents plus Anderson were downstairs.

She heard another cacophony of activity from the den with crashing and yelling. Her heart dropped, fearing the worst for Mason and his family. Forcing air into her lungs, Kennedy tiptoed to the stairs. The agent lay in an awkward position at the bottom, so she moved down the steps with as much stealth as she could. She kept her eye on the doorway that appeared to lead to the den and the back of the kitchen. This was the first time she had been in this area of the house, but the layout seemed straightforward.

No one appeared in the doorway before she had completely descended the stairs. As she looked down to step over the fallen agent, a figure rushed through the doorway.

"Drop your weapon!"

She dropped the gun and almost peed her pants as the man in black approached her with his own gun drawn.

"Kennedy, thank God you're okay."

She did a double take. Officer James Walker stood in front of her. Just then, Kennedy's awareness all seemed to return at once. The smell of gun powder, the blaze of the sun through a window behind James, and the sound of sirens outside... They assaulted her senses and flooded her with a mix of relief and dizziness.

"Come on, let's get you checked out." As he took Kennedy's arm to guide her to the den, two more officers in tactical gear rushed past them up the stairs to assess what danger might be left to deal with.

They passed through the den where Bartlett police officers had the three agents handcuffed and face down on the floor. Anderson had also been handcuffed, but she was shouting obscenities as one officer led her out of the room.

Mason, Ronnie, and Becky were nowhere to be found. James encouraged Kennedy to have a seat in the kitchen, but she refused to sit. Her frantic eyes searched for the man she loved and his parents. "Where's Mason?" she asked with a voice she almost didn't recognize as her own.

"He's outside. Come on."

The blinding sun, along with the swarm of activity, made another wave of dizziness overtake Kennedy. She stumbled down the stairs of the porch into a sea of emergency vehicles. "Come on, you're okay," James urged her to keep going, continuing to offer support to keep her upright.

An abundance of ambulances, fire trucks, and police cars were lit up all over the property like unseasonal fireworks. Focus eluded Kennedy in the swirl of sirens until she heard a familiar voice. "Ken... Ken..."

She searched every face until she found the one she

was looking for. Mason lay on a stretcher, allowing a medical technician to assess his lower leg. Forgetting her dizziness, Kennedy ran to Mason, almost knocking him off the stretcher with her aggressive embrace. Regardless of his injured leg, his arms felt strong around her. He whispered sweet nothings in her ear, while tears flooded her face.

Finally, she backed away enough to make eye contact. "Where's your parents?"

Officer Walker, still standing nearby, chose to answer, "They're together in the other ambulance, getting checked for shock."

Another officer approached her before she could choose to visit Becky and Ronnie in the other ambulance. "Kennedy Hughes?" After she nodded, he continued, "I'm Police Chief Tony Lawrence. We have some questions for you."

Before the questioning could begin, another officer exited the house, laughing. "Chief, you're not going to believe this." Several EMTs exited the house, pushing two stretchers. "The president got shot in the nuts!"

Kennedy watched as the two men she shot were loaded in other ambulances. "Chief Lawrence, those are the bad guys!" she exclaimed, pointing her accusing finger in their direction.

A swarm of police officers escorted the men into the waiting ambulances. Kennedy felt a small amount of relief that she didn't kill anyone, even though she probably wouldn't have lost sleep either way. The disabled agent from the bottom of the stairs, along with the two unconscious ones, had been wheeled out on stretchers as well.

"Go check on my parents," Mason said, shooing Kennedy away.

She moved in a trance towards the ambulance. The EMT wrapped a blanket over Kennedy's shoulder when she approached the open doors of the vehicle. Ronnie and Becky sat on the side of a stretcher with a blanket wrapped around them both. When they saw Kennedy, they both jumped up to pull her into a group hug. The tears never really stopped, but the floodgates opened again as she soaked up the warmth of the embrace.

When they finally released the hug, Kennedy asked, "Where's the girls?"

Becky answered, "They're safe. They aren't here."

The police chief had followed Kennedy to where she was. "Ms. Hughes, I understand you shot the president of the United States. You're going to have to come with me for questioning."

Becky answered on Kennedy's behalf, changing the direction of the conversation altogether. "Chief Lawrence, do you remember I was your science teacher in high school?"

"Um, yes, Ms. Dean, but that doesn't change anything here. We have a lot to sort out. You're going to be questioned as well." The chief tried to maintain his authority over the scene.

"Young man, I respect your position, and I know you need some answers. I just think the nanny cams we have hidden all over the house will answer many of the questions you never even thought to ask. Take the next couple of hours to watch the videos. We'll all come by the station after we get treated here."

Chief Lawrence must have trusted her because he moved on to bark orders to other officers on the scene. Officer Walker escorted Kennedy back to where Mason waited on the stretcher.

"It's just a flesh wound. The bullet went right through the side of my leg. The loose-fitting camo pants didn't give that agent a good target." Mason laughed as he tried to step down off the stretcher. "James, how did the police know to come here?"

"Man, I told you a storm was brewing even though I never would've guessed the president was involved. I knew it was trouble when I saw the Suburban parked in front of your parents' house this morning. I told Chief Lawrence that everything might come to a head regarding the missing girl, her murdered mother, and the house fire. He got our SWAT team together by the time Ms. Dean sent me the 911 text, and it's a good thing he did."

While James filled them in on his suspicions, a small army of black SUVs pulled into the front yard with sirens blaring. As quickly as vehicles were put into park, black suits rushed out of the vehicles and projected their authority over the scene. Kennedy figured this must be the CIA or whatever alphabet agency investigates crimes involving the president. The ringleader of the crew found Chief Lawrence to catch up on the events so far.

Within fifteen minutes, Kennedy found herself being transported to the Bartlett Police Station, along with Mason and his parents. No one asked questions to begin with. They were simply shown into a small conference room that offered eight chairs, one table, and a pot of stale coffee. Knowing that their conversations would be overheard, the foursome stayed quiet for at least two hours. That gave Kennedy's heart enough time to restore a normal rhythm rather than accelerating and skipping random beats as it had done all morning.

Finally, the door opened. Chief Lawrence entered the room with two suits right behind him.

Suit number one spoke first, "Good afternoon, everyone. It's been quite an eventful morning, and we're slowly putting together the pieces of this unexpected puzzle." He inhaled deeply as he looked at each of the four people in his audience. "I'm Special Agent in Charge Brad Shenk. I've spent the better part of the past two hours reviewing the camera footage from inside your home, Mr. Dean. While it helps us sort out the events of this morning, it leads to a complex problem never anticipated. Given the evidence we have on camera, we aren't going to hold you here any longer, but we expect all of you to be available for questioning as the investigation continues. Do you all understand?"

Four heads nodded in agreement.

"The only mystery I need some resolution for now has to do with the little girl. Where is she?"

"She's safe." Becky said, not offering even one extra syllable in explanation.

"I can accept that for now, Ms. Dean. Eventually, we'll want to get a confirmed DNA sample to prove paternity, and then the girl will become a ward of the state. You'll have to turn her over once I determine she isn't in danger."

"I'm filing to adopt her as soon as that happens. She'll stay in my custody," Kennedy replied with more confidence than she felt. There were certainly laws and rules that had to be followed, but she doubted anyone would be fighting for custody over Joy. She would maintain her position and fight to keep the girl with her no matter what.

"Those are bold words from a woman who just shot President Crawford in his testicles," Agent Shenk retorted, suppressing a smile.

"I've never shot a gun before; I was aiming for his heart."

"He would probably have preferred a bullet to the heart. Anyway, I'm letting you go for now. I have all your contact information, and we'll be filling in the blanks over the next few weeks. I'll call each of you as I need you."

Police Chief Lawrence gave Kennedy and her entourage a ride back to the house. Investigators and forensic specialists still abounded, collecting evidence and taking pictures. It was the parents' turn to pack a bag so they could stay elsewhere until their home was investigated, cleaned up, and turned back over to them. From there, Mason drove them to Chief Rice's house to trade vehicles back. The sweet fire chief offered canned Cokes and packs of crackers to the weary foursome. Kennedy was already running on fumes from the events of the day, but she was still desperate to see Joy and Gracie.

Once they all buckled into the red Suburban, Mason asked, "Okay, Mom, where's the girls?"

"Oh, I don't actually know where they are. I knew those guys might try some torture, so I made sure no one knew where to find them." Becky touched her bruised cheek while she answered. Kennedy's fingers reached for her own bruised cheek, thankful that was the only physical assault she experienced. It could've been so much worse.

"I'm too tired for games right now. By the time I pull into this gas station and fill up, I better have an address to where my daughter is."

Becky sent a text, which got a reply almost immediately. After Mason took his position in the driver's seat again, they headed to the adjacent town of Lakeland.

The drive only took twenty minutes, but Kennedy was on pins and needles by the time they entered the gated community. When they parked in the driveway of the house that looked more like a fortress, Kennedy's heart rate elevated again. Two weeks ago, she didn't even know Joy existed. Now, only a few days without her felt like an eternity.

The petite blonde who answered the door had a quick smile, but her green eyes were wary and discerning. "Welcome to my home. I'm Jenna." She reached out to shake hands with the four visitors before leading them inside. The view of Garner Lake outside the wall of windows in the back of the house impressed Kennedy, but the real beauty was inside the house. Gracie and Joy had created a blanket fort in the living room.

Within this fort inside the fortress, the girls giggled, while a dalmatian and Milo sat between them. Ginger watched the action from a kennel inside the fort as well.

Gracie was the first to look up. "Daddy!" She ran straight into her father's arms, and Joy wasted no time jumping into the arms of her mother figure. Kennedy's heart felt like it might explode from the outpouring of love. Her tears were relentless these days, releasing years of pent-up emotions.

With Joy still in her arms, Kennedy sat on the couch. Through her tears, she looked up at Jenna. "Who are you? I owe you a debt of gratitude."

"Pennie is my best friend. She told me this was life or death, and she isn't one to be dramatic about things like that."

"I don't understand. Pennie didn't know where to find them. How did they get here?"

Ronnie spoke up this time, "I spoke to Pennie's brother, Officer Walker. I knew we could trust him, and he coordinated a safe place for the girls to stay for a few days. We could tell this conspiracy was fixing to unravel. The safest plan for these girls was to put them in the hands of someone who couldn't be quickly traced through our immediate friends and family. Officer Walker picked the girls up yesterday morning, not a moment too soon."

Just the idea of so many people working together overwhelmed Kennedy. She really had been missing out on having family and friends for so many years. She didn't do anything to deserve the outpouring of support, but they offered it anyway. Mason. His parents. Officer Walker. Pennie. Jenna. Her vicarious family was growing by the minute. And she imagined she would need all the help she could get to raise a child.

"Well, the girls have had fun here, but Dolly and I are ready to have our quiet home back. Why don't y'all go enjoy some family time."

The four adults and two children ate Chick-fil-A around Kennedy's coffee table an hour later. She still wasn't hungry, but eating was necessary. Gracie and Joy talked about their adventures at *Aunt Jenna's* house. Not just about the blanket fort, but they enjoyed everything from bubble baths and face masks to curled hair and homemade bracelets. They showed off freshly painted fingernails and toenails. Apparently, Aunt Jenna taught them a lesson in being pampered little girls. They were so enthralled with the tales of indulgence, they never even asked why BB and Kennedy had handprints on their faces.

During the course of the day, all sense of time had been lost. Kennedy was surprised to see what the clock had to say. Five thirty. Her level of exhaustion convinced her it was bedtime, but the blur of activity convinced her it was noon. Maybe five thirty was a good compromise.

When the girls finally stopped talking to take a breath, Papaw jumped in, "Mason... BB and I are going to stay at your apartment if you're going to stay here for the time being. We need to get some rest."

"Let me get out our bags and booster seats, and you can just take the Suburban. The garage opener is on the visor. I think we all need some rest."

After getting his parents on the road, Mason came back in and collapsed on the couch. Kennedy joined him and found some cartoons for the girls to watch. The most amazing part of the day for Kennedy was how the girls never knew they were in danger. They simply watched their cartoons, completely oblivious to the crisis of the day. Maybe that was part of being a parent. Shielding children from the vile realities of the world for as long as possible. Protecting their innocence. Joy had already been exposed to some wickedness, but it was time to let her thrive under the care and protection of someone who loved her and had no interest in using her as a pawn in some blackmail scheme.

By nine, the girls were ready for bed. Bathing, hair drying, and book reading were all checked off the list by ten. Kennedy still had a few chores to finish. Her bedding was all in the dryer, and a load of clothes remained in the washer. She had barely been home that week, and floors didn't sweep themselves. Going to bed with a dirty house was something Kennedy could never do, so she expended the rest of her nervous energy scrubbing countertops and toilets. Mason must have known she was working the events of the day out of her system; he wisely stood back and offered to help here and there.

When she finally ran out of nooks and crannies to clean, Kennedy felt thoroughly exhausted, physically and mentally. Midnight had just passed when the adults finally moved to the bedroom.

"Will they be okay sharing a bed tonight? Joy just has the twin bed," Kennedy asked as she cuddled against Mason in her own bed. Milo didn't join them since he opted to sleep on the floor next to Ginger, where he could be close to his favorite tiny humans.

"They fit in the bed just fine. Plus, this is still an adventure for them." He pulled Kennedy closer to his side where her head could rest on his shoulder. His fingers gently stroked her hair.

Kennedy felt like her own adventure was just beginning, if only she had more energy. She relished the simple contact, lying against his bare chest and feeling the loving way his fingers made her scalp tingle. She savored the moment. The safety and security of his arms.

"I hope you don't mind us staying here. I'll have to get some clean clothes tomorrow for me and Gracie. These pajama pants won't make it another day."

"I don't think I ever want to wake up without you again. I got kind of spoiled the last couple of days," Kennedy managed to say even though she was drooling a little from the light petting.

"I'm glad you said that. Listen…" Mason said as he sat up.

Nothing good happened after midnight. Kennedy knew this. She didn't feel like talking anymore. She hated that he chose this moment to sit up, taking her comfy, safe place with him. He turned on a lamp and reached for his wallet on the nightstand.

Kennedy's mind had a little trouble focusing on what was going on. Was he trying to find a condom? As eager as she was for his physical attention after the last week, there was no way tonight was the proper time for it. Feeling disappointed, she lay back on her own pillow while he fumbled with his wallet. If she turned him down, would he stick around? Would he respect her more? Or pull away from her?

"Ken, everything about our relationship has been unorthodox." He rolled back towards her, lying on his side as he spoke. "Times of adversity reveal a person's true nature. You've been so brave, so strong, and so selfless the past ten days. You've risked your own personal safety to protect Joy even though you were never obligated to do so. Even before that happened, you bothered to wake up in the middle of the night to take in an orphaned bunny. You have such a pure and sincere soul. There's no one in this world who would be a better influence for my daughter, and there's no one in the world I'd rather wake up to every morning. Ken, I love you. Will you please marry me?"

The ring he held in his open hand glistened in the light of the lamp. Kennedy gasped and shot up from her pillow to get a better look at the ring. The oval-shaped solitaire sparkled between the tiny diamonds set in the gold band. She lightly touched the mesmerizing jewel with her index finger to see if it was real.

Mason must have noticed she wasn't comprehending, so he took her hand and slid the ring onto the appropriate finger.

He repeated, "Kennedy, will you marry me please?"

She turned her face towards him, but she couldn't find any words to respond to his amazing request.

"Speechless again?" His gorgeous smile managed to outshine the ring.

Kennedy nodded, hoping to convey everything she felt through mental telepathy. Accepting her unspoken affirmation, Mason brushed his lips lightly against her before pulling her into another embrace. They fell asleep for some peaceful slumber for the first time in over a week.

THURSDAY, FEBRUARY 24

The lazy morning refreshed Kennedy. She enjoyed getting back into her routine of feeding her animals, and she was pleased to see her seedlings were still growing strong. Gracie and Joy played board games. Mason took the Jeep to get some clothes and toiletries from his apartment. The girls instantly fell in love with *Aunt Pennie* when she came over to check on them. The fact that she brought cans of slime and bottles of bubbles probably helped.

Over their dinner of delivery pizza, Mason broached the subject of them all living together. Gracie was thrilled over the idea of having a sister. Plans were made for Gracie to occupy the third bedroom, and she quickly agreed to keep Pickles the rat as her roommate. Kennedy and Mason made plans to marry later that week and combine their homes in preparation to adopt Joy.

Becky and Ronnie came over after dinner to drop off the Suburban. Becky pulled Kennedy to the side, while the girls showed Ronnie their new cans of slime. Standing in the tiny kitchen, the grandmother stuck her hand in her purse, rifling for something. "I watched the videos from our cameras last night," she said quietly while studying the contents of her purse. "I didn't know when I gave you that rabbit's foot, it would save your life. I guess it had a little more luck in it than I expected." Finally grasping the item that had eluded her, Becky pulled out another blue rabbit's foot.

Kennedy accepted the lucky charm with a smile. "Now

that all the danger's in the past, I hope I don't need any more luck."

"Since you're wearing my grandmother's ring, and you just gained two daughters in the package deal, let's hope this rabbit's foot wards off any danger in the future. Mason told me you aren't going back to work... that you intend to be a full-time mother and wife. You have a full family now, Kennedy."

A full family. A soon-to-be husband. Two daughters. Friends. She didn't need the blue fuzzy talisman. That midnight call ten days ago may have brought trouble, but the midnight proposal last night made it all worth it. For a family, the trouble would always be worth it.

EPILOGUE

The next few weeks would reveal quite a bit about the nation's new president. Robert Crawford had been a womanizer over the years, a lifestyle that remained hidden thanks to hush money, threats, and cover-up efforts of Pamela Anderson. She admitted everything with the offer of reduced charges regarding her part of the scheme.

Paternity did prove that Crawford was Joy's biological father. The results were immediately sealed from the original test Marla Jamison requested to find Joy's father through the DNA database. She must've suspected a powerful man in a high-rolling position was involved, and she enlisted Destiny's former friend Autumn Gibson to help with her investigation. Of course, they didn't make it far before becoming the next two fatalities in the cover-up endeavors.

Everyone who associated with Robert Crawford over the years had been promised great things. His bodyguards who used to be US Capitol Police were put through the Secret Service training on a fast track. Pam Anderson and Jordan Atwood became advisors once Crawford made it to the White House. Their legacy would only last those first couple of months as the shocking truth was uncovered.

Despite overcoming all his indiscretions over the years, and the political obstacles that hindered independent candidates, Robert Crawford became the most powerful man in the free world. This only made his fall from grace seem farther. From his hospital bed, Crawford resigned as president, relinquishing the duties to his more conservative running mate. With presidential immunity behind him, Crawford was swiftly charged with multiple counts of conspiracy and abuse of power.

Attorneys compelled Crawford to release any rights to Joy, and temporary custody was granted to Kennedy without delay. Mason and Kennedy married and moved into her house the next week to start what they hoped would be a normal existence, free of any political drama. The decision to quit working never brought an ounce of regret to Kennedy. Full time motherhood suited her perfectly.

With Joy's limited social experiences, Gracie helped her new sister adapt to school and other normal routines for six-year-olds. With Kennedy's limited social experiences, Mason and all her new friends helped her adapt to the normal routines of being a wife and mother.

Ever since that fateful call on Valentine's Day, Kennedy learned a lot about hope, life, gumption, and love. And a little luck from a rabbit's foot couldn't hurt either.

BOOKS BY THIS AUTHOR

A Pennie Saved

Book 1 in the Pennie Nichols Mystery Series.

A Pennie For Your Thoughts

Book 2 of the Pennie Nichols Mystery Series

Cost A Pretty Pennie

Book 3 of the Pennie Mystery Book Series

Made in the USA
Columbia, SC
20 January 2025

51205679R00135